This story, written as realistic fiction,

may have actually happened.

Hans-Peter

David Poland

outskirts
press

Outskirts Press, Inc.
http://www.outskirtspress.com

ISBN: 978-1-9772-3245-8

Outskirts Press and the "OP" logo are trademarks belonging to Outskirts Press, Inc.

PRINTED IN THE UNITED STATES OF AMERICA

Chapters & Pages

Dedication

To all of us who are quite sure we don't know what's really going on.

Chapter One
Money Off-the-Record

While this story is now known to most everyone on the planet, I was there as it developed. In fact, I was a participant at several key moments. My contributions were small, but I was there, beginning to end.

My given name is Traypart. It's a name that I cherish, a name that no one else has ever taken. It is mine alone. When I started my career in journalism, I took the fictitious family name of Artamus because it's pleasant and arouses no suspicion whatsoever.

Many years back, just before I came to southern California, my father advised me to never be completely open with anyone, and if at all possible to never deceive anyone, either. He went on to say that both honesty and integrity are ultimately personal pleasures, but only if they are genuine. I am quite certain his observation captured a fundamental truth; and even to this day, I continue to puzzle over its subtleties.

And so I came to California to report on aerospace and to keep track of the endless possibilities of improving spaceflight, and to ponder how the human mind might in fact be maturing.

From my perspective, this story starts the Tuesday morning Ruthiebell called and asked me if I could stop by her office. As you may know, Ruthiebell is the Science and Technology Editor for the *Los Angeles Herald Express*. Often the newspaper would publish one of my articles in their Sunday edition. It was very unusual for her to call me; usually I would hear from her secretary. She herself would customarily communicate by email.

In these 'millennial' times, office visits were rapidly disappearing. We were both older than the Internet and enjoyed doing things the old way.

We both also knew that nowadays our friendly government was copying every email and every telephone conversation that anyone ever made. We never talked about 'Surveillance.' We suspected using the 'S' word would raise a red flag for the eavesdropping software. As I pulled in to park at 140 11th Street, I wondered if she might have something truly confidential.

Her office had the feel of the twentieth century and I liked it. When I entered, she left her desk and we sat in comfortable chairs off to the side. She was very bright and a bit crafty. I knew this part of her office was meant to make the visitor feel like a friend and an equal. "I hope your drive across town was pleasant," she said as though she had no agenda.

"Yes, it was. Everyone on the road was well behaved. I was wondering, as I drove, if you were interested in another follow-up on the Boeing 737-Max story?"

"No. I think my readers have grown tired of reading about that one." The coffee table before us had thick elegant cookies and sparkling mineral water as well as coffee cups and saucers. She rather thoughtfully drank some of her coffee. "Have you been keeping up with Hans-Peter?"

"No, not recently. I last saw him about a year ago when he presented his newest titanium alloy. As you may recall, he did that one at sunrise and it was very poorly attended."

"So I heard, but I have a copy of the article you wrote for *Aviation Week*. I was hoping you learned a lot more than what you wrote about. When you were there, did Hans have his big central hangar open?"

"No. He had set up a big tent near that hangar and he had his new alloy out on a table. At the end of that tent there was a kitchen. Everyone that showed up got a good hot breakfast." She seemed to cringe a bit when I started to talk about his breakfast. "Let me guess. You're not interested in that breakfast."

"Have you heard the rumor that he's developing the next generation rocket engine out there?"

"Yes, but that rumor is at least ten years old and its never been verified."

"When you were there," she said. "I was hoping you might have seen signs of engine development inside his hangar. This rumor to me is very important. We're old friends, Traypart. I want to give you some off-the-record money to investigate that rumor in a very quiet way? Would you do that, for me, with absolute confidentiality?"

"You can trust me, but I don't want to mess around with anything that involves the National Security Agency or Navy Intelligence."

"Neither do I," she said. "I'm sure he sells metals to the black world, but as far as I can tell he's not dealing with the NSA. They either don't know about his rocket engine, or they don't care."

"But then we don't know anything about it either. He talks about metals, not rockets. What exactly are you looking for? If your money is off-the-record, then this conversation is also off-the-record. Right?"

"Right."

"So tell me: what are you looking for?"

"Everyone knows he has three old F-111s," she said with reasonable certainty. "I think he's modified the best one to carry his rocket to high altitude. Then at altitude, he's going to fire it and fly into space."

"That's very unlikely. Everybody knows he has two old F-111s behind his hangar, but they've been back there for years returning to nature."

"Those two are just for spare parts," she countered as though saying the obvious. "The one that counts is inside being refitted."

"Okay," I said, "but you need to get going about 17,500 miles per hour to get into Low Earth Orbit. You can't put enough fuel in an F-111 to get that far; it's not big enough."

"I knew Hans in college," she said with a hint of pleasure. "Now listen, what I'm going to tell you I have never told another soul. You must never repeat what I'm about say. Can I trust you, or should we stop right here?"

"You can trust me, but if you've been keeping this secret since your college days, why let it out now?"

"I'm not letting it out now," she snapped. "I'm only telling you and you're not going to repeat it."

"Then why tell me at all?"

"Because I'm running out of time, and I need some very qualified help."

"Okay," I said reluctantly. "So way back in collage he was talking about rockets and F-111s."

"Way back then," she repeated, "he told me he was thinking about how to blend a nuclear reaction into a liquid fuel rocket engine. Do you think that's even possible?"

"Nuclear fuel?" I had to smile. "Yes, it's possible, but nobody's even talking about nuclear fuel. Anything nuclear is highly regulated by the government. Is that why this conversation is totally confidential? Do you actually think he knows how to do that?"

"Yes," she said, "and I don't want you telling anybody about my speculations. I think Hans-Peter is about to rewrite aerospace. So do you think it's possible to supercharge a liquid fuel rocket with a nuclear reaction?"

"Yes. That's a very interesting question. Between you and me, I don't know why someone hasn't tried it before now."

"That is," she said, "in the white world, but we don't know what's going on in the black world."

"That's very true. How do you want to start?"

She went back to her desk and brought back an envelope that looked stuffed with something. She sat back down and opened it up. It was stuffed with hundred dollar bills. She counted out two thousand dollars, then stuffed them back in the envelope and handed it to me. "There's more where that came from."

I took it. "You're serious. I like the assignment."

"Good," she smiled. "No emails and don't ever mention this on the phone. Can you do that?"

"I can."

"In a day or two, Hans will announce another open house. He's going to show off his newest product, and I will be there. You plan to be there too."

"I hadn't heard."

"You will," she said, as though she knew things others didn't, "and be sure to be there."

As I drove back to my office, I knew Ruthiebell might be very close to the truth. This book, however, is not about her, or me for that matter. It's meant to tell the story that's already being denied as impossible.

Working in aerospace journalism brought me face to face with Hans-Peter long before anyone in the reading public even knew his name. As far as I can tell, he was the first one to say that if a camel is really a horse designed by a committee, then surely the Space Shuttle was really an aerospace plane that was designed by another committee. We haven't heard much about the aerospace plane concept for the last twenty years; so let me refresh your memory. An aerospace plane is an airplane that can fly fast enough and high enough to get all the way up and into orbit; and that was exactly what Ruthiebell thought Hans-Peter was going to do with his rebuilt F-111.

The truth is, I love to watch the human enterprise of flying faster and higher. I would be chronicling the progress of aerospace even if no one ever bought my copy, but of course that's not the case. Editors recognized my technical insights from the very start and started publishing my stuff. Hans-Peter was one of my first readers, and he initiated our acquaintance.

How fortunate I was to have such an interesting man reach out to me. He gave me that first call back in the mid-eighties when everyone knew that a 'low cost space transport' would be the key to an ongoing space program. Hans-Peter had seen my editorials suggesting that while the Space Shuttle would be an interesting step forward, the real future in space would go to the first aerospace plane.

Back then; we met for a midweek lunch. Early in the conversation I realized he hadn't called me to hear his thoughts for a new configuration. He wanted to hear everything I had learned from other interviews that I hadn't put in my editorials. He seemed to know my dad's advice and wasn't showing me much of what he knew. With the advent of classified information, nondisclosure had become the order of the day. In Hans-Peter's case, however, I don't believe he was protecting and hiding government secrets. I believed he was hiding his own unpublished thinking.

Unlike my usual interview, he wasn't looking for some free PR by appearing in my next editorial. Hans-Peter wanted to talk about the physics and chemistry of hypersonic flight, rather than show me his dazzling drawings of what he thought could fly at hypersonic speeds. He said that now that supersonic flight was routine, the next step toward a true aerospace plane would be to make hypersonic flight also routine.

What I remember from that luncheon was that for Hans-Peter, hypersonic flight was the halfway step to orbit. He left the impression with me that he had radically new ideas for propulsion, and then he asked me to not ever quote any of his thinking in my editorials. In fact, he went on to say he'd rather I never mentioned our conversation to anyone.

Over the years I have honored his request for confidentiality, but I have thought about what he said. My best guess was that he found a way to use nuclear energy. Needless to say, Ruthiebell's confidential speculation about nuclear energy fired up my memory. I didn't tell her how much of Hans-Peter's thinking I already knew. I was keeping his request for secrecy. I realized he was telling me that he really wanted to find a better way to fly into space. At that moment I felt he had obliquely confided his real goal. I knew I had just heard his defining dream, and I determined not to ever betray his goal to anyone. I believe such a dream is sacred.

It was back in the year 2000 that he announced the formation of a company he called Titanium Composites. He and his associates took over the eastern half of Norton Field, formally Norton Air Force Base, located in San Bernardino, California. When the Air Force moved out, they left a long heavy-duty runway and a number of enormous hangars. I was quite sure that he and his friends were doing things that others were not even trying. The following year, the Inland Empire Airport Authority took over the western half of the old Air Force base and built a civilian airport. The new airport is now open, but as of this writing, no airline has yet scheduled a flight there.

Hans-Peter's friends included some of the best aerospace people I knew of, and every few years they would show off their newest product at an open house. I would always drive out and report on it. I would make a serious effort to show how important their advancements were in my editorials, but I never mentioned his collection of old F-111s.

I knew Hans-Peter liked what I wrote, but with time he seemed to be less interested in any kind of publicity. The work he and his colleagues were doing with titanium alloys was extremely important, but only to a very narrow readership. To make matters much worse, he started having his open house events at sunrise. Very few people were willing to drive out to San Bernardino before sunrise to see a piece of metal. His events were very poorly attended, but as I said, I always made sure to be there. My attendance was a mixture of moral support and curiosity. I didn't know when it would happen, but I was sure this man had something spectacular up his sleeve.

Sandy Koop was still in her twenties. She had majored in journalism with a personal agenda. She had grown up in a family totally preoccupied with the Roswell crashed weather balloon incident and wanted to write with such clarity that there would be no more room for conspiracy theories.

As an undergraduate, she encountered the idea of archetypes and dream analysis in an introductory class to psychology. Her eyes were opened and she then determined that everything from the Loch Ness monster to little green men from Mars were archetypes the unconscious generated to work out experiences the conscious intellect – the conscious intellect is a fancy way of saying a person who is wide awake – had encountered during their day. As a journalist she was aiming to set the record straight.

There was no question in her mind that for the decade starting now, in this year 2020, the most important issue was the environment. Anything, including swamp gas and weather balloons that distracted from the environmental crises, was in fact a treason against all of humanity. Her plan was to cut her teeth on general reporting and look for an opportunity to focus on the environment.

She had just landed her first significant job, and was now the newest reporter for the *Los Angeles Herald Express*. The *Herald* still printed a daily paper, but the website had grown international and was where most of the action was.

As fate would have it, Ruthiebell was tied up with the newspaper's bankers the day of the open house. She reasoned that since I would be there as an informed observer, she could send a rookie in her place and get a totally uninformed observation as a contrast.

Sandy knew that being asked to drive to San Bernardino before sunrise to look at a piece of titanium was the bottom of the barrel, but she was puzzled when Max, her supervisor, told her that Ruthiebell had told him to give her the assignment.

Sandy knew of Ruthiebell, but she had never met the woman. She asked a few questions and learned that she might be the only reporter to show up. Unknown to Sandy, several other hardy souls, including myself and another man named Keith Wiley, were also planning to attend.

Out on the high desert, considerably north and east of Victorville, the Air Force operated a desert environment Forward Operations Base, an FOB, for A-10 tactical aircraft. The American A-10 was designed to support ground troops and its weapons can destroy any tank an enemy could deploy. The base had been set up in 1992 shortly after the initial victory of Desert Storm. At that time everyone knew that a victory in the Middle East could be very short lived. The Pentagon had set up the FOB in California to refine desert operational skills. The official name for the base was never used. The officers and personnel called the place Cactus Patch, and they liked it that way.

The place was not very big and was meant to be very much like a temporary desert airstrip. There were three large Quonset huts set up to protect the aircraft, – two A-10s in each one – but no other permanent buildings. The personnel lived and worked from tents, which they set up and took down from time to time. The supplies were flown in on C-130

Hercules transports, just the way they would be to an FOB.

In the operations tent, the night before Hans-Peter would make his new product announcement, a corporal had been working through the night and was following the live video post from Sandy Koop on his cell phone. She liked to attach her smartphone to the dashboard of her car and talk to her growing number of followers as she drove. She would talk about what she thought would entice her viewers to read her news reports.

For the corporal, the very sound of her voice aroused a deep longing. She was a millennial like he was and he had fallen in love with her. At least once a week he would get a chance to see her driving out on an assignment. This morning she was driving through the dark, griping about the sunrise assignment she had to cover out at Norton Field. She seemed clueless about how important Titanium Composites was to the world of high-temperature metals. As the corporal watched and listened, he realized something was afoot. Suddenly his secret love affair had turned into real surveillance. He was in fact doing his job.

The base commander was a major and the corporal knew he was one to rise very early. He called the major's office and was not surprised when the first ring was answered. "Major Hayes."

"Good morning, sir. This is Corporal Tabby in operations. Today there will be some activity down at Norton Field that might be of interest to you."

"Really. What's going on down there?"

"I'm listening to a reporter driving out to Norton to cover a sunrise product rollout. Titanium Composites has invited the press to come out and see their newest product.

"That's gotta be Hans-Peter," answered the major. "He's the only one romantic enough to pull a stunt like that at sunrise. Does the reporter have any idea what they're going to roll out today?"

"No sir."

"How many planes are operational?" asked the major.

"Five."

"Who are the next two pilots on the roster?"

"Potash and Woodburn."

"SMOKY and RAINDROP," said the major. "Good, I think it's time for a drill. Hit the alert and start your clock now!"

"Yes sir." A pulsating horn sounded rudely breaking the tranquility of the desert night.

"I'll fly the lead. You notify those two pilots. They had better meet me in the locker room and pronto. I want three planes without any ordnance on the rails. Do we have planes with recon pods already loaded?"

"Yes sir, but only SMOKY's hog."

"Have them get recon pods on the other two aircraft, and no ordnance. Then get those three A-10s rolled out to the flight line and tell the flight line guys I want the tanks up to at least two-thirds capacity."

"Yes sir."

"Get our people moving corporal. The clock's ticking. I'm on my way to suit up. Those other two pilots better be there. Let's see how fast we can respond. Write this one up as a tactical recon drill."

"Yes sir, and best of luck."

When Sandy came to the gate, I had just gone through. She showed her press card and was welcomed in. She was directed to park where I was, behind a tent near a large hangar. When she parked, she saw my car and only three others. We were unloading our equipment. She joined us and we were all escorted to a place fairly near the hangar. We were then told not to try to photograph inside the hanger. In fact, we were told to cap our cameras and put our electronic devices in a pocket or our bag. They also told us that we couldn't have anything in our hands until the hangar doors were closed again. Needless to say, I was wondering if they were about to roll out a modified F-111.

Several security men stood by us to make sure the request was followed.

When the first rays of sunrise could be seen, the great doors opened and they rolled out an astonishingly sleek new aircraft. This was no rebuilt F-111. As it rolled out, I tried to look back into the hangar for a rocket engine. There was a lot of equipment in there, but the lights were off and I couldn't see what it was.

Sandy was awestruck by the new airplane. She instantly knew she had the biggest story of the day and quite possibly the month. Fascinated by the new airplane, none of us had noticed Hans-Peter, come up behind us. He was close enough to hear what we were saying. As soon as the big doors closed, all five of us started taking pictures and making videos.

Sandy was one lucky rookie, and she was the first one to notice someone standing behind us. She had never heard of Hans-Peter before this assignment, but she had a reporter's intuition and she had found an old photo of him on the Internet. She turned and looked at him. "Would you be Hans-Peter?"

"Yes. I don't believe we've ever met."

"I'm Sandy Koop with the *Herald Express*, and that must be your airplane?"

"Yes, that's our airplane and we think it's unlike anything that's ever been built before."

The other reporters and I turned to meet Hans-Peter. He extended his hand to me. "Hello, Traypart. I had a hunch you'd drive out for this event.

As you can see, we're doing a little more these days than forging titanium parts."

"It's spectacular. It's truly spectacular," I said. "The skin looks like bare metal to me. Are we looking at buffed titanium?"

"Yes. The entire plane is made of our newest titanium alloy. It's something you've never seen before."

"It looks like it can fly even faster than an SR-71. What do you call it?"

Hans-Peter didn't answer me directly, but said, "Five of you. I see five; so very good to see each one of you here this morning. We have your names and affiliations noted. As the program develops, we will give each of you first access to coverage. Those other journalists that are still at home sawing logs will not get the same access we will give each of you. Let's step inside the tent and I will make the first official announcement. When we get inside, we'll give you plenty of time to set up your equipment before I speak."

Good grief, I thought. Ruthiebell's F-111 idea was close and even more reasonable than what we were looking at. No one except she and I had ever guessed that Titanium Composites was working on their own airplane, let alone something bigger and more awesome than an SR-71. His airplane looked much too good to be true.

When everyone was inside and ready, Hans-Peter stepped up to the speaker's platform. The side of the tent facing the airplane was open. The platform was on that side and from inside we could see the airplane behind Hans-Peter. He told us the new plane had been named the Rebel, and it was designed to challenge the hypersonic velocity range. He then reminded everyone that hypersonic flight started at Mach 5 or about two Mach numbers faster than the SR-71s had typically flown.

A Mach number for an airplane in flight, as you may recall, is the ratio of the airplane's speed to the speed of sound at its present altitude. As you know, the speed of sound is a little different at different altitudes. It slows down as you climb up higher.

To get things started, Sandy spoke up before I could. "You've built the most beautiful thing I've ever seen. Now, exactly how fast will it go?"

"We don't know for sure. For starters we're shooting for at least Mach 7."

"That's hypersonic," blurted out Keith Wiley. "That means you think you've beat the thermal problem. Will you be circulating fuel through the skin to keep it cool?"

"No, we won't need to do that. We've put a lot of thought into managing the extreme temperatures. For starters, we do have a better skin than the SR-71 did, but we have also worked out a new kind of solution that I'm rather pleased with."

"How can that be?" asked another reporter. "Your new titanium alloys are good, but they can't be that much better than the old ones. Would you tell us more specifically how you're approaching the thermal problems of hypersonic flight?"

"That's a very important question, but we feel it is best not to talk about the details at this time."

"Yeah, okay," said Keith, "but talking about details, your engines don't look big enough to push that thing even supersonic, let alone hypersonic. Are we really looking at a full-scale mockup? Is that what you just rolled out here today?"

"No," answered Hans-Peter. "The aircraft you're looking at is complete and ready to fly. In fact, we could fire it up today."

"By saying you 'could fire it up today'," asked Sandy, "does that mean you won't be starting it up for us?"

"Yes, that's correct. We're not going to light the engines today."

"Have you scheduled the first flight?" asked the other reporter.

"Yes," said Hans-Peter with the beginning of a smile. "The Rebel will take to the air in just ten days. We will roll her out again at sunrise and take her off in the cool morning air."

Not again, thought Sandy. Doesn't this guy know that sunrise is a good time to be in bed asleep? She wanted to suggest an 11:30 rollout, but thought it would be better to keep her mouth shut.

I couldn't help but ask, "If it's ready to fly, why don't you fire it up right now and let us record it taxiing? We'll get ten times as many hits if they can see it moving under its own power. You have shown us the Rebel, now let us show it to the world in a way that will attract the audience it deserves."

"You're probably right, Mr. Artamus," answered Hans-Peter, "but we've burned up most of our jet fuel in static tests. Today we don't have enough fuel for a taxi run."

"When will there be a taxi run?" asked Sandy.

"We're not planning any taxi tests. When we roll it out for its maiden flight, then you can watch it taxi. We are planning to take off west, fly north along the Cajon Pass, and then out and around the San Bernardino Mountains. When we get all the way around the mountains, we'll put it back down here."

"With all due respect," asked Keith, "don't you think forgoing the traditional taxi tests raises safety issues for your neighbors? Norton Field isn't exactly out in the middle of the desert."

Hans-Peter seemed to be tiring of the questions. "We have a great deal of confidence in our design. For now, I think I'll pass on any more questions. I'd like to thank each of you for coming out. Over there we've made up a hot breakfast for each of you. Please stay as long as you like." Hans-Peter then left with one of his security men.

Sandy took her hot breakfast to a table big enough for six. Keith Wiley and I joined her without sitting very close. Of course, I had known Keith from other reporting encounters, but I had never met Sandy.

Then suddenly Keith said, "I don't believe that BS about no jet fuel. Why do you think that guy won't run a set of taxi tests like everyone else who's ever built a real airplane does?"

"Not at Kitty Hawk," said Sandy taunting him just a little.

"Right," answered Keith gruffly. "So now we have the second exception to the rule. Oh, and by the way, the world has changed a little since then. "

"Well, for starters," I said, "we saw them roll it out of the hangar, so they know they can at least roll it that far, but that doesn't mean a thing. After their static tests they may have taxied it around the field late at night when no one was watching. We really don't know what they've actually done. We only know what he just told us. I'm sure what he told us is true; it's just not complete."

Keith looked at Sandy and me and shook his head. As he stood up, he said, "If you two are aviation journalists, you should know better than that. If that thing is really ready to fly, and by the way, I don't believe it is; they should fire it up and let us see it roll under its own power. You know I'm beginning to wonder if it's really an airplane or just a very convincing prop for a new movie."

"Oh, come on, Keith," I said. "You should know better than that. Surely you can tell that's a real airplane by just looking at the landing gear and the tires."

"I think there's something fishy here," he said and then walked away.

As soon as the gate was opened, people started coming through. Visitors were allowed to walk as close to the plane as they wanted. A little later on, when Sandy was standing by the front landing gear being photographed with people she had never met, the sound of military jet engines could be heard coming out of the east.

Everyone looked up and saw three A-10s fly fairly low over the field in a tight formation. They made a lot of noise for planes no bigger than they were. As everyone watched, the A-10s banked off to the north and started to make a very big circle. Due north were the mountains. The three planes climbed and broke formation as they turned. As they finished the long turn, they were each flying their own course. One by one, they dropped down much lower and flew back over, giving their recon cameras an ideal vantage. West of the field, they regrouped and flew off north and up the Cajon Pass.

Within just a few hours, Keith revealed to the world that he was quite sure the Rebel was only a mockup constructed for a new movie. He told his Internet followers that this was obviously just a crafty new way to market a new science fiction movie, and nothing more. The possibility that it wasn't a real airplane didn't seem to dampen the Internet enthusiasm.

While Titanium Composites didn't bother to reply, the people who had stood under the airplane did. The people who had been there said the movie idea was dead wrong and posted their many photographs of the aircraft and its very convincing landing gear. Numerous websites began to debate Keith's movie idea and agreed that if it was a prop, it was the most realistic movie prop ever built.

Later on that day, the company announced over the Internet that in ten days, at sunrise, the Rebel would have its maiden flight. The company went on to say that, while the company grounds would be closed to the public, the land and road south of the runway and the entire Santa Ana River Wash were always open to visitors.

Once the announcement had been made, Keith prepared to file a formal complaint with the County of San Bernardino arguing that a titanium foundry, with no track record of aircraft design, had no right to expose the citizens of San Bernardino to the hazard of an experimental airplane crashing down on their heads. He insisted that the Rebel be banned from attempting a takeoff or, if airborne, attempting to land at Norton Field until its flightworthiness had been established and certified.

While he knew the Rebel was a real airplane – the words 'movie prop' were just a sound bite used to attract Internet hits – he hoped being the champion for human safety, would put his name of the front page.

Sandy had sent everything she had about the Rebel, pictures and text, to the paper electronically. She knew her stuff was already dominating the paper's web site and was sure it would be on the paper's front page tomorrow. Rather than go home, she fought her way through the evening traffic back to the office to see what the swing shift was doing with her story. She was sure that the Rebel rollout would be the most important technology story for at least a week and probably even longer.

When she walked to her table, it was fifteen after seven and a middle-aged woman was sitting in her chair scanning her text and pictures from San Bernardino. The woman was expensively better dressed than the others. Rather than come up from behind her, Sandy went around and approached from the front. She put her pack softly on the table.

The woman looked away from the screen and pleasantly and said, "You must be Sandy Koop?"

"Yes ma'am. Would you be Ruthiebell?"

"Yes," she extended her hand. "I knew you had hired on. So nice to meet you." As they shook hands, Ruthiebell continued. "How were you treated out at Titanium Composites?"

"Very well. They treated me like the other reporters. Actually, I liked them. I have the feeling they are all very good people."

"I've heard that's true," said Ruthiebell thoughtfully. "Did you meet Hans-Peter?"

"Yes, I did, but only briefly."

"How did he look?"

The question startled Sandy. She was expecting, 'What did he say.' Sandy knew in an instant there was some history here. She must proceed with caution. "Oh, he looked just fine. I think he's very proud of his new airplane."

Ruthiebell was pleased with that answer and said, "A man named Keith Wiley is making trouble. He's using the Internet to say they must be stopped. We must find a way to discredit Keith Wiley and help Hans fly his airplane."

Chapter Two
Claudius and Eleanor

The next day Keith Wiley went to the county offices to file his complaint. He recognized many of the bureaucrats from the day before when the Rebel had been rolled out. It seemed that at least half of the county employees had driven over to see the Rebel for themselves. He started at a general information counter on the first floor. The man he talked to informed him, saying, "I have never handled a flightworthiness challenge before, but for starters, I think you have the wrong terminology. The regulations talk about 'airworthiness' and not 'flightworthiness'."

"I'm here with a concern about safety," said Keith, using a tone of voice meant to enlist the clerk as a colleague in the quest of public safety. Then he asked, "Has Titanium Composites filed an 'airworthiness' document with the county?"

"I really don't know. If you would like me to look, I will need a written request and then about three days to comply." The clerk could see Keith's building frustration, and tried to be sympathetic. "You know I may be the wrong person to talk to. Why don't you try your request down the hall at the office marked Miscellaneous Grievances?"

Inside the office, a clerk promised that someone higher up would call him, but she was very vague about when he would get this call. He tried to make her understand that if nothing was done within the next few days, those upstarts out on the field would expose the citizens of the county to the worst hazard since the last earthquake.

"Oh my," she said, "we mustn't let that happen. Are you some kind of rocket-scientist?"

"Well, no ma'am, I'm a career aviation journalist and I've been around this kind of technology for many years. I've been out to the Mojave Air and Space Port to report on taxi tests for the Stratolaunch Heavy-lift aircraft. "

"Oh, well, why didn't you say so? Just between you and me, I think that Rebel is the prettiest rocket ship that anybody ever built. I mean, you gotta say it's got the right stuff."

"Yes ma'am. It is very pretty." Keith somehow knew that explaining that the Rebel wasn't a rocket ship wouldn't help his cause. "It's my understanding that an aircraft must have an airworthiness decal before it can fly out of Norton Field."

"Well, that sounds about right to me," she said, "but the criteria for airworthiness for an individual aircraft type are listed on the aircraft type certificate. We can only determine the airworthiness for an individual airplane by checking its certificate." She thought for a moment. "It might be the other way around. You know, I've really never done one of these before."

Cautiously, Keith asked, "Did they file a certificate for the Rebel?"

"I don't know. If they did, they wouldn't file it with me. You know, come to think of it," she said. "I seem to recall if they fly VFR, that is Visual Flight Rules, they don't need to file a flight plan at all."

"You got to be kidding," objected Keith. "Nobody flies a hypersonic thing like the Rebel VFR."

"Well, I really don't know. Maybe you should go over to the airport and talk to those FAA people. Their office is right there near the control tower."

Before he left, he did get her name and what he thought was the direct phone number to her desk. He couldn't get, or she wouldn't give him, the official email address for that office.

When Keith found the FAA office, no one was there. As he looked around there were no aircraft taking off or landing. In fact, the whole airfield looked deserted. There was, however, a phone number and an email address for the local FAA posted behind the glass of the door, and the phone number to the county office he had just visited.

As the days passed, Keith found everyone he contacted to be very courteous and totally noncommittal. It became pretty obvious that all the bureaucrats liked the publicity the Rebel was giving San Bernardino. They really weren't much interested in what he had to say.

He was beginning to doubt the wisdom of telling the world that the Rebel was a movie prop. He was enjoying the Internet activity, but he also knew it was degrading his credibility.

He had made his best effort to warn the county of imminent danger; what more could he do? If he circumvented the county officials and went directly to the regional FAA, he knew the county would never talk to him again. The ten days were evaporating like steam.

Sandy was at her table in the open space at the *Herald*. She didn't yet have a desk. She was admiring her photo of the Rebel that was printed on the front page of the newspaper. It was her best photo of the Rebel, and it showed off all of its astonishing titanium splendor. She looked over at the row of private offices and wondered which one of the empty ones Ruthiebell would give her. Max had the best one, but he didn't have access to Titanium Composites like she did. She smiled. She was one lucky rookie.

"Why aren't you typing? Daydreaming is worthless if don't put it on paper." It was Max. He had startled her. She hadn't heard him come up from behind. "The Rebel is yours," he said, "I got no choice. But this is what I want you to do. I want you to work a UFO angle into the Rebel story. Have you ever heard of Nikola Tesla or Hermann Oberth?

"Tesla was the guy that invented alternating current. I never heard of Hermann Oberth. Why should I care? The Rebel is an 'identified' hypersonic aircraft. It's not a UFO, we know who built it."

"Both Tesla and Oberth are real historical people, and they both talk about UFOs. Oberth is the old man that taught von Braun how to build rockets back in Nazi Germany. Now listen, this is the angle I want you to take. First, read about Tesla and Oberth and you'll learn they both said they had help from 'beings from other worlds.' And of course those 'beings' came here in UFOs. So this is the angle. You need to educate our readers about Tesla and Oberth, and then hint that Hans-Peter must be getting some otherworldly help just like they did. Think about what you saw out there. There's no way some little titanium foundry out in San Bernardino could have the money to do something NASA couldn't even figure out."

"That's ridiculous," protested Sandy. "I never heard anything about Tesla talking about his friends from outer space. If I start writing about how little green men told Hans-Peter how to build his airplane, my career will go up in smoke."

"Look, it's not as far out as it sounds and I'll help you."

"But it's insulting. You want me to say Hans-Peter can't design his own airplane. I write stuff like that and they'll cut off my special access to the Rebel project even before it gets off the ground."

"You got a point there. We don't want to lose our access. I heard that Hans-Peter is only recognizing the five reporters that showed up at sunrise. Do you know who the other guys were?"

"I only met two of them. Traypart Artamus sat at my table for breakfast. He's 'old school' and a perfect gentleman."

"Yeah, yeah, yeah, I know the guy. Who else did you meet?"

"The other guy was Keith Wiley, and he's nuts. He thinks the Rebel is a prop for a movie.

Max smiled. "Yeah, I saw his post. He is nuts, but he's fun to read. He used to work for me until he went overboard one day. We relocated him out the front door. Now listen, I'm not being totally crazy here. What I want you to do is push the journalistic envelope. Just hint that Hans-Peter might be a running dog for a UFO full of aliens." They both laughed.

"That's even nuttier than what Keith Wiley is saying," she said. "Hans-Peter has been around for years. Everyone knows he's a leading expert for titanium and he has some very good people working for him; and as far as UFOs go, have you ever heard of Carl Jung and his interpretation of archetypal symbols?"

"The guys that talked about archetypal symbols all worked for Project Blue Book and they were boring as hell."

"You know, I came back here last night and I found Ruthiebell at my table looking at my screen."

"So you met the boss," said Max. "What'd she have to say?"

"That she had seen what Keith Wiley was posting about stopping the Rebel. She told me she wanted to find a way to discredit Keith, and help Hans-Peter. She wanted to use editorial journalism to help the Rebel test program get started and she didn't say one word about UFOs."

"Yeah, yeah, yeah, that's very interesting," said Max. "Have you ever read one of Ruthiebell's books?"

"No. I didn't know she wrote a book."

"Books. Ruthiebell has written several books. She cut her teeth investigating UFO sightings out in the Midwest, out among some of the big ranches."

"I thought she got started with some kind of a film about nuclear energy."

"Yeah, she did that too, but go look at her books. Ruthiebell is a credible journalist with many fine bylines. She took an MA from Berkeley in journalism. Take a closer look at Tesla and Oberth. Those guys were also very real. You might also look at how much money it takes to develop an airplane up from scratch. Do some background reading and we'll talk again soon."

"Before you go let me get this straight," she said. "You want me to say that the only way Hans-Peter could build the Rebel on his reasonably limited budget, was if he had some help from outer space aliens."

"Yes, but don't be too obvious, and put just a pinch of drama in your writing. When people pick up your copy, they won't be able to put it down. Tease them with just enough information to make them want to see your next article."

"Are the space aliens supposed to be green?"

"I don't know. Go read Ruthiebell's books, then you tell me; and another thing you're going to learn is that our boss, the very respectable editor of science and technology, is the godmother of the UFO subculture."

"I didn't know we had one."

"What? A subculture, or a godmother?" he asked with irritation.

"Either one or both, actually," she answered.

"Oh cut the crap. Everyone knows about UFOs." He tapped her photo that was on the front page. Look, you brought back one dynamite photo, but your writing is so flat and technical that when I read it, it puts me to sleep flat on the floor. You sound like that Traypart guy who writes for *Aviation Week*.

"Wait a minute Max. The *Herald Express* prints Traypart's stuff. He's one of us."

"They only put his editorials in the Sunday paper. He's not a reporter like you and me. We're not writing for a bunch of specialists, we're writing for the man on the street and all those brain dead millennials. They want to be entertained and so do I. I like to be entertained. So this is what I want you to do. You go look up Nikola Tesla and Hermann Oberth and get one of Ruthiebell's books. I don't care which one, but I want you to do it today. Then we'll talk about it tomorrow."

"But Ruthiebell wants me to find a way to discredit Keith Wiley."

"No problem. Work that into the story too."

Three days later and realizing he was getting nowhere and losing time, Keith went directly to the regional office of the FAA. The Federal Aviation Administration was very professional and gave him an appointment the day after the maiden flight was scheduled. When he told them their calendar was exposing innocent people to an avoidable disaster and therefore they would be on record for willful negligence, they transferred him to Claudius Thud, the Supervising Regional Manager, who listened carefully to his story. Mr. Thud wouldn't comment on anything Keith said about the county's possible negligence, but he did say that safety was always a reasonable and timely concern. Mr. Thud went on to assure him that he would look into the matter himself and give him a call the day before the maiden flight.

Seriously doubting the government would actually do anything, Keith thanked Mr. Thud for looking into the matter, and started to plan to be out there at sunrise. He knew that whatever happened, it would be a big story.

Out on the high desert, a couple of days later, Major Hayes had just finished reading a letter from the FAA informing him that his A-10s had been filmed flying too low over Norton Field. It was lunchtime and the major walked over to the mess tent. The mess tent was large and there was a wide-open space separating the officers from the enlisted personnel. The officers had about a quarter of the space and the enlisted personnel were given the rest. Major Hayes sat with his officers at a long table. His pilots were all lieutenants and both his Medical Officer and his Aircraft Maintenance Officer were captains.

Speaking to the major, the Medical Officer said, "When I picked up my mail this morning, did I see a letter from the FAA?"

Major Hayes groaned under his breath, "Yes. They reviewed some of the film the reporters shot of our recent recon drill over Norton and decided we were flying too low."

"Did they file a formal complaint?" asked the other captain.

"No. The FAA examiner, somebody named Claudius Thud, wanted to encourage us to keep our A-10s a little closer to the regulation airspace."

"That was it?"

"No, he went on to sign the letter wishing the personnel of Cactus Patch every success in achieving their objectives."

"I didn't think anybody outside this place knew we called it Cactus Patch," said Lieutenant Collins.

"Neither did I," said the major.

"Sounds like we have a friend over at the FAA," said the Medical Officer.

"Well, hopefully. I've never heard of this guy. The name Thud is new to me. Let's not take anything for granted." The major then looked down the long table making eye contact with several of his pilots. "So we all need to pay closer attention to the regulations."

The men at the table ate quietly for a few minutes and then Hank Potash raised his hand toward the major. The major acknowledged him with a nod. "Does that mean our next flyby is canceled?"

"No," said the major thoughtfully. "This will give us a chance to flyby the field while observing all the regulations. We'll show them we can do it with total compliance. This time the trick will be to get there just when the new airplane is taking off. I'd like you to be just a couple of hundred yards behind that new bird when it takes to the air. That will give us some recon worth having. "

"Do we know their exact takeoff time?" asked Collins.

"Not exactly," said the major. "They said it would be a sunrise takeoff, but if I know Hans-Peter, he'll open the doors to the hangar at sunrise. We know the time for tomorrow's sunrise, but we can only guess how long it will take them to get from the hangar to the runway."

"So we need to be there just after sunrise," said Lieutenant Collins. "So if they're delayed we can fly a big circle until they're ready to takeoff."

"Yes, exactly," said the major. "However, San Bernardino is a rather complicated airspace. What are the two biggest obstacles you face if you want to circle Norton Field?"

"At the lower altitudes we must pay attention to the final approach to Ontario Airport. Ontario is not that far west of San Bernardino; planes on that final approach are pretty low," answered Collins. "And with several scheduled airlines flying in and out of there, the place can be pretty busy."

"Yes," said the major. "That's the most pressing concern." The major then focused his attention on Hank. "And what's the less pressing concern?"

"I would say the big commercial aircraft locked into their approach to LAX. They're quite a bit higher, but with an A-10 we can climb up there pretty fast."

Another pilot who hadn't said a word raised a hand toward the major.

"Raymo," said the major with a smile. "Has your careful analytic mind spotted something we have missed?"

"Yes sir, if I may." Raymo's voice was clear, but very cautious. "If you get there early, and need to kill some time, the only real option is to circle to the north, but you must remember the mountains. Most of the range goes up to 6,000 feet and several of the peaks are quite a bit higher."

"Good point, Ray. Do you feel any apprehension about flying this sortie tomorrow?"

"No sir. I've been looking forward to it, but I think we should fly the mission with at least minimum ordnance. We don't need ordnance on the wings, but I think we should have a full load of ammunition."

"I don't see why, lieutenant, we are not in a war zone. In fact we're pushing the regulations by flying down and taking a close look."

"Our world isn't as peaceful as it used to be. What if some enemy comes by and tries to destroy that new airplane? If I don't have any bullets, there's nothing I can do," said Raymo showing concern.

The major considered Raymo's question for a moment. "9-11 changed our world, no question about it; and I trust you guys, but if no one is carrying ordnance then there can't be an ordnance accident. So that's my decision for tomorrow's sortie. No ordnance." Then the major considered Lieutenant Raymo. "Is the old RAINDROP up for a recon sortie?"

"Yes sir. I've committed the maps to memory," answered Raymo. "If we fly a holding pattern, Lake Arrowhead will be our northern landmark."

"Well, actually Lake Arrowhead will be your northern landmark. I've been asked to fly down to the March Airfield with one other A-10 that day. Martinelli and I will leave at about Zero Six Hundred Hours, and they told me to plan and stay for two days. So for the Norton flyby there'll be just three planes; you and Potash, and I'm putting Collins in my place. Now, keep in mind that the only thing we know for sure is that they will be taking off to the west. That will put the sun to their back and make it easier for you to follow them off the runway."

"And then we'll turn with them and follow them up the Cajon Pass?" asked Raymo.

"That's what I'd like you to do," said the major, "but remember that thing looks a whole lot faster than anything we can do."

"With all due respect," said the Captain of Maintenance, "that's a bit of an understatement. A-10s are tactical and subsonic. That chunk of polished titanium is supposed to be hypersonic." The captain's remark was taken with some humor.

"Oh, golly," answered the major. "Are you telling me if they turn up the wick on that thing, we won't be able to keep up?"

"Yes sir, that is my considered opinion." The captain's voice conveyed the humorous absurdity of the comparison. Everyone laughed.

After finishing a short piece for a Canadian magazine I took a look at Keith Wiley's web site. Just as I thought, he was still hammering away at the County of San Bernardino for letting the unproven Rebel make a maiden flight over a populated area. I thought his absences of criticism of the FAA was rather conspicuous; but then Keith's a crafty guy. He knows which bridges not to burn. Unfortunately, his objection was reasonable. Fortunately, I knew the Senior Flight Controller for Norton Field. She is Ms. Eleanor Scribble. I gave her a call.

"Hello, Traypart," she answered. "I knew you'd call me after you learned about the Rebel. It's been awhile. I enjoyed your post for the Rebel."

"You don't miss much."

Eleanor laughed. "Oh, come on. You know there's not much going on out here. Let me guess. You want to know if Keith asked me to stop the Rebel's maiden flight. You know generally, we don't approve or cancel flight plans, we just file them; and if they're flying VFR, they don't even need to file one."

"It's good to hear your voice again, Eleanor, and as usual you've cut right to the heart of the matter. Did Keith make that call?"

"He did, but since Hans hadn't filed a flight plan yet, we had nothing to talk about. I tried to be wonderfully polite and totally noncommittal."

Imagining the conversation made me smile. "Do you have the authority to stop the flight?"

"Yes, I do," she answered thoughtfully, "but I need sufficient grounds. Hans-Peter has a very exciting new airplane, but Keith Wiley has a very reasonable objection."

"May I ask what you're planning to do?"

"Not really my friend," she said, "but I've talked briefly with my boss in LA. He said Keith came to his office with a formal complaint. When Hans gives me his flight plan, we will have the right answer for him."

"Are you going to let him fly?"

"That's not for me to say at this time. So why are you so scarce? Next time you're out here, let's do lunch."

In the early evening the day before the Rebel would attempt its maiden flight, and several hours after Keith had decided he wouldn't be hearing from the FAA, Claudius Thud gave him a call. "Hello. I am calling for Mr. Wiley. Is he available?"

"Yes. This is Keith Wiley speaking."

"Good evening, Mr. Wiley. This is Claudius Thud calling from the FAA. I apologize for calling after business hours. I was unable to call earlier. Do you have time now for a brief conversation?"

"Yes, of course, Mr. Thud, it is good to hear from you. I've been hoping you'd give me a call today. Did the FAA make a determination on the Rebel's proposed first test flight?"

"We have determined that your concern is well-founded and establishes legitimate grounds to bar the Rebel from making its planned flight."

"So Hans-Peter finally filed a flight plan?" asked Keith.

"Yes," answered Claudius. "He filed yesterday afternoon. There was not enough time today to contact Titanium Composites, but I was able to talk to the senior flight controller for Norton Field. Her name is Eleanor Scribble, and she understands the need to cancel the planned flight. She said she wanted to review the Rebel's flight plan tonight and be out on the field tomorrow at sunrise to stop Hans-Peter. I am planning to drive out tomorrow morning with a Federal Marshal and assist Ms. Scribble in blocking the flight. The marshal and I will be out there before sunrise. I know that you are one of only five journalists that were invited back inside the gates for the maiden flight. Were you planning to drive out tomorrow for the event?"

"Yes, of course, but now you're telling me nothing is going to happen."

"Not exactly, I've only said that the flight plan they have filed has been cancelled."

"So you're saying they can still fire up the engines and give it a taxi test and even speed it down the runway."

"Yes, and it would be in their best interest to show off at least that much of their plane's capability. As you have said, no one has yet seen their plane taxi under its own power. When the marshal and I meet Hans-Peter, I'd like you to be there. Your thoughts initiated the rejection of their planned flight; I would like you to be present when we discuss the possible alternatives. Ultimately, I would like to help Titanium Composites accomplish their objectives, and your insights may prove helpful."

"Thank you, sir. If you would like me to be there, then I will drive out. Are you planning to encourage Hans-Peter to demonstrate a powered taxi roll? You know if you can get him to do that, I'm sure I could get some great video."

"That's one of several options I will discuss with Hans-Peter, but I would like to meet you inside the gate before I meet him. I don't want tomorrow to be a total loss for anyone."

Mr. Claudius Thud, as before, was very pleasant in saying goodbye.

Sandy Koop had called Titanium Composites on behalf of the *Herald Express* and got permission to bring out two photographers.

She had taken the time to look up Ruthiebell on the Internet and was intrigued to find that she had been trying to make some sense of the UFO phenomena for the past thirty years. Sandy also learned that Ruthiebell had taken a masters degree from UC Berkeley in journalism just like Max had said.

The night before the first flight, I had slept fitfully and was glad to be up and out of bed. It was now three-thirty a.m. I peeked out the window between the blinds and saw the full weight of night still covering the landscape. At this time of day I knew I could get to Titanium Composites in only an hour or possibly a little less. I had planned to leave as soon as possible and have breakfast in San Bernardino at a place I knew near the gate.

California freeways are very safe and fast when you are sharing them with just a few other people. By my watch, I was at the coffee shop in forty-eight minutes. This was fine; the drive had given me enough appetite to enjoy a steak and eggs. I wondered how many people were making their way out to the Santa Ana Wash to watch the Rebel take off. Each one of them, I reasoned, would eventually learn that Keith Wiley had caused the flight to be cancelled. Today he was making more enemies than he could count. I wondered if things like this were happening on other planets out in space.

In the predawn darkness, the personnel at Cactus Patch had the three A-10s for Potash, Woodburn and Collins pulled forward of their large Quonset hut hangars. SMOKY, RAINDROP and CALLBIT were near the A-10s with the captain of aircraft maintenance. The ground crew was standing by. The captain was the most senior officer present and he was keeping an eye on the time. He had determined to fire up the aircraft and start the sortie fourteen minutes before the sun broke the horizon. "Mount-up gentlemen, the time is near."

My breakfast had been very good, in fact better than I expected. Outside the night was starting to lighten. It was time to go. I realized I should have asked Eleanor to meet me here for breakfast. A missed opportunity, but if this place had made a lousy breakfast, that wouldn't be any good either.

Once through the gate, I spotted Keith Wiley parked about forty feet away and standing by his car.

"Hey Traypart, good to see you. Did you hear I got the maiden flight of that big movie prop stopped? But even so I think the FAA is going to let them taxi it today anyway."

"So you decided it is a real airplane," I said.

"I've decided it's the best movie prop that's ever been built; and it may even be able to fly, but you can bet it'll never go supersonic."

A big unmarked government car came through the gate. The man driving looked like a Federal Marshal. The car pulled up next to us and Mr. Thud lowered his window. Keith walked over and spoke to him. Mr. Thud told him to follow his car to where they would park near the hangar. When they drove over, I followed. As we parked, a personnel door to the hangar opened.

Hans-Peter and his pilot came out to meet us. They were both wearing pressure suits and looked ready to fly the Rebel. "You're Claudius Thud of the FAA," said Hans-Peter, "and ten minutes ago Eleanor told me you've cancelled my flight?"

An open jeep from the control tower pulled up. Eleanor Scribble got out carrying what looked like several maps. "Hello, Claudius, I see you brought along your strong right arm from the Marshal's Office."

The Marshal was carrying a pair of binoculars and recognized Eleanor with a polite nod. His weapon, a 357 magnum, was out of sight.

She looked at Hans-Peter. "Can we step inside?"

Inside! After being prevented from photographing through the hangar doors ten days ago, at the rollout, I was actually being invited inside. Ruthiebell wanted me to snoop around for a rocket engine and now I had the chance. Hans-Peter held the door open for Ms. Scribble and invited all of us in.

I followed them inside. Not far from the door was a large table. The woman spread out her maps and then opened her folder and put the three-page flight plan for the Rebel on top of the maps. "This is the flight plan that was filed," she said. "It is correctly written and I filed it." She looked at Claudius. "Is there anything wrong with this proposed flight?"

"Yes," answered Claudius. "Mr. Wiley here has pointed out that it is unreasonable to fly an unproven prototype aircraft over a populated area, and the FAA is in total agreement."

"Okay," said Eleanor, "but that's only the case for a westward takeoff. Look here. She pointed to her map. If they take off east, they'll be mostly over the Santa Ana Wash and that land is empty for several miles. If they go down out there, they'll only be hitting rocks and sand."

"I've also been looking at those maps," said Claudius, "and I agree." Claudius now focused his attention on Hans-Peter and his pilot. "At this time in the morning do you think you can take off directly into the rising sun? Can you handle an easterly takeoff or would you like to wait an hour or two?"

I was amazed. Claudius and Eleanor seemed to have worked out an alternative. Good thing I brought my equipment.

"The sun is no problem," said the pilot. "I've flown other aircraft out of here going east at sunrise. It's a piece of cake."

"You want us to take off east and then as we turn south-east to avoid the mountains, you probably want us to stay north of Interstate 10 as we gain altitude," said Hans-Peter as he fixed an inquiring stare at Mr. Thud.

"Yes, and I'd like you to stay at least a mile north of Interstate 10 at all times."

"No problem," said the pilot. "There's at least three or four miles between Interstate 10 and the mountains."

Mr. Thud opened his own folder. "Well, of course you'll need another flight plan." He took out a new flight plan. "Eleanor faxed a copy of your original flight plan to me, and I've written up a new plan that I can approve." Claudius looked at the pilot. "What I can approve is an eastern takeoff and then a long turn out over the high desert. The flight plan I've written up for you will keep you at least twenty miles north of the approaches to both Ontario and LAX. I would like you to fly out over

Joshua Tree and then turn due east. When you reach 24K of altitude, you can then go through your 'performance testing' checklist. When you return, I'd like you to come back over the same course. That will mean you'll come in over the Santa Ana Wash again and land going west. Would that in any way be a problem for you?"

"No, sir. I would enjoy flying that course." The pilot looked very carefully at the document, then he spoke to Eleanor. "If I sign this thing will you sign it off?"

She returned his inquiring look with, "Well, sign it and see what happens." The pilot signed and dated it; then she signed it off. She looked at Claudius, "Will you initial each page and date it?"

"Yes, ma-am."

Two of the men from within the hangar came over and one of them said, "The sun just broke the horizon, shall we open the doors?"

In a subtle way, I tried to look back into the hangar, but the lights were off in the back and many things were cover with tarpaulins. We were leaving and I had seen nothing unusual except all those tarps covering, or were they hiding things. Why was Hans-Peter covering things up inside his hangar?

As the doors opened, Claudius left with Eleanor. It was clear he was going to watch from the tower. The marshal left the big car parked by the hangar and rode out with me to the runway. The rising sun had burned off the darkness and as we drove, we could see a significant crowd south of the field along the Santa Ana Wash. There were literally hundreds of cameras set up and trained on the runway.

Inside the fence, I saw that Sandy had taken the very best spot with her photographers from the newspaper. They were not far off the runway.

Back inside the hangar, two others dressed in pressure suits climbed aboard the Rebel before Hans-Peter and his pilot reached the aircraft.

Later on I would learn that the fourth place in the Rebel's cockpit was for an observer, and Hans-Peter had given it to a friend.

The hatch was closed and the tow tractor began to pull the Rebel out into the cool morning air.

Chapter Three
With Everyone Watching

The morning was cold by California standards and the air was crystal clear. I had parked, as close to the runway as I thought would be safe. The Federal Marshal and I were outside leaning against my car. I had a good camera and he had a good pair of binoculars. From our vantage point, I could see the large crowd that had gathered along the dirt road on the south side of the runway.

As the plane rolled out, the crowd began to cheer. I looked up at the tower to see if I could spot Claudius and Eleanor. I couldn't. Through my telephoto lens, I tried to look past the airplane and photograph the inside of the hangar. My best effort yielded nothing more than spotting the large objects covered with tarpaulins that I had seen when inside. The ground crew closed the hangar doors as soon as their aircraft was completely outside.

The sleek new airplane was pulled away from the hangar and turned so its jet exhaust was pointed away from the building. The tractor pulling the Rebel was disconnected and the two men that had walked out near the main landing gear ran over and hopped onboard. The Rebel was left parked alone as the tractor with its long pull bar vanished around the side of the building.

The crowd along the road fell silent. Light from the rising sun danced along the Rebel's shadowy titanium skin. It sat motionless. It hadn't been painted 'iron ball' black like an SR-71. Its titanium skin, buffed out smoother than silk, was all bare metal. Titanium doesn't have a mirror shine like chromium-plated metal. The buffed skin reflected the rising sun with several hues of deep gray. In the cool morning air, the profile of this aggressive bird redefined what was possible. It was truly built to challenge the hypersonic frontier.

Nothing happened for the longest seven minutes I can remember, and then, simultaneously, the two outboard engines noisily fired and began to spin up. The crowd cheered again and began to wave.

I couldn't help but yell out, "Yes! Fly that thing!"

With the two outboard engines heating up smoothly, the two inboard engines fired up.

High overhead and coming out of the east, we heard the noise of three A-10s. In just a minute or less they flew high over the runway and turned north toward the mountains. Their appearance didn't look like a coincidence to me.

Back on the ground, brakes were released and the Rebel began to roll forward. Then I saw it! Today Hans-Peter was revealing yet another one of his secrets. As the Rebel moved toward the taxiway, I could see that the tail cone of the fuselage, which we saw just ten days ago, was missing. Where the tail cone had been, there was a nozzle protruding out a few inches and it was the same size as the jet nozzles tucked into its wings. I couldn't tell if it was another turbojet engine or perhaps the exhaust nozzle of a ramjet.

If it were a ramjet, I would have guessed it would have been rectangular and not round like a turbojet. You probably recall NASA's unmanned hypersonic X-43. Its engine was a supersonic ramjet, or what they call a scramjet, and its top speed was recorded at just over 7,300 mph or about Mach 9.6. The scramjet powered X-43 holds the world speed record for a breathing engine and it was rectangular and not round. Whatever Hans-Peter had built, it had to be something special to power this new aircraft up into the hypersonic velocities.

Reaching the taxiway, the Rebel turned west and headed for the west end of the runway. As it taxied west, I could see the A-10s off in the distance flying to where I thought Lake Arrowhead was. They pulled a long fast turn and then came screaming back down heading for the Field.

"Hey there CALLBIT, that shiny airplane is going the wrong way," radioed Lieutenant Hank Potash.

"Affirmative, SMOKY. That for sure westerly takeoff looks like it got turned around," answered Lieutenant Collins. "What do you think RAINDROP?"

"Taking of to the east puts them over open ground. It keeps the test flight away from the population. My money says they'll take off east," answered Raymo Woodburn.

"Got it," said Collins. "We'll finish out our turn over that freeway interchange and chase the Rebel into the sun."

At the west end of the runway, the Rebel turned without stopping and spun up to full power. The four engines roared, showing off their lack of any kind of sound suppression. The Rebel hadn't been designed to drop in and out of commuter airports. It was not very civilized, at least not at takeoff.

The sleek titanium beast accelerated much faster than I expected. The noise shook the crowd, and they loved it. At mid runway the Rebel was airborne, clawing into the sky more like a fighter than a plane of its large size. It climbed steadily over the Santa Ana then it turned southeast toward Oak Glen. The rising sun created photography problems for everyone, but there was now no question that the Rebel could fly and fly well.

Then from out of the west and no more than 150 feet off the ground, came the three A-10s burning up the cool air as fast as they could. They aligned with the Rebel's course and were trying hard to catch her. I was impressed by how well they held their formation as they flew over.

The crowd went nuts cheering for the A-10s as the gutsy little tactical aircraft scrabbled after the Rebel. It was a great show, but in just one minute, the Rebel and her escorts were disappearing into the rising sun.

The marshal had put down his binoculars and was watching me. When I stepped back from my camera, he said, "There's nothing more to see. Let's go up to the tower and listen in to what they're getting over their radio."

I drove over a little faster than I should have and then we climbed the stairs as quickly as we could. There was a sheriff's deputy blocking the door. The marshal whipped out his badge and we were admitted.

"You didn't lose any time getting here," said Eleanor.

"Well of course not," I answered. "How well can you hear the Rebel?"

"We're getting the full telemetry stream they're sending back to their own people," she said with a hint of pride. "And look here, we've got their flight instruments on this screen in real time, and overhead we can hear their chatter. You should sit over here near the screen. I'm expecting some first class writing from you about all this."

She let me sit down at the best place I could ask for. Immediately I realized that a camera in the cockpit was displaying the four crewmembers and their activities. I knew Hans-Peter and the pilot, but I hadn't seen the other two on the ground. I got the impression one of them was a woman. They were all wearing pressure suits and helmets, which made it pretty hard to tell who was who.

Over the speakers we heard Hans-Peter. "San Bernardino, this is the Rebel, do you copy?"

"We copy," answered Claudius who was sitting at the controller's station. "We also have a patch into your telemetry. Would you confirm your data? We read your speed at 382 knots and accelerating, your heading is 135 degrees south-east and your rate of climb is at 2,200 feet per minute."

"Roger that San Bernardino, 390 knots, 135 degrees, and a climb rate of 2,200 feet per minute are the numbers our instruments are now showing."

Claudius called back to the Rebel. "Your rate of climb is slower than I was expecting. Is there a problem?"

"No. There is no problem. Now that we're airborne, I'm holding the turbo machinery at 2/3 power. I'm comparing our real flight data with the performance we calculated when we designed it."

"Is your bird doing what you predicted?"

"Yes, it looks very close. We are now over Oak Glen and starting our turn to 90 degrees due east. I believe we are consistent with our flight plan. There are no anomalies; however, I see something on my aft-looking radar. Are we being followed?"

"Affirmative Rebel. Three A-10s came over Norton Field shortly after you took off. Your course is correct, and they are shadowing you. Do they present a problem or a distraction in any way?"

"No, San Bernardino. They are more than welcome to come along. Let them know we like their company."

"I can see a crew of four," I said to both Eleanor and Claudius. "I presume that would be the pilot and copilot up front, and an engineering station behind the copilot. That must be where Hans-Peter is, as both flight engineer and flight commander. Is that fourth seat for an observer?"

"Yes, they're carrying an observer," answered Eleanor. "The observer's name is Cathy Bear. She is a Forest Ranger who has worked here in the San Bernardino Mountains for many years. She's an aerospace enthusiast and has requested more than one tour of Titanium Composites. She's very bright and rather old school. Hans-Peter liked her and knew she would be ideal for the safety PR that he would need to counter the kinds of problems that Keith Wiley was bound to create."

"Hans-Peter must have had tremendous confidence in his airplane if he was willing to take a passenger on the maiden flight," I answered.

"He had enough confidence in the Rebel to go up in it himself," replied Eleanor rather flatly. "I'm sure Cathy understood the risks. She probably thought if he was willing to go up, so was she."

San Gorgonio stands 11,503 feet in altitude and its snowcap is breathtaking at sunrise. The mountain dominates the landscape. As they flew east the summit stood above them. Their flight plan didn't call for flying over the mountain, but rather around it. When they passed the mountain they kept climbing steadily at 2,200 feet per minute.

Now beyond San Gorgonio they headed north-northeast over the Big Morongo Canyon. They were climbing steadily and looking for the Joshua Tree landmark.

Sandy and her two photographers were still with their big van by the runway. The photographers were sending their videos back to the newspaper. No doubt, Ruthiebell was the first to review them. Two women from Titanium Composites had come over in a jeep with coffee and breakfast burritos, and a special frequency radio. All five of them were listening to the chatter from the Rebel. The burritos were great, scrambled eggs, chorizo, a little rice and a few white beans. I know what they were because they sent some up to the control tower and I had one.

Down on the field, Keith Wiley walked over to Sandy's van carrying his camera still attached to its tripod over his shoulder. "Man, I was down wind of you people and I could smell food. You folks got some extra?" There was plenty and Keith was given a burrito.

Sandy recognized him. "So you still calling the Rebel a movie prop?"

"The best! It's absolutely the best prop ever built."

Two women from the company grimaced a bit and considered pouring the coffee over his head.

"Get real Keith!" said Sandy. " There was nothing pale or wimpish about the sound of those jet engines. That thing took off like it owned the sky."

"Yes. It took off very nicely, I'll give you that," said Keith, "but that's nowhere near supersonic. They won't even try for the sound barrier for at least six months. That will give them time to explain why their four little jet engines can't do it, and they'll probably make up some other reasons as well. You mark my words. That thing is nothing more than a movie prop."

One of the company women held up her hand to quiet Keith. Then they all listened to the radio. "Greetings A-10s, this is the Rebel aircraft, do you copy?"

"Loud and clear, Rebel. This is Lieutenant Collins flying lead. We heard you tell San Bernardino you liked our company. You're looking very fine, but a bit slower than we were expecting; and at some point I would guess that you're going to climb a little faster than you are now."

"What'd I tell ya!" blurted Keith to Sandy and the others. Sandy's group was listening to every word over their special radio. The two women from the company waved him down again to be quiet.

"Try to stay with us lieutenant," answered Hans-Peter, "we're just warming this thing up. Are there three of you?"

"That's affirmative, Rebel. We are three."

"What can you tell me about the color around the exhaust nozzles? Do they all look about the same?"

"Yes, that's affirmative, Rebel," replied the lieutenant. "There is no color on the nozzles. The exhaust plumes for the four wing engines all look the same, but your central engine looks cold."

"That's correct lieutenant. The central engine has not yet been lit."

"We A-10 guys heard you won't see any color on those nozzles till you go a lot faster. In fact we heard you won't see any color until you go at least Mach 2."

"Not quite. The fire inside a jet engine is enough to make the nozzle glow even in a ground test. But on the other hand, skin heating doesn't start until about Mach 2.2 or so. Today we won't be going that fast," answered Hans-Peter. "We're now making our turn to Joshua Tree and heading due east. Please tag along if you can."

"Happy to tag along Rebel. So far keeping up with you is no problem. Are you sure that thing can go supersonic?"

"Yes lieutenant, I'm quite sure. You know I worked on the A-10 about twenty-five years ago. Back then we were looking at the possibility of reconnaissance pods for the ordnance rails. Are you guys carrying recon pods?"

"That's affirmative, Rebel. Today's flight is a recon drill. We are all carrying reconnaissance equipment."

"I know you can see the ground. How well can you see us?"

"No problem Rebel. I'm tracking you as we speak."

"That's great! When we get home I'd like to see your images."

"You'll need to talk to the commanding officer. To see our photos, you'll probably need to show him a 'need to know'."

"But you're filming my airplane and I'm in it!"

"Sir, I don't make the rules."

The pilot of the Rebel spoke to Hans-Peter. "This thing feels great. It's more responsive than I thought it would be. How do your gauges look?"

"Perfect. So far we're meeting all the criteria for a rocket burn. I think we can do it. I'm starting the pressurizing sequence for the LOX and the fuel right now. If the tanks pressurize correctly, then we'll fire the rocket as planned for a short burn when we get to 36,000 feet."

"Very good," answered the pilot. "I'm ready when you are."

I knew it. Back down in the control tower we all heard those words. That center nozzle was round because it's a rocket and not a ramjet. I knew Hans-Peter hadn't shown his full hand.

"A rocket?" said Eleanor. "He's talking about a rocket burn. Claudius, did you put a rocket engine burn in the flight plan you wrote up for him?"

"No, I didn't. Did you see a rocket test burn in the flight plan Hans-Peter filed with you?"

"I don't remember anything about a rocket burn," said Eleanor defensively, "but there was some vague wording about 'performance testing' at 36,000 feet. We just heard him say he was going to fire the rocket at 36K if his tanks pressurize correctly. If he lights off a rocket engine, will he be in violation of his flight plan?"

"I also saw the 'performance testing' words. In fact I put them in the flight plan I wrote, but I didn't write anything about a rocket. I thought he was talking about the performance of his airplane. I had no idea he was talking about a rocket. I hope to God he's not carrying a tank of liquid oxygen."

"We heard him say he was pressurizing his LOX tank,' said Eleanor. "LOX is liquid oxygen, what else would he be carrying."

"He could be carrying nitrogen-tet."

"That's not any safer. It's very toxic and nasty in other ways."

"But at least it's not cryogenic," replied Claudius.

"If the rocket's built into the airplane," she said, "then he's testing his airplane's performance. Right?"

"Of course it's built into the airplane," said Claudius, "but he didn't say the word rocket anywhere in his flight plan. If he had, I would have remembered it."

"So if he lights it, is he in violation?" pressed Eleanor.

Claudius was slow to answer. "No. If he lights it, and I hope it doesn't blow himself to smithereens, we'll call it 36K 'performance testing'."

Flying due east and rapidly leaving the California airspace, the Rebel took a transmission. "Rebel aircraft, this is Lieutenant Collins. The A-10 group has turned due east with you, may I ask about that central engine?"

"Our central engine is a rocket," said Hans-Peter. "You're looking at the nozzle of a liquid rocket engine."

"Very good. I thought I overheard that. Does that mean your jet engines were never meant to push you through the sound barrier?"

"That's correct lieutenant. The jet engines are meant to get our full mass off the ground and up to an altitude of about forty thousand feet. Think of them as taking the place of the huge launch gantry they built for the Space Shuttle."

"Rebel, those jets can also be used to move you from place to place in between tests. So you don't need to ride on the back of a 747."

"Yes, exactly," said Hans-Peter. "That's good observation, may I ask your name?"

"Yes sir. My name is Raymo Woodburn and my callsign is RAINDROP."

"Good to meet you RAINDROP. Listen up A-10s; when we reach 36K, we are planning two short test burns. Would you care to take up an escort pattern and give those recon pods a workout?"

"No problem Rebel. We're here to gather data. What pattern would you like?"

"Let one aircraft take a position off each of our wingtips. Please fly 100 feet off, thirty feet high and about even with our nose. I'd like to be able to see the two planes. I'd like the third plane to take a position about 200 feet aft. Please align with our fuselage, but get about 100 feet higher than we are. I don't want the third man to be in line with our rocket blast."

"Rebel, this is SMOKY off your starboard. Is this where you want me?"

"You're looking SMOKY. Please hold that position."

"Rebel, this is RAINDROP, I'm off your portside."

"Looking good lieutenant. Please hold that position. Lieutenant Collins, do you copy?"

"Affirmative Rebel. This is COLLBIT. I'm on your centerline, 100 feet high and 200 feet aft. I'm also reading an altitude of 29 thousand. Are you still 'go' to light your rocket at 36K?"

"Yes, CALLBIT, that's the plan. Is CALLBIT the callsign for Lieutenant Collins?"

"Yes, Rebel. CALLBIT's my callsign. How long until rocket ignition?"

"A-10 group, I'm pressurizing the rocket tanks as we speak. I will fire in just a few minutes."

"Rebel, this is RAINDROP. May I ask what your rocket will burn?"

"Today we're burning JP-4 and LOX, that is the same jet fuel the turbos are burning and liquid oxygen. That's a good question lieutenant. Have you read about rocket engines?"

"Yes sir, I have; and if my memory is any good JP-4 and LOX are not the most energetic propellants around."

"That's true lieutenant, but they're fairly easy to handle. Are you familiar with specific impulse?"

"Yes sir, I am."

The copilot's voice was heard next. "We just crossed 30,700 feet and mark our flight time 7 minutes and 20 seconds."

"So how much specific impulse do you think we'll get out of JP-4 and LOX?"

"Oh, I don't know, at 36K maybe 290 seconds," answered Woodburn.

"That's a very good guess. I hope to get about 284 seconds at that altitude."

"We're crossing 31,800 feet and climbing," said the copilot.

"Stand by A-10s. The tank pressurization looks good. I'm releasing the safety stops. The ignition buildup is only 4 seconds long, then I will hold at a constant minimum thrust."

"What angle do you want?" asked the pilot."

"Let the rate of climb go to 10,400 feet per minute. Remember the first burn is only 20 seconds long. At the end of that burn, we want to be at 40K. Bring the jet engines up to full power, now!" said Hans-Peter.

"Understood," said the pilot, "and the jets are coming up to 100%."

"We just crossed 34K," said the copilot, "and the speed is increasing."

Back down in the control tower, Claudius broke the intense silence. "Oh my God he's going to light a rocket on his first flight in an unproven airplane."

"His flight time is at 11 minutes even," said Eleanor with total cool. "Let us mark the rocket ignition time."

Hans-Peter uncovered his ignition switch. "Okay, here we go. I will light in 18 seconds, 16 seconds, 14, 12. 8 seconds, 6 seconds, 5, 4, 3, 2, Fire. I show ignition. We have fire and 1, 2, 3, 4, and now minimum thrust"

"Very smooth," said the pilot. "No boot in the butt. How much thrust do you see?"

"100,000 pounds, just as planned."

"You've got fire in your rocket nozzle, Rebel. This is the following A-10. You're flying away from us. We can't keep up."

"Thank you A-10. Combustion is confirmed. We can feel the rocket. What does the flame look like?"

"It's beautiful; almost clear. I can see a little red and in other places a little blue, but it's very clean. I can also see three very distinct Mach diamonds."

"That's great! Did you get it on film?"

"I don't know, Rebel; I'm trying as we speak."

"The copilot reported, "We just passed 500 knots and we are

accelerating. We're probably over Arizona. I think we lost our friendly A-10s."

"Affirmative Rebel. The A-10 group is on your course, but you're flying away from us very fast. In fact, I feel like we just stopped."

"We just went supersonic," reported the copilot.

"Okay, we're holding at the planned test thrust. The rocket looks good." Hans-Peter said nothing for a few seconds. "That's it; the first burn is now over."

"Our speed maxed at 608 knots. Read that as Mach 1.060," called the copilot.

"My systems are all still 'GO,'" said Hans-Peter. "I'm initiating the second burn now."

"What angle do you want?" replied the pilot."

"As you feel the power, take what it will give you, but don't let it stall."

"Understood."

"We're now climbing fast," said the copilot. "We just crossed 42K."

"A-10 group, this is the Rebel. Do you copy?"

"We copy Rebel, but not clearly. Your rocket engine is creating a lot of radio static. We can no longer see the rebel. We can only see your rocket flame. Rebel, do you copy?"

The static became more intense. CALLBIT said nothing more as the rocket engine burned.

"CALLBIT this is RAINDROP. Their rocket will burn out in less than a minute."

When the radio went clear they heard, "A-10s this is Rebel we have flameout. That's it, no more power. You should be able to hear us now. We are coasting straight up. Can you still see us?"

"That's a negative Rebel, but my recon pod is still tracking you."

"A-10s, our radio link is very good. We will coast up another three miles and then start to fall back home."

"Congratulations Rebel. I don't know of another maiden flight that ever broke the sound barrier. We need to head for home. Best of luck for your safe return and landing. This is Lieutenant Collins, A-10 group out."

The telemetry coming back to the airfield from the Rebel was excellent. Everyone at Titanium Composites was listening and so were many other people who had the right kind of radios. "Well, they just admitted they went supersonic," announced Eleanor. "They didn't put that in their flight plan, either."

"Thank God their rocket worked correctly," said Claudius. "And yes, we know about their speed from our tracking system. I'm showing their max speed at 868 knots, or you can make that a supersonic 998-Miles Per Hour. At their altitude the speed of sound is 658.9 MPH; so we'll record that as Mach 1.514, and that's supersonic without question."

Inside the Rebel, the passenger spoke to Hans-Peter and the crew. "I feel weightless. Is that possible?"

"Yes Cathy, right now we are all weightless," said Hans-Peter. "We'll be weightless as long as we coast up and as long we are in free fall. We've had good constant air pressure since we took off. I'm lifting the faceplate on my helmet. Would you like to unbuckle and float free?"

Even before she answered, one could hear her shoulder straps and seat belt unbuckling. "Yes indeed." The cockpit area was roomy enough for her to float free. Rather than lift her faceplate, Cathy took off her helmet and stowed it. Her black and white communications carrier assembly, better know as a 'Snoopy Cap,' held her hair in place in the zero-G environment. Directly behind the cockpit was an open cabin space. Cathy gently pushed herself aft.

"I'd also like to try out zero-G," said the pilot.

"Sure Angelo, give it a try," said Hans-Peter. "Why don't you float on back and answer any questions Cathy might have." The pilot also took off his helmet and stowed it.

The interior of the Rebel was roomy enough to comfortably accommodate a crew for a very long flight. Up front, the cockpit area had room enough for the crew of three and a passenger. The two seats behind the pilot and copilot were slightly elevated and gave the flight engineer and the passenger an excellent view out all of the windows. The aisle between the back two seats was a full three feet wide. There was also enough headroom to stand up in the aisle. While there was a wall, or more correctly a bulkhead, behind the back two seats. The aisle between the seats gave access to the aft-cabin.

Continued aft, one passed the double door hatch. Cathy had taken a number of trips on airliners and didn't remember any double door hatches. She reasoned that at supersonic speeds you might need two doors. A few feet further along, the passageway opened into the aft-cabin that was slightly larger in diameter than the cockpit. It was more than twenty feet long and there were three windows on each side and one on the ceiling. The cabin was empty and so very inviting, that she floated back into it.

"T-C Control, this is the Rebel. Do you copy?"

"Loud and clear. We show your velocity approaching zero. What altitude are your instruments showing?"

"Our altimeter is indicated a max of 83,670 feet. We are at zero velocity and starting to fall. What max altitude did you record?"

"Radar data showed a max of 83,700 feet. The margin of error may be a bit more than 50 feet. Your altitude confirms the rocket engine delta-V. Congratulations."

Aboard the zero-g Rebel, and now more or less in the center of the aft cabin, Cathy realized she was trapped within the gravity void. When she reached up, she couldn't quite touch the ceiling; and when she stretched out her legs, they didn't quite reach the floor. When she tried throwing her arms up as fast as she could, she put herself into a slow spin.

"You're a pretty fancy gymnast," said Angelo from his secure place in the doorway.

"There's nothing to it," she said scornfully. "So how do I get back down to the floor?"

"You need a small compressed air jet. You just shoot it in the opposite direction you want to go," he said rather indifferently.

"Oh darn. You know, I just don't happen to have one of those. Now what?"

"You're in luck. I have one."

"That's lovely, Angelo. Why don't you come on up here and give me a hand and we can go back down together," she answered rather indifferently, as she slowly turned head over heels.

Hans-Peter's voice came over a speaker. "You two need to come back to the cockpit. We're falling fairly fast and pretty soon we'll be feeling some turbulence and some gravity. As we're coming in, I'd like you to get your helmets back on."

"The air's getting thicker," said the copilot, "I'm initiating our 180 degree turn."

"Very good," answered Hans-Peter. "This thing is falling a little faster than I thought it would. I'm starting the inboard engines only. We're light enough now without the LOX to fly on two engines. Let's try to hold at 40K."

"I can feel the two engines, but we're still falling. I'm bringing them up to 7/8."

Back in the aft-cabin Angelo had just started to shoot his compressed air gun when the Rebel started to turn. The force of the turn threw them both softly against the wall and farther apart.

"Nice try Angelo," said Cathy, "but now I've got hold of a handgrip. In fact I'm starting to feel some gravity."

"We better get back up front." Helping each other, they moved back up front as quickly as they could.

"This thing doesn't feel right," said the copilot. The drag from the two dead engines may be more than you thought."

"Okay, I'm firing the two outboards. Try to slow our descent. I'll do the calculation. We want to be at 15 K when we get back to Joshua Tree."

"I'm correcting our course to 240 degrees west. Hey, this thing feels a lot better with four engines. What speed do you want?"

"Give me a minute." Hans-Peter calculated a rate of descent and speed to put Rebel on an ideal course. The four turbojets had no problem holding 350 knots and the descent was essentially a very long approach to Norton Field. With the Rebel settling into a very ordinary transport mode, Hans-Peter and his copilot both took off their helmets.

With San Gorgonio Mountain now off to the starboard, the Rebel turned west-northwest and flew toward Oak Glen. With its speed diminishing, they turned onto magnetic 237 for their final approach to Norton Field.

Out on the Santa Ana Wash, most everyone who had come was still there waiting and watching for the return of the Rebel. In the tower we had a precise fix on the Rebel. It was now over Oak Glen. The telemetry showed the landing gear doors open and the gear lowering into place. A minute later, everyone along the runway could also see it. I went to the windows to watch. The sleek titanium craft was coming down the final approach as though it had landed here a dozens of times before.

The main gear of the Rebel hit the deck smoothly and the craft rolled perfectly straight down the runway. The moment the nose gear touched down, thrust reversers on the jets revved up and slowed it down.

By the end of the runway, the reversers on the Rebel had shut down. It didn't stop; it turned and headed for its hangar. The landing was right out of a textbook and the crowd cheered again.

The hangar doors were not opened as the Rebel taxied over. The ground crew came out before the Rebel came to a stop. When the Rebel had stopped, I watched all four flight crewmembers deplane. The ground crew then took over the aircraft. They closed the Rebel's hatch and then left the airplane parked outside.

The marshal and I grabbed our stuff and left for the hangar. Once again I drove a bit too fast. The marshal didn't mind. We were both eager to hear what Hans-Peter had to say. I was sure that Claudius and Eleanor would be close behind us in her jeep. Today there would be no open house at Titanium Composites, and so everyone out on the Santa Ana wash started to leave. I knew, however, that Sandy and her group would be coming along, and of course Keith Wiley. I was sure I'd also see those other two reporters that had special access.

The event appeared to have been a flawless maiden flight. There were now at least a hundred people ready to post what they saw in every conceivable place on the Web. Any trace of obscurity that Hans-Peter may have once enjoyed was now gone forever.

Chapter Four
It's Like a Gatling Gun

The Rebel's maiden flight had been a spectacular success. No one had expected a rocket engine hidden inside the fuselage; and no one was expecting the Rebel to break the sound barrier the first time out. For everyone watching and listening, the excitement was electric. From my vantage, however, the flight raised several important engineering questions.

A hypersonic airplane should not be rocket powered. Rocket engines burn up their fuel much too fast. A hypersonic airplane should be powered by a scramjet engine, like the engine that powered the X-43. Otherwise the airplane will not have a meaningful range.

I had also noted that Hans-Peter had never said his Rebel aircraft would 'cruise' at hypersonic speeds. What he said was that Mach 7 was a performance goal. Recalling conversations I had had with him years ago, I was sure his Rebel was really an aerospace plane. While I knew that speculation would make a great editorial, I determined to keep his secret until the time was right for a full exposé.

The Rebel had landed not more than fifteen minutes ago. The marshal and I had left the control tower and headed over to where the Rebel was parked. We wanted to get inside the hangar and hear everything Hans-Peter would say. We were anxious to hear his first remarks. When we reached the hangar, the marshal's big official car was still parked there with two other cars. Those two cars belonged to the other two reporters that came out for the rollout ten days ago. They were the only other reporters Hans-Peter said he would let in. There were only five of us from the press that were given access. Since Sandy showed up today with two photographers, our number had grown to seven.

As I parked, Sandy pulled up in the Herald Express van with her two cameramen. Keith Wiley followed her in his car. When I looked back at the control tower, I saw Eleanor and Claudius in Eleanor's jeep heading our way in a hurry. The few of us who were allowed inside the gates were gathering quickly.

Inside the hangar, they had spread several large Persian carpets in the space where they usually parked the Rebel. There were tables with rather classy upholstered chairs. At the end of the carpeted area was a raised platform for the crewmembers. They were still wearing their pressure suits and were sitting no more than a few inches above us. They were raised just enough to make it easy to hear what they had to say and easy for us to photograph them.

Hans-Peter stayed seated and studied us for a moment before he spoke. "I see all five of you who were here for the rollout. Thank you for coming back today. I look forward to seeing how each of you will write up the Rebel's maiden flight. At this point, there is no question that the Rebel can fly; and let me say this up front, I had nothing to do with those three A-10s that came along to check us out. I look forward to seeing the data and images they collected. It was very nice to have their company. Since our flight ended only twenty minutes ago, this meeting is more like a debriefing than a report. To start, I'd like to give the floor to Sandy Koop of the Herald Express. Sandy, do you have a first question?"

I could see that Sandy was not prepared to be center stage, but she got it together quickly. "Two of your employees came out to our van with a special radio and let us listen in on your flight. Is it true you actually broke the sound barrier?"

All four of them smiled. They couldn't hide the pure joy of their first flight. "Yes, we did," answered Hans-Peter. "Our instruments showed our top speed was Mach 1.51 or about one and a half times the speed of sound. That's the maximum speed we attained just as our rocket shutdown. At that speed, we were coasting almost straight up; but with no power, gravity started slowing us down. We coasted on up to about 83,000 feet or about 15.8 miles before gravity took over and started pulling us back down."

"And then with no more power," continued Sandy, "you were weightless!"

"Yes indeed," answered Kathy Bear, "we were weightless as soon as the rocket engine stopped pushing us. They let me unbuckle and float back into the cabin. It was just like the old videos of astronauts floating around inside the Space Shuttle. Zero-G is more fun than anything I've ever done. I hope someday everyone can try it."

"If the Rebel aircraft is meant to explore the hypersonic frontier," asked Keith Wiley, "why didn't you fly level for speed instead of wasting your energy on climbing for altitude?"

Angelo the pilot answered. "The premise of your question is correct. If I had leveled off at, say, 60,000 feet, more of the rocket energy would have gone into speed rather than altitude, but this first flight was planned to prove the rocket engine integration and give us some time at very high altitudes. On this flight we were not pushing for high speeds. Hans-Peter directed the copilot and me exactly what to do, and he was there with us. What we were doing may have sounded spontaneous to you over the radio, but everything had been planned out beforehand."

"We heard you call out a maximum rocket thrust of 100,000 pounds to your crew," continued Keith. "Is that the maximum thrust you can get out of your rocket engine?"

"A good question," said Hans-Peter. "The rocket we fired is throttleable and has a lot more potential than what we saw today. In fact, today the engine was just loafing. I wanted to see how the Rebel would handle at the 100,000-pound thrust level. From what we have seen in ground testing, I think the engine can give us about twice that much or about 200,000 pounds if we turn it up."

"I believe I heard you tell the A-10 pilots that you were burning LOX and JP-4. Have you considered a more energetic fuel than JP-4?" I asked.

"Yes. That's a very insightful question from my old friend Traypart Artamus. As you all may know, Mr. Artamus is often printed in *Aviation Week*. The rocket we fired today can be modified for both other fuels and other oxidizers. Keep in mind that today we were only carrying about 27% of the rocket propellant mass that the Rebel can carry. As we test the Rebel, we plan to carry more propellant mass and go much higher and much faster."

Claudius Thud of the FAA spoke next. "At what altitude do you plan to fly hypersonic; and what is your velocity target?"

"The first milestone is Mach 7 at 120,000 feet. That's our first target."

"I'd like to add, just as a reminder," said Claudius. "You are required to put anticipated performance numbers into your flight plan. As you know, there are many planes in the sky; and we at the FAA need reliable performance numbers to keep the airways safe. The flight data we gathered for your maiden flight is not exactly what we were expecting from your flight plan. In a day or two we need to talk about that. Your next flight plan had better give us a much better idea of what you are going to do."

"Yes sir," said Hans-Peter. "My office will look forward to hearing from you for that conversation."

"Do you have plans to try other types of rocket engines?" asked one of the reporters who hadn't yet spoken.

"Yes," said Hans-Peter. "We have built our fuselage to accept a modular rocket engine and fuel tank assembly. The aft fuselage has a disconnect bulkhead that allows us to change rocket assemblies with very little work. The rocket assembly we used today is just like the one over there on that dolly."

When I looked, I realized they had uncovered one of the large objects that had been under a tarpaulin. It was now out of hiding and they were showing it off. It was a least part of what Ruthiebell wanted me to find.

"Do you mind if we photograph it?" asked one of the other reporters.

"No, not at all. It's a very conservative design. There are no company secrets built into it. Please note that the rocket assembly is modular. In fact, we plan to use that rocket assembly for our next flight. We plan to swap it for the rocket we used today. Pulling the whole assembly out gives us the best possible way to examine it post flight."

"Rocket engines are great for a big boost of power," said Keith, "but you can't maintain that kind of power for very long. So even if you can cruise at Mach 7, you can't do it for very long with a rocket. So what's the point of a short hypersonic cruise? We already got that kind of data from the X-15."

"We understand how rockets work Mr. Wiley," answered Hans-Peter, not sounding the least bit challenged. The two photographers and several others gave Keith some muffled laughter. "As we gain experience with the Rebel's flight characteristics, we plan to test several entirely new types of rocket engines. We have some very encouraging static firing data that we want to test at altitude. If any of you remember the work of Arbit and Clapp, back in 1969 they gave us the first tri-propellant engines. We're picking up rocket design where they left off."

"Well Mr. Hans-Peter," said Keith, "I for one don't remember much of anything from 1969. What kind of a specific impulse do you think you can get; or better yet, what kind of impulse have you seen?"

Hans-Peter took his time considering the question and then said, "We have demonstrated over a 700 seconds of specific impulse."

I knew it! And as they say, I knew Hans-Peter had an ace up his sleeve. Most of us listening knew he just said something outrageous, but I knew this man never made inflated claims. Was he about to change the world?

Before Keith could speak, that other reporter asked, "That would be truly amazing. As I recall, back in the eighties, the National Aerospace Plane was said to be achievable if someone could build an engine with 1,200 seconds of impulse. Do you think the performance of your new engine can grow up to 1,200 seconds?"

Hans-Peter looked at the reporter carefully before he spoke. "We haven't met, but I believe you're Nigel Turing of the Associated World Press."

"Yes, that's my name and affiliation," answered the reporter.

Hans-Peter smiled a bit, "We have actually demonstrated more than 800 seconds of specific impulse right here at sea level."

"That's insane!" said Keith. "If you're flying that kind of an engine and something goes wrong, it'll blow up like an A-bomb."

"Oh come on Keith, you're getting carried away," said Eleanor rather angrily. "Today he flew JP-4 and LOX. If those propellants fail, you'll never get an A-bomb. Do you care about the real technology, or are you just here looking for dramatic sound bites to sell your copy?"

"That's not what I'm talking about. He said he's got a tri-propellant that can give him a 800 seconds of specific impulse at sea level!"

"Every time you open your mouth," objected Eleanor, "your words get more dramatic. You don't care about the technology. You just want to sell copy."

"Sell copy! You're telling me I'm just selling copy!" yelled Keith. "I'm not just selling copy. People have a right to know the truth."

Claudius Thud of the FAA stood up. "Be quiet Mr. Wiley. I now have the floor." Keith looked like he had just been slapped in the face. "All of us at the FAA want to congratulate the crew of the Rebel. It was a pleasure to be here and share the excitement of your first flight. In the future however, and I mean starting right now, we at the FAA will expect clear disclosure of what kind of equipment and which propellants each test flight will be using. I have every confidence in Eleanor Scribble's discernment and I expect you to keep her informed of every development. If you have questions, let Ms. Scribble help you."

The marshal had never taken a seat. He had been standing behind the group and now moved to open the door for Mr. Thud. Claudius raised his hand with a friendly wave. "I'm off now, best of luck."

First thing in the morning, Sandy got to Max's office just as he was walking in. "Your front page story for the Rebel's first flight was dynamite, it's getting more hits on our web site than all the other stories put together. Come in. Please come on into my office. Why didn't you open up the angle of some possible UFO contact? Boy, now that would give them something to talk about "

"Obviously, the story didn't need the UFO angle," she said, "and there's not one shred of evidence for UFO contact, either. Look, I'm no rocket scientist; but when . . ."

"Stop right there dearie," said Max, "you sound like you're brain dead. Only the uninitiated talk about 'rocket science.' Rocketry is a branch of engineering; therefore one who designs and builds rockets is a 'rocket engineer'."

"Right," she said. "I'm supposed to learn the difference between science and engineering from somebody who believes in UFOs? Give me a break Max. UFOs are Jungian archetypes anyway. They are not real objects some real engineers designed and other real craftsmen have made."

"You got to be open minded. You got to look at everything."

"Okay, so I'm no 'rocket engineer.' But, I did a lot of listening and I didn't hear anything that even vaguely suggested your UFO angle. Max, on this one I think you're dead wrong, and I can even say you're drastically misdirected. You're on your way to be laughed of the planet."

"Dead wrong? Distractingly misdirected? So now my only total greenhorn reporter, a woman with only one good story under her belt, is telling me I got it wrong. So what's next? If you'd listen to me, you could play the UFO thing for weeks. So what are you going to write about while the Rebel is on the ground? They may not fly it again for weeks, or even months."

"The A-10s, remember the A-10s? They flew over for the rollout and then ten days later they came back and chased the Rebel when it took off. When they flew over, the crowd went crazy. Those gutsy little airplanes stole the show. I want to go out to their base with a photographer and do their story."

"Not bad. I like it," said Max. "You got an idea there. Where do you have to go to get their story?"

"You can't drive there. They came from a 'Desert Environment' training base. The only way to get out there is in an airplane."

"I like it, that's even better. You want to take an airplane ride?"

"Yes. When can you get a charter out of Burbank?"

"Oh no. No, no, no. That's not the way you do it. Remember, we need drama. Besides they probably won't let a chartered airplane land on their base anyway. I'll call Mrs. Rumble downstairs; she can get you and the photographer on an Air Force transport. When you go, you better pack your bag. The flight home may not be the same day. Now go back to your desk and write out the very best questions for your story. I want to see them before you leave. Mrs. Rumble will call you when she gets it worked out. The lady is dynamite, she can do anything."

Out at Cactus Patch, Corporal Tabby had been rotated onto the day shift. At the moment absolutely nothing was happening. While he was keeping an eye on his monitors, he was also trying to find Sandy Koop's web site on his smart phone. With pleasure he recalled the night he watched her drive out to Titanium Composites for the Rebel's rollout. Reporting the rollout to the major before it actually happened had earned him some seriously good points.

He knew that he and Sandy were the same age. He was sure she would instantly see what a great advantage it would be for her to have a friend like him who was career Air Force. Oh yes, he thought, a good friendship could lead to a real romance. How on earth could he possibly meet this lady? He could go down to Los Angeles and have lunch at the coffee shop nearest the *Herald Express* building. He would wear his dress uniform and appear to be there coincidently. He imagined running into her when the place would be so crowded they would have to share a table. He was sure that he and Sandy were meant for each other. He knew if something was meant to happen, it would happen.

The phone rang on Corporal Tabby's desk. "Operations," he said rather flatly.

"This is Mrs. Rumble of the *Herald Express*. Have I reached the operations desk for the 'Desert Environment' A-10 base here in California known as Cactus Patch?"

Tabby's heart exploded. His mouth went dry. His mind flashed. This was a practical joke. Not to be fooled by his buddies, he checked the caller's number and origin on his monitor. The call was coming in from 11th street, in downtown LA. It was the real thing. He cleared his throat, "Yes ma'am, you have reached the Patch Cactus, I mean the Cactus Patch here in California. How may I help you?" He knew he was turning red as a beet.

"There were A-10 aircraft that escorted the new Rebel Aircraft on her maiden flight. Did those aircraft originate at your field?"

"Yes ma'am, they did." Tabby had regained his composure.

"We at the *Herald Express* were delighted with the escort your A-10s extended to the Rebel and her crew. We would like to send a reporter and a photographer out to Cactus Patch to write up your side of the story. When may we come and what arrangements would you like me to make for their trip?"

"May I ask which reporter you are sending?"

"Does that make a difference?" asked Mrs. Rumble.

"No ma'am. I was just curious, I do read your paper."

"When can I send our people out?"

"Any old time." Tabby realized he couldn't say that. "That is, if it were up to me. May I have your phone number? I will take your request to our commanding officer and then call you back. To be clear, you would like to send one reporter and one photographer to our base for an interview. Do I have that correct?"

"Yes, that is correct and may I have your name?" asked Mrs. Rumble.

The next morning, Sandy and the photographer were driven to Long Beach Airport to catch an Air Force C-130 cargo plane that had stopped at a commercial terminal to pick up supplies for Cactus Patch. They were told the plane would leave at seven a.m. They were there at 6:30 sharp and by her watch they left at 9:47. She seemed to recall someone saying, 'hurry up and wait.'

They were only in the air thirty minutes. The high desert by air is not far from the LA basin. As the C-130 touched down, Sandy remembered Mrs. Rumble. Sandy had no idea that anyone like her worked for the newspaper. She would remember Mrs. Rumble's name.

Corporal Tabby had contacted the pilots of the C-130 and learned that Sandy was the reporter onboard with a photographer. He had managed to get a haircut yesterday afternoon just in case they were sending Sandy and today he was wearing his newest uniform. His teeth were also as white as the driven snow from at least five brushings. He met his CO and was now walking with him to meet the C-130 as it was landing. "Sir, I learned from the flight crew that the reporter's name is Sandy Koop, and that she is one of the few reporters that was allowed on site for the Rebel's first flight."

"Very good corporal, that's helpful." As the major spoke, he took a closer look at Tabby. "You're looking very sharp this morning. Is there something I missed?"

"No sir, not that I know of. I dressed to help make the best possible impression for our unit."

"Yes, I see. That was very thoughtful."

"Thank you sir."

The corporal and the major had reached one of the of the Quonset huts that protected the A-10s. The big door was open and they stood just inside, in the shade. As the C-130 taxied nearer, the lieutenants and the two captains showed up and stood just behind the major and the corporal. Looking around, Tabby realized that most of the enlisted personnel had also showed up and were standing perhaps another twenty feet behind the officers. When the C-130 came to a stop, everyone rather quietly walked closer behind the major and Tabby as they went outside to meet the cargo plane. No one could remember a civilian ever visiting Cactus Patch before, let alone a reporter from a big newspaper with a photographer.

In Tabby's eyes Sandy looked more beautiful than she ever had on the web. Her photographer was an older guy reminiscent of a hippie. He was no competition. They were now close enough for an introduction. Tabby was so close he could touch her. Her beauty took his breath away. He couldn't make a sound.

The major could tell that his corporal seemed to have lost his voice and extended his hand. "Good morning, I'm Major Hayes, the commanding officer; and I understand that you are Sandy Koop of the *Herald Express*." The major then spoke with an even friendlier tone of voice. "Was I correctly informed? Did I get your name right?"

"Yes Major Hayes," she said taking his handshake.

It was gone! Corporal Tabby's chance to speak to Sandy was gone. He could only step aside.

"And you must be the photographer," said Major Hayes. "May I ask your name?"

"No problem dude. They call me Milo Schotts and I want to thank you for a really nice ride out of the city in your big airplane."

There was a bit of laughter among the personnel; and the major himself seemed to enjoy the introduction.

"You're more than welcome, Milo," answered the major. "Come along inside and let's take a closer look at an A-10 Thunderbolt II." The major introduced them to his officers as they looked at the aircraft. He let his captain of maintenance answer many of the questions.

Around the front of the A-10, the photographer reached up and touched the seven-barrel machine gun protruding under the nose of the airplane. "Look at this, Sandy," he said. "What'd I tell ya? They put the biggest Gatling gun ever built on this thing."

"I thought the Gatling gun was used in the Civil War," objected Sandy.

"You're both right," said the major. "Richard Gatling invented the first rotary cannon for the American Civil War. The weapon he's pointing to is a Gatling 'type' rotary gun that can be thought of as the great-great-grandson of the Civil War weapon."

"Do all the A-10s have one of those?" asked Sandy.

"Yes," answered the maintenance captain. "Keep in mind that the A-10 Thunderbolt II is an anti-tank weapon. The rotary gun we are looking at has a 30-millimeter bore, and its projectile is so powerful it can penetrate the armor of any known tank. There's nothing electronic here. It's basically an old fashioned gun that throws its heavy bullet very, very, hard."

"You have just made a point about, 'nothing electronic,' but I'm not sure I'm following you," questioned Sandy.

"What I'm saying is that missiles and even bombs nowadays are smart. They have electronic computers that tell them what to do. So, if an enemy can develop 'countermeasures' that can confuse the electronics, the enemy can send the ordnance the wrong way, or even worse, send them back at you. With the A-10, its canon projectiles are so dumb they can't be confused. They go where you point them."

"Hot Damn," said Milo. "If you see some of those creepy little green men in a UFO, for sure that's the gun to get'em with."

Milo embarrassed Sandy with his dumb comment. Looking about to escape the moment, she made eye contact with Lieutenant Woodburn. The lieutenant seemed to be paying close attention to Milo and agreeing with him. Her eyes shot back to the major looking for a thread of sanity.

The major could see her embarrassment and took over the conversation. "We don't have any UFOs in our ID silhouettes," he said with a bit of humor, "but Mr. Schotts is making a good point. If we have a sophisticated adversary, with sophisticated electronics, there's nothing they can do to stop a burst of A-10 fire."

No one knew what to say next. Corporal Tabby stepped forward, and spoke with a good clear voice. "Major Hayes, it's just a few minutes before noon and I know our chief has something special for our visitors." Tabby finally managed to compose himself and said the right thing. Sandy was relieved to change the topic. Sandy looked directly at Tabby with an unspoken thank you.

I did it, thought Tabby. I just made contact!

"Yes, of course," said the major graciously. "Thank you corporal." The major then shifted his attention to Sandy. "It will be some time before the C-130 will be ready to go back. Would you care to join me for lunch? We have a place set for you." The major then asked Corporal Tabby to escort the photographer to a lunch with the enlisted men. That meant he had worn his newest uniform to host a burned out hippie. Not the best assignment.

The major had the long table usually set for the officers separated into two. One of the tables was set as far away from everyone else as possible. The major sat at the head of the table with Sandy at his right side with the two captains. On the other side of the table facing Sandy were the three lieutenants who had flown the reconnaissance sortie.

As soon as they sat down, Sandy picked up the interview again and said, "I was on the field when the Rebel took off and I saw the three of you come overhead trying to catch that amazing airplane. Shortly thereafter two TC people brought us a special radio and we could hear everything. She looked first at Lieutenant Collins and read the nametape on his uniform. "You were the man flying lead who first spoke to Hans-Peter?"

"Yes ma'am. I was the one who flew lead."

Then looking at the man sitting next to Collins, she read Woodburn on his uniform. "And you would be Raymo Woodburn, the one they call RAINDROP?"

"Yes ma'am, they call me RAINDROP."

"You sounded like you know all about rockets. Would you like to be an astronaut?"

"No," answered Lieutenant Collins. "Raymo here wants to be a fireman when he grows up, don't ya Ray?"

Sandy and the two captains had to concentrate to stifle their enjoyment of such a speculation.

The major cleared his throat, "I'd like to hear Lieutenant Woodburn's answer."

"No thank you," said Raymo. "The Air Force and national defense are my calling. At the moment our nation can't put a man in space, but even if we could, I like it right here. This is where I want to be."

"That's certainly admirable," said Sandy with genuine respect, "but then why the interest in rockets?"

"There's a lot of crazy stuff in the sky these days. I figure if I know what human technology looks like, then I won't ever be fooled by some crackpot calling in about a UFO."

"I had no idea that the Air Force was on the lookout for UFOs," said Sandy as if to tease the lieutenant.

"That's not what the lieutenant said," corrected the major. "I would imagine you have encountered a crackpot or two in your line of work."

"If you can believe it, the newspaper gets a call almost every day about a sighting or an abduction. I learned that a few years back the paper hired a man who had actually been involved with Project Blue Book. He determined that all of the smartphone videos that people were sending us were nothing more than 'Computer Graphic Art'."

"And what did he say about the abductions?" asked Lieutenant Woodburn rather seriously.

The lieutenant's tone startled Sandy and she proceeded with caution.

"I really don't know. The man they hired was an older man and he retired some time back. Nowadays, the paper sends all that kind of stuff to one of the UFO 'disclosure' groups."

"Including the abduction stories?" pressed Raymo. "You have to admit that after Betty and Barney Hill, there is at least something out there to think about."

"Yes, there is something there to think about. I'm sure the paper sends every one of those stories to one of the very best special interest groups," answered Sandy trying to disengage from the topic.

The next day, back at the *Herald Express*, Sandy conned Max into giving her a private office so she could watch all the crazy UFO postings Ruthiebell had put up on the Internet and take notes without distraction. Max helped her move into a vacant office that didn't have a door. He sat down in one of the extra chairs, and showed her where to find Ruthiebell on YouTube.

Ruthiebell's latest post came up first. It was titled *Extraterrestrial Machinery Hidden Inside the Moon*. Max had never seen it. "Oh come on Max," said Sandy. "This can't be real journalism. The title assumes that extraterrestrials are real and have visited our moon Luna. This is not journalism. This lady has found a way to make a fast buck off a public that wants to be entertained."

"That's not a bad thing," said Max. "I like to be entertained when I read."

"Listen, Max. Those guys out in San Bernardino have built themselves a very real airplane," she said. "The *Herald Express* is not a comic book; it's a real newspaper. The Space Shuttle Orbiters are all sitting in museums. This country can't put a man in space. Hans-Peter is 'pushing the envelope.' Did you ever hear that phrase? They are 'pushing the envelope'."

"Have you forgotten who is working for whom?" said Max rater flatly.

"Have you forgotten who is one of only five that has access?" Sandy was cut off by the old-fashioned telephone ringing on her desk. She answered it, "Hello, Sandy Koop, how may I help you?" As she listened, her face relaxed into a receptive professional. "No, I didn't, but then we have had some trouble with incoming emails. I would love to come out, however. May I bring a photo crew?" As she listened, Max could tell it was something big. "That's great. You can count on us, and thank you for the call. We'll be there for sure."

"So what was that all about?" grumbled Max.

"That was Titanium Composites. I've been invited out, with a crew, for their next flight this coming Tuesday."

"Very good, I liked the way you handled the call. Did they say if they were going to try for Mach 7 at 120 K?

"No, they didn't say; and I didn't think it was a good idea to push them for more information while they were inviting us out. I didn't see any point in sounding rude."

"You're a reporter Sandy. You should always be pushing for more information. I'm going back to my office, but would you please watch some of Ruthiebell's stuff on the Internet. She talks about the UFOs in a very interesting way. I also happen to know that she and Hans-Peter have some history. She might be out there for that next flight. You need to learn something more about UFOs. When you read her stuff, you learn something about her; so get yourself busy."

Chapter Five
Ruthiebell's Strategy

The day after the Rebel's first flight, I wrote a letter of congratulations to Hans-Peter and complemented him on how much better his airplane performed than any of us expected. None of us were expecting the rocket engine tucked away inside the Rebel's fuselage; and while the FAA seemed a bit perturbed by its omission in his flight plan, they were very supportive of the program. I put my letter on fine cloth paper and folded it in half into an oversized envelope. I knew that Hans-Peter remembered the world before the Internet and would appreciate an old-fashioned letter. I drove over to a courier and paid for same day delivery.

Having tipped my hat to the bygone twentieth century, I was pleased to receive a phone call from Hans-Peter that very afternoon. He liked my brief letter and apologized for not being able to give me more time the day of the flight. He invited me to drive out to his place after the rush-hour traffic for the conversation we had missed and to plan to stay the night.

I left at seven p.m. and found the freeways still moving slowly, but starting to loosen up. I would have written to Hans-Peter even without Ruthiebell's somewhat clandestine assignment; and I would have preferred driving out for this interview without her off-the-record money. My own curiosity would have led me to try for this interview. Since the *Herald Express* had been printing my stuff for years, I wasn't sure why Ruthiebell wanted all the confidentiality. As I drove out, I decided not to mention the *Herald* or Ruthiebell. I really didn't know what her objectives were.

Hans-Peter had four acres in the foothills near Norton Field. The area had been subdivided into four-acre parcels that all opened onto a wide equestrian trail. The homes were mostly in Spanish architecture. His home was about seven thousand square feet and was looked after by Mr. and Mrs. Maltby. The Maltbys lived on the first floor in the back near the garages. Hans-Peter lived in a suite of rooms on the second floor at the other end of the house. He had lived this way for more that twenty years and the Maltbys were more like family than servants.

Hans-Peter wasn't an equestrian. He didn't keep horses, but he did enjoy the sight of his neighbors riding by on the trail; and in particular he liked to watch the occasional carriage go by pulled by one or two horses. Several times in the past, he had barbequed beef and pork in his backyard and his neighbors had come over on horseback through the back gate. He had both a barn and a small corral in his backyard to accommodate his visitors.

This was a weeknight and I had imagined him in his study analyzing his maiden flight data. As I pulled onto his property, I realized I had no idea what the flight objectives might have been for the maiden flight. What his airplane had accomplished may have been a disappointment. I would assume nothing. Over the years, I had driven out three times for a Saturday barbeque, but I had never been an overnight guest. I was pleased. Hans-Peter was treating me like a friend.

Mr. Maltby answered the door and recognized me from my last visit. He showed me every courtesy. Not long after I was settled into my room, up on the second floor, Hans-Peter tapped on my door. He took me downstairs to the table off to the side of the kitchen for pie and ice cream.

"I was very much aware of you the day of the flight," he said, "but dealing with the problems in the flight plan kept me from giving you some time."

"I was rather impressed with the way Eleanor and Claudius fixed the problem," I answered.

"And of course I was pleased that we didn't crash down on the Santa

Ana Wash." We both laughed.

"I don't think any of us watching were expecting the rocket engine built into your airplane. I'm guessing on following flights you'll be getting a lot more performance than you started with?"

Hans-Peter almost smiled. "That rocket engine performed beautifully, but it was only JP-4 and LOX. Do you remember the tri-propellants?"

"Yes, but nobody has talked about tri-propellants since Arbit and Clapp. Have you built one?"

"Yes, I have and I've found a way to get a lot more energy out of my fuel. In fact I've been ground testing one for over two years. Traypart my friend, I would rather you didn't print anything of this until I demonstrate it in flight."

"No problem. By letting me know what you have, that will give me time to consider how best to educate my readers." We both laughed again.

We talked for about two more hours and he confirmed that he had actually demonstrated more than 1,700 seconds of specific impulse with his secret rocket engine. That is a much bigger number than anyone has ever achieved. Keep in mind that most rockets deliver between 280 and 380 seconds of specific impulse. I wasn't sure if Ruthiebell would grasp the game-changing significance of that number, but I determined I'd keep my promise to Hans-Peter and not tell her until after he flew the engine. I also learned that he was planning to try for 100 miles of altitude on his next flight. This was something I would tell Ruthiebell, and not tell anyone else. That was much more altitude than anyone was expecting. She could have the altitude number for her own secret.

Toward the end of the two hours, Mr. Maltby came back with a bottle of very expensive brandy and two glasses. He left them with us and left without a word. When the door had closed, Hans-Peter said, "That's his way of saying it's time to hit the sack. He knows I have a full day ahead of me."

We each drank a little. It was very good. Then just as we got up, Mr. Maltby returned and spoke to me. "Mr. Artamus, may I show you to your room?

The next day, I enjoyed driving back into LA, and as I climbed the stairs to Ruthiebell's office, it dawned on me that the topic of her books, namely extraterrestrials and UFOs, was the reason for all the secrecy. Even at this time in the twenty-first century, UFOs are still not a subject that credible people discuss openly.

"Hello there Traypart," she said looking up from her desk. "Please close the door as you come in." She left her desk and took one of the comfortable chairs. "I heard Hans received you at his home last night. I'm impressed. What did you learn?"

How could she know that? I thought it best not to ask. "As you know, he's going to fly again in a few days. What I learned is this time, he's going to open up the throttle of his rocket engine and try for an altitude of 100 miles. He asked me, however, not to talk about the rocket engine until after the flight."

"Ye, he's finally doing it," she said. "I knew he was going for orbital space. What velocity will he have when he gets up there?"

"Well, that's just it, he won't have any at all. His rocket will push him up most of the way and when he stops coasting upward, he should be at about 100 miles, but then he will start falling back down. He will touch space, but I'm afraid he won't stay there very long."

"Very unsatisfactory, Traypart. That's not good at all. It would have been much better if, when he got up there, he had enough speed left over for a dynamic-soar around the world as he came back down, but 100 miles is enough for what I need. Did you tell anyone about going out to his place?"

"No. Mr. and Mrs. Maltby continue to keep his grand house and they are the only ones that knew I was there. Why on Earth does that make any difference? The *Herald* prints my aerospace copy, and so obviously I interview aerospace people like Hans-Peter all the time. That was nothing out of the ordinary. Why all the secrecy? What are you not telling me?"

"You've read my books?"

"Yes, of course. Given your topics, it's amazing that you can keep your job. Nobody considers UFOs mainstream science and that's probably why you never print anything in the *Herald* about ETs. So, is that it? Has one of your anonymous informants told you Hans-Peter may be flying into a UFO event?"

"Not a bad guess Traypart, but the answer is both no and yes. Nobody has told me anything about an upcoming UFO event, but I know from friends that there is a tremendous increase in UFO sightings going on right now. If Hans can get his airplane up that high in the next couple days, I'm sure he will have at least one close encounter. Now listen Traypart, I trust you. You're a good engineer in your own right. Do you think he can do it? Don't give me the details. Just tell me, is his airplane reliable enough that you would be willing to fly in it on his next flight?"

I couldn't help but smile. "Yes. I think he knows what he's doing. Do you have enough clout to get me onboard the next flight?"

"If I could get you onboard, would you take the assignment?"

"Yes, I would. If you can get me onboard, I'll give you back your money. I think Hans-Peter is making history."

"Excellent. If you are that willing to go, then I am willing to go. Now you keep your trap shut and you can keep my money. He let Cathy Bear from the Forest Service fly as an observer, so there's no reason he can't let me fly as an observer. Between you and me, I think Hans will have the first solid alien contact ever undeniably recorded, and I want to be there."

"That all sounds great, but let's be realistic," I said. "If right now there are an unusually high number of sightings, why are we not getting reports and pictures from the International Space Station? They're already in orbit. They should be right in the middle of it."

"The extraterrestrial mind is incomprehensible. You know that as well as I do. For years, many researchers have said if the UFOs wanted to make contact with the ISS, they would have done it by now; and of course they haven't. Nobody has a clue what their agenda is. The ISS is old news; it's been flying for years. Hans' airplane is something new; it should attract their attention on its first flight up into space. It's time for an uncontestable event, and I want to be there. I think Hans has built the right kind of airplane, and now is the right time for contact."

"Okay. I love your energy. You've truly got the right stuff, but wanting something to happen won't make it happen. Ultimately there may be nothing more out there than weather balloons and swamp gas. So, I gather my real assignment was to find out how high the Rebel aircraft would fly on her next flight, and whether or not I thought it was safe enough to fly in myself. Was there something more to my assignment?"

"Yes. Do you think you can get yourself into their mission control room the day of the flight? I want somebody I can trust keeping track of the swamp gas."

I shrugged slightly. "When I had breakfast with Hans-Peter at his house, he invited me back and said he would give me a place in his mission control room. I'm already planning to be there. Are you sure you can get that observer's seat?"

"I haven't tried yet," she said. "I wasn't sure I wanted to go up a brand new aircraft with only one flight to its credit. Listen, I want you to go back to his place and volunteer. You guys are apparently friends and you're technically competent. I'm sure if you go out, he'll let you help him; and don't let him know we're working this story together. If you see something that isn't right, you can tell me before I go. But you have to be out there to know what's going on."

"I'm already halfway there. He likes my technical writing."

She stood up. "Okay, go do it and don't tell him you're on assignment. Get going. Run along. I've got work to do. Please close the door on your way out."

When I reached the bottom of the stairway, Sandy Koop was there. She saw me and stopped. "Mr. Artamus, great to see you. I knew you wrote for the Sunday paper, but I didn't know you ever came by. Can I have a few minutes of your time?"

"Sure. I'll make a little time for you. What's up?"

She put her hand behind my arm and pulled me along. "Come on back and I'll show you my new office."

When we reached her office, Max was inside sitting in her chair and reading her work in progress on her computer screen. Max looked up at me. "Well look what blew in off the El Segundo beach." Max stood up and shook my hand. "Hello there Traypart, it's been way too many years and, look at you, you haven't aged a day."

Upstairs, Ruthiebell switched the monitor on her desk to the hidden surveillance camera in Sandy's office. She could see and hear everything. She liked Max; he conveniently lacked conformist rationality. His provocative statements and questions usually pulled unexpected information from whomever he talked to. As she watched, Max took one of the chairs off to the side. Sandy took the chair at her desk.

Max hardly waited for me to sit down before he said, "So what's our star Sunday journalist doing down here amongst the Nibelung?"

"I want some of your gold," I said, as though he had some.

Sandy heard echoes of Wagner. "I gather," she said, "you two have met?"

"Yeah, yeah, yeah, I know this guy," said Max. "I understand you're one of the lucky five that have access to Titanium Composites?"

"That's true, but then so does Sandy."

"Yeah, yeah, yeah, two lucky ducks in the same room. So what are you doing here? Why aren't you out there reporting on the Rebel? Send me some good stuff. You know I'll post anything you give me."

"Max, I'm a contributor, not an employee."

"So why are you here? Go out there and contribute something."

"Sandy caught me in the lobby and asked me for a few minutes." I then looked over to Sandy. "I'm here. Did you have a question?"

"In all your aerospace reporting, did you ever hear stories about an old Nazi engineer named Hermann Oberth?"

"Yes. He was one of the old men that taught von Braun rocketry."

"What'd I tell ya, what did I tell ya," interrupted Max. "If you had done your homework, like I said, you would have learned that on the Internet."

"Max, I found Oberth on the Internet," she said rather flatly, "but I didn't see anything about him and UFOs."

"Sandy, I've also heard some of that UFO stuff," I said. "There are several places where Oberth is quoted as saying, 'we had help from beings from other worlds,' but I've never seen the quote in what we could call orthodox history."

"So what's that supposed to mean?" she asked.

"It means," snapped Max, "the 'beings' came to Germany in UFOs back in the thirties and forties and helped the Nazis build the V-2 rockets. Our government, including FDR, knew about it; but it was so scary they classified it top-secret and hoped and prayed it would just go away."

Sandy focused her attention on me. "That can't possibly be true. That's just a big fat Rhineland urban legend. Some of their people, just like some of our people, have nothing better to do than make up stories."

"Oh well," I said, "some urban legends have a thread of truth, and of course, some don't."

"Listen to the man," said Max. "He couldn't bring himself to say it's not true. He left the door wide open for real UFOs."

"You listen to the man," snapped Sandy. "He didn't say it was true."

"So what's it going to be Mr. Traypart Artamus?" said Max. "Sandy here seems to be giving you more credit than she's giving me."

Upstairs, Ruthiebell liked the way Max was pushing for the truth.

"I've never written about UFOs," I said with a shrug. "That would make me, more than likely, unqualified to comment on the subject. I need to get going now. I will keep an eye out for how you handle the subject in your copy. Best of luck." I then left the *Harold* building as quickly as I could.

From her private office, Ruthiebell called Titanium Composites. She hadn't called Hans-Peter in years and thought it likely that none of his current employees would remember her. She represented herself truthfully as an editor from the *Herald Express*. Under the official heading of the newspaper she had sent several emails commenting on the rollout, and congratulating him on the Rebel's first flight. She hadn't heard from Hans-Peter. Someone else in Public Relations had replied to each email with appreciation and courtesy.

It took several minutes to get through to Hans-Peter. Her call caught him off guard. He hadn't talked to her in years. He didn't know about her emails. His people in PR read incoming emails. The pressures of the first flights had eclipsed his active memory of her. Although he recognized her voice immediately, this wasn't the right time to renew an old friendship. When she pressed him for an interview, he first checked to make sure she was still with the newspaper. Then, in an effort to end a phone call he didn't have time for, he invited her out to his place for dinner. When he was off the line, he asked his secretary to call the Maltbys and have them prepare for his dinner guest.

Ruthiebell wrapped up her morning work and drove home for lunch. She gathered her things and was on the freeway eastbound by 2:00 p.m. Traffic was bad, but she managed to get to Hans-Peter's home just after 4:00 p.m. The Maltbys received her and gave her a place in the library where she could work for an hour or two before dinner.

She had the tenacity to succeed in journalism. She also had the tenacity to go wherever she wanted. She knew the house and the Maltbys very well and was pleased to be back in the familiar old library. Mrs. Maltby came in for a brief conversation and didn't leave until she was sure that Ruthiebell had everything she needed.

Ruthiebell wondered if it was even possible to revive the old friendship she once had with Hans; she had mixed feelings about getting involved again. Being back in his comfortable old library aroused an old affection for him she had been denying for years. No, she thought, that's not what this, is all about.

Inside the big hangar, Hans-Peter was pleased with the final installation of the tri-propellant rocket engine. In fact, the final preparations of the Rebel were slightly ahead of schedule. As he walked away from the assembly area, he started considering what he could remember of his old, long past, relationship with Ruthiebell.

He remembered painfully that when he had mentioned marriage, she let him know that nothing was more important than her career. She left him soon thereafter. She had been a big part of his life when they were both young. He wondered if her hair was now gray or silver.

He reasoned she was looking for the unpublished story behind the

Rebel's maiden flight, or she might be here to remind him that UFOs are often seen at very high altitudes. He had read her books and when they were young, they had talked often about UFOs. He really liked her, but she could be impossible. Along with her better than average intelligence, she had a tendency to see the world only from her own perspective. Several others had pointed out that she could be rather hardheaded.

When Hans-Peter drove home, he parked in the garage and came in through a back door. Mr. Maltby met him and told him that Ruthiebell was in the library; and that the table in the small dinning room was set for two and dinner was ready whenever he was.

"Please show her to the table while I wash up a bit and grab a clean jacket.

The small dinning room was more elegant than the large one, and Hans-Peter knew she liked being there. As he walked in, the sight of her made him feel twenty years younger. Her hair was still jet black, not a strand of gray. She threw a disarming smile and he fell for it. As he sat down, his intellect kicked in and reminded him she had left him. He asked her about her drive out.

"I still live near Griffith Park," she said, "and the traffic made it a little over two hours. The time in the car gave me a chance to replay all the audio posts I had collected about your Rebel's maiden flight. Sounded to me like you had a roaring success."

"Yes." He liked her choice of words. "The flight was everything it was planned to be."

Then lacking any subtlety, she asked, "Who is Cathy Bear?"

He knew she had no business asking such a question. Ruthiebell had left him years ago. Should he even bother answering the question? "Someone had to fill the great hole you left in my life," he said insincerely, and then realized that was the wrong thing to have said.

She knew he was teasing her by his tone; or was he? "Your own company said she was a local forest ranger with an interest in aerospace technology."

"That's true. She's been looking after the local forest for more than twenty years. I don't know the details, but she may now be the senior ranger for the whole area. I like the woman and since I'm right next to her forest, her friendship is a real bonus."

"Does she live with you here in this lovely big house?"

"You left me, as I recall. Is that question any of your business?"

"Hans, I do care about you, and I had always hoped you'd have some wonderful friends."

"How thoughtful," he said. "And is there a forest ranger in your life?"

Ruthiebell had mastered that form of feminine charm that could melt the male ego. It was not with words. It was with expressions and very carefully planned eye contact that went along with whatever she was saying. "No. I've missed out on any close encounters with a forest ranger. I've also missed our many conversations about new approaches to space transportation. Would I be hopelessly optimistic if I speculated that your Rebel airplane is really an aerospace plane and you're using hypersonic flight as a cover story?"

Hans-Peter shook his head, not so much to say no, as to express his amazement at her insight. They had been very close friends and she really did know many of his thoughts. Tempting as it was, however, he had no real need to confide in her. "Have you lost interest in Cathy Bear?"

"She's truly lovely. I watched the debriefing video of your first flight several times. I enjoyed her words about the zero-G experience, and of course I want you to have lovely friends." She took a piece of bread and thoughtfully buttered it. "You taught me that Low Earth Orbit starts at 17,500 miles per hour at an altitude of one hundred miles. Of course, the speed of sound changes with altitude, so if you take its speed to be an average of, say, 650 miles per hour as you go all the way up, then orbital velocity could be thought of as about Mach 27. One third of that is Mach 9; and they also say that hypersonic flight starts at Mach 5. Do you think the Rebel can get up to Mach 9?"

"That's a rather well-informed question." Hans-Peter took another swallow of his beer.

"So I deserve a rather well-informed answer?" she pressed.

"The answer is yes, and I think I can do even better than that. For now I have said that my first hypersonic target is Mach 7. If you're still the discreet professional you used to be, I'd rather you didn't say anything more."

"That's fine Hans," she said with genuine sincerity. "Are you going to try for Mach 7 on your next flight?"

"No. Our first flight was so successful that next time I want to try for 100 miles in altitude. As you may recall, we only made it up to about fifteen and a half miles on the maiden flight."

"So, next time you're going for the LEO altitude. Can you get up there with just LOX and JP-4?"

"No, not with the propellant mass ratio we have. Next time we're going to fly a modified high performance rocket engine." She could see a little pride and pleasure come across his face. "We're going to fly something no one has ever seen before. I've found a new way to increase rocket performance, but this is not the time to talk about that."

"So, have you finally figured out how to put a tiny little pinch of nuclear reaction inside a rocket engine?"

He found her insight disconcerting, and tried hard not to let it show. She couldn't possibly know what she was talking about. He answered with calm disinterest. "That's a pretty wild idea. Did you dream that one up on your own?"

"No Hans, it's your idea. You explained it to me forty years ago."

"Are we that old?"

"Yes. We are that old, and I regret not staying much closer. Let's not change the subject. When we were close, you were thinking about how to put a small nuclear reaction in a rocket engine. As I recall, you never told anyone about it. You only told me about it when we were home and alone. You asked me not to even mention your ideas to anyone, and I didn't. I never wrote about it in any of my books, and I never told another soul."

Hans-Peter was trying to remember the old days with her. "I forgot that I had told you about it. Thank you for keeping my secret. So why didn't you come out with Sandy Koop when we had our rollout?"

"You didn't announce it was a rollout. If you were just going to show off another titanium alloy, Sandy wouldn't need my help. I've been an active technology reporter for years and I've kept your secret. I made you a promise and I've kept it. You can trust me. Now, more to the point, you've let it be known that the Rebel has interchangeable rocket engines. Do you have a nuclear hybrid sitting in your shop?"

"Oh my," he said, half under his breath. "Yes, I do, but I'm not ready to talk about it. Your memory is much better than I would have ever guessed."

"Will you fly the nuclear engine on your next flight?"

"This is starting to sound like a cross examination."

She made eye contact with the beginnings of a gentle smile that radiated all of her feminine charm. "Hans, I have kept your secret for forty years. I have carried it in my heart."

He narrowed his eyes wondering what he should do with her. She was sharp as a tack and he really liked her, but?

Before he answered she said, "Your people have invited my reporter

Sandy Koop out for your next flight. Have you also announced your 100 mile altitude objective?"

"No, but between you and me, I'm going to put it in my flight plan."

"That should give Cathy Bear more time to float around in zero-G."

"Yes it would, but Cathy said she couldn't make the next flight. Her job looking after the forest is pretty demanding."

Ruthiebell could hide her thoughts as well as any poker player, but Hans-Peter could tell she was very interested in that vacant seat. Of course he must act like he hadn't a clue. "What do think of my butternut squash?"

"It's lovely and just perfect and one of my favorites. I think I'll have a little more. Were you planning on putting another observer in Cathy Bear's now vacant seat?"

"Oh, I don't know. If we leave it empty, that will lighten up the airplane a little and we might get slightly better performance," he answered without being entirely serious.

"That's ridiculous Hans. Given the weight of the Rebel at takeoff, the weight of one more crewmember will be undetectable."

"That's probably true, Ruthiebell. Did you have someone in mind?"

Before she spoke, her face lit up with the expression that said, 'am I not here?' Then she adopted her no-nonsense business tone of voice. "I would like to fly with you on the next flight. With my established place in journalism, I think I can make an important contribution to your public relations. I've noticed that Keith Wiley is raising all sorts of problems for you, and I've dealt with people like him before. In fact, I've dealt with him before. I know I can help you."

"Years ago, you wouldn't even go up in a private airplane with me. Why the change of heart?"

"Back then, most of my life was still before me. Things are different now."

"Oh that's reassuring. So now that your time is running out, you'll give me a little of what's left?"

"Not exactly. Don't say things like that. Do you have someone else in mind for Cathy Bear's place?"

"No, not really," he said.

"I can help you Hans. I'm ready to get involved," she answered with all the enthusiasm of a college kid volunteering for something new.

"That all sounds great," said Hans-Peter, "but you come with some baggage. Some rather considerable baggage."

"What are you talking about? Many people have thanked me for the even-handed way I've handled UFO stories."

"So tell me, are some of your anonymous friends extraterrestrials?"

"No, not yet anyway. You'd think with all the stuff I've written about them, some ET would drop in on me; but it hasn't happened. And as you know, I've talked to hundreds of very credible people who have had direct experience with ETs."

"So, next time out, you want to come along in case some ET in a little UFO comes by and tries to give us a few words of wisdom?"

"Yes," she said impatiently. "Of course, and that's your next flight. You're going high enough for a close encounter."

"You don't give two hoots about me. You're just here to get yourself in space and talk to the next passing ET. Tell me, do you only want a one-way ticket?"

"Don't talk to me that way. Don't you tell me what I care about and what I don't care about. There's never been anybody in my life like you, but our careers literally went in different directions. What are you going to do, if you do make contact? I can help you. I think it's time we start working together."

"You know, I've actually thought about that. Not that I expect it will happen, but I have thought about what I would say to an ET. Years ago, long before we met, I bought a copy of Caruso Phillip's Roswell book. If you recall, we met in a library when we were both trying to get better information about Betty and Barney Hill. If I ever encounter an ET, I know how I would handle my part of that encounter."

"So you think you're ready. You may know how to build a pretty good airplane, but you don't know a tenth of what I do about ETs. Hans, if you make contact, you will need my help!"

"That's a nice thought, but it's extremely unlikely that we'll see a UFO. The flight won't be very long. A UFO would have to have perfect timing. I don't think any ETs are watching me, or my Rebel aircraft; but you, on the other hand, have been in the middle of ET reporting for more that thirty years. If ETs are watching the Earth, why haven't they contacted you?"

"I don't know," she said with exasperation. "Lately I've been asking myself that question a lot. Maybe the right time and place will be with you on you next flight."

He could hear her exasperation and knew she was being totally honest with him. "As I said, the next flight will only touch LEO and then it will fall back."

"Well, like you said," she continued. "I haven't been flying with you before. So maybe it's high time I went up in an airplane with you."

Chapter Six
Simultaneous Agendas

After my rather enlightening meeting with Ruthiebell, I went home and packed for the next week in San Bernardino. The River Blossom was a very acceptable motel that was not far from the gate to Titanium Composites. I called and made a reservation. I didn't bother calling Hans-Peter; I knew the gate at TC was open to me. What an interesting assignment, and I had money in my pocket.

Right about 7:30 p.m. I hit the freeway eastbound. As I drove, I recalled the first time I met Hans-Peter. It was over a midweek lunch and I came away with the idea that he was going to focus his resources, both intellectual and financial, on building an aerospace plane.

I was still intrigued by Ruthiebell's insight. She seemed to know his unpublished objective as well as I did. Apparently we both thought he would someday rollout a highly modified F-111. While everyone else was surprised to see the Rebel airplane rollout, instead of samples of a new alloy, Ruthiebell and I were not.

The Rebel was, however, much more than we were expecting. In the debriefing after the maiden flight, Hans-Peter had told Nigel Turing of the Associated World Press, that he had demonstrated 'more than 1,200 seconds of specific impulse' in a tri-propellant engine that he has not yet flown. The next night when I was Hans-Peter's guest, he had told me off the record he had demonstrated more than 1,700 seconds. That meant he actually had several hundred more seconds of impulse than he needed to get into orbit. I hadn't told Ruthiebell about the world changing performance he told me he could get, but I had told her about the 100-mile altitude objective he had for that next flight.

As I drove into San Bernardino, I realized I had missed dinner. So before going over to the Rive Blossom Motel, I went to the coffee shop that I had tried for breakfast the day of the Rebel's first flight. As I walked toward the door, Eleanor Scribble of the FAA was coming in from the other direction. I really didn't want to see her right now, but there was no escape.

"Hello Traypart," she said cheerfully. "Are you traveling alone?"

Obviously I was, and there was no way to avoid the senior FAA official for the city of San Bernardino. "I am. Would you care to join me?"

"I would," she said with a scheming smile. "I knew sooner or later you would ask me out, and tonight's the perfect night. How fortunate to run into you. I need to talk to someone like you about Hans-Peter. Let's take my favorite table."

When I had breakfast here a few days ago, I had no idea she came here often. She definitely took the best table in the house. "I'm guessing you really want to talk to someone like me about Hans-Peter's airplane and not about the man himself?"

"Well, that's a reasonable answer, but in this case I think the two are rather closely entwined." She didn't say any more. She left the statement and her question hanging in the air. It also seemed that she was flirting.

"The roast beef is a very good choice," I said. "Do you often eat this late?"

"I never eat this late. This coincidental encounter is so opportune, I must assume it was meant to be."

I wondered whom she thought could have possibly meant us to have dinner together. Perhaps the new Rebel aircraft wasn't her primary objective. I said nothing.

"So what are you doing out here this late?" she asked. "Surly you're not planning to drive back into LA tonight."

"I have a room over at the River Blossom. I'll be here until the Rebel's next flight."

"Then I'll be seeing a lot more of you for a few days." Her words seemed to imply there would be opportunities to improve our acquaintance, but then she said, "Do you have any idea how Hans is going to keep his aircraft skin from melting at sustained Mach 7 flight?"

"No, I don't. That's a very good question," I answered, hoping Eleanor's questions wouldn't get around to what Ruthiebell and I were speculating. "Do you think he and his buddies have figured out how to make an alloy that's tough enough and nonconductive enough to endure sustained Mach 7 flight?" I asked.

"I have no way of knowing that sort of thing. You're better at this than I am. When you just restated my question, you added the word, 'nonconductive.' That means if the skin can stand up to all that heat on the outside, it must also keep it from getting inside and cooking the crew. I'm sure a qualified engineering type like yourself knows that stuff better than I do."

"But I'm just a reporter. I'm not an engineer."

She looked at me as though I was trying to sell her the Brooklyn Bridge. "Right," she said. "Your modesty is rather suspect, but then you're a man of several mysteries. We met twenty-five years ago in LA at an FAA open house for the press. Do you remember?"

"Yes, I remember that day. Back then nobody knew what was going to happen to the old Norton Air Force Base."

"And back then you looked just like you do today. Why don't you age a little like the rest of us?"

"I do age. It's just that some families show their aging a little slower than others. And look at you. You look great. Father time has hardly made any progress with you either." That wasn't quite true, but I knew she loved to hear it.

Her eyes narrowed a bit. "More to the point, Traypart, I also happen to know that you were Hans-Peter's houseguest just the other night. I'm sure the Maltbys treated you splendidly. Did you and he discuss the titanium alloy he built the Rebel out of?"

"San Bernardino is more of a big town than a small city isn't it?"

"Yes, it is, and I'll not repeat a thing you tell me. I'm not a writer, so I'm not trying to scoop your story. I like Hans and I want to help him. Remember when Keith Wiley tried to stop his first flight? Claudius and I found a way to make it happen; and you were there. The more I know about what he is doing, the better I can help him. So you can help him by letting me know what you learned."

What she was saying was true, but I wasn't going to breathe a word about his tri-propellant rocket engine or what Ruthiebell and I were guessing about Low Earth Orbit. I had to tell her something real or I'd lose the professional side of our acquaintance. She really was someone worth knowing. "Has Hans-Peter filed his next flight plan yet?"

"No. I haven't seen it yet."

"Just between you and me, he's not going for Mach 7 next time out. So he won't have to worry about the hypersonic heating problem. He's after the altitude of Low Earth Orbit. He wants to touch 100 miles before he falls back. I have told you what I know because I trust you. If you divulge this conversation, you will ruin my relationship with the man. So where do I stand with you?"

"Not a word," she said like a cohort in a conspiracy. You can take me out this coming Saturday night. "I won't say a word," she continued, "100 miles really is the beginning of space. Things at that altitude can orbit if they have enough speed; and orbital space is where the Johnson Space Center comes in. I will determine if the JSC has authority over flights to that altitude. I'll work the problem before it happens."

After dinner in the small dining room, Ruthiebell and Hans-Peter stretched their legs by walking around the first floor of his home. While I was, shall we say, dealing with Eleanor during our unanticipated dinner, Ruthiebell was dealing with Hans-Peter during her cleverly contrived dinner. Of course, Hans-Peter thought the dinner was his idea, but Ruthiebell had calculated the right time of day to call him when she knew it would be easer for him to invite her to dinner than talk to her.

As they walked along, Hans-Peter said, "Cathy Bear's interest, given her position with the Forest Service, has been very helpful in avoiding zoning problems."

Ruthiebell knew Hans-Peter's home from many years back and tonight she seemed to be rediscovering it. Mr. Maltby had lit the fire in the living room and as warm and inviting as the fireplace was, they had moved along and settled back in the library where she had left her papers and computer.

"So you gave her a ride in your new airplane to make her feel indebted to you and your company?"

"No, not at all. That's a terrible thing to say." He could tell his answer made her feel like a fulltime conniver. "So is that remark supposed to give me a better way of understanding what kind of a person you have become? It really has been some time since I saw you last. Perhaps I don't know you anymore."

"No, not at all." She could recover as fast as any politician could. "That's the kind of thing Keith Wiley would put on his web site. I can help you deal with that sort of thing. So how would you handle that remark without me?"

"I'd just tell the truth. She's a neighbor with a genuine interest. She's been stopping by once a year since we started the company. There were a number of years that she brought several others from the Forest Service and we would set up a luncheon for them inside the biggest hangar. What I'm saying is that our ordinary Public Relations also lead to a better relationship with one of the federal organizations near by. Should I expect some editorial criticism from your newspaper 'exposing' the neighborly relationship between Titanium Composites and the U.S. Forest Service?"

"No," she said in an instant, "but if somebody like Keith Wiley throws that at you, I can help you deal with it."

"Let's forget Keith Wiley and Cathy Bear. You're obviously not here to talk to me. You're here for a ride out to an alien encounter. Let's talk about what UFOs mean if they are real. Let's talk about your agenda."

"Don't be so sure about what I'm here for," she said, regaining her confidence. "I never married and neither have you, but you're going to fly to the edge of space in a couple of days, and I want to be with you. We can talk about other things when we get back."

"So for now I'm your chauffeur?" he said in a way that was meant to tease her.

"Oh come on Hans, you know perfectly well that some of the older astronauts are saying that all human space flights have been followed by UFOs," she answered impatiently. "Right now, our own time is strangely difficult. We can't possibly know where the next UFO will land. They can show up anywhere, any continent, any country, or even anywhere out over the ocean; but since they like to follow human space launches, your next flight to the edge of space will attract them. Hans, you're going to make contact whether you want to or not."

"So I'm just bait. Just put the Rebel on a hook and you'll catch a UFO."

"That's not the best way to say it, but you're on the right track." She was not joking and proceeded as seriously as she could. "I think the time has come for contact and I want to be there with you. You and your crew and your beautiful airplane are going to chauffeur us both up there."

"Are you sure you want to make contact? Look what happened to Betty and Barney Hill. The ETs they encountered didn't exactly have them over for tea and cakes."

"So you think their story is authentic?"

"Yes, I do. I think it's a true story because it happened long before faking alien encounters became a national pastime. What makes you think you're going to be treated any differently than they were?"

"Because I'm going to initiate contact," she said patting her chest with great confidence. "That's why I must be onboard, on your next flight. In all the alien encounter stories I know, people act like deer stunned by the headlights when the UFO gets close. When you start to get up there, say above 70 miles, I want to call out assuming we are being followed. You can show me how to call out over several different radio frequencies at the same time. If we initiate the contact, then they might just talk to us. Of course I'm not sure about the tea and cakes."

"That's almost reasonable," he said, "but ETs are famous for not cooperating. What makes you think they'll understand and give you an answer?"

"If they're smart enough to get here, they should have no problem figuring out our language. Hans, I really believe your Rebel airplane is going to be followed just like everybody else. Every time they launch a Soyuz spacecraft, you can bet some stealthy UFO is following them up into orbit."

"But if the ETs in the UFOs do nothing more than watch and listen, then they might as well not be there. It doesn't make any difference."

"It does make a difference, Hans. Even if they're up to their old tricks, and don't bother to answer us, we need to know they are there. Since they came here, it's a given they're smarter than we are. We must think about how to approach an intellect that's significantly smarter than we are."

"Is it possible that we're so dumb that they would consider talking to us the way we consider talking to gold fish?"

"Yes, but I was hoping you would compare us to dogs," she said. "There really is some communication between dogs and people."

"That's not much better," he said. "I don't want to run around like a dog and catch a Frisbee in my mouth. So when you talk to your dog, what do you expect to learn? I think the question here is what would people of much greater intelligence be interested in? Can we even comprehend what sorts of things they think about?"

"We can't know until we talk to them," she said impartially. "Our only real question, that is the only meaningful question, is why did you come here in the first place?"

"For starters our planet is beautiful. The photographs that came back from Project Apollo were much more beautiful than anyone was expecting. If you had a technology that would let you traverse the galaxy, I think you would visit all the most beautiful planets."

"Okay, and then what?" she asked.

"They would look for whatever was valuable to them," he said.

"Like pure gold?"

"No, that would be really disappointing. If they can figure out how to fly across the galaxy, but can't figure out how to transmute mercury down into gold they need to go back to school."

"Why did you say down into gold?" she asked. "Don't you mean up into gold? Gold is more valuable."

"I'm talking about atomic weights. Gold has one fewer proton and several fewer neutrons than mercury; so, its atomic weight is a step down from mercury. We Earthlings already understand the transmutation of elements. We just haven't figured out a cheap way to do it. Think about it. What would you be most interested in, if you had perfect health, an unlimited life span, and all the physical comforts you needed? What would you do with your time?"

"Explore the galaxy," she said. "What else is there?"

"From our perspective, that's a good answer. I think it also implies that there is no end to knowledge. So as the ETs get smarter and smarter, they would have to look harder and harder for something new; they would always be on the lookout for something new. Taking pictures and leaving footprints is nice enough, but I think they would be looking for what they don't know. If they can get here, they already know more than we do, but given the complexity of DNA, there's probably no way to predict all the forms life can take. They are doing the same thing that Charles Darwin did when he sailed aboard the HMS Beagle back in 1831. They may be exploring to find as many genetic possibilities as possible."

"Like what, for instance?"

"Within the kingdom of the plants, they may be looking for the perfect rose."

"Oh my dear Hansie, you're still a hopeless romantic. I don't think the perfect rose ever crossed an alien's mind?"

"Okay, but what I said is not as simple-minded as it sounds. They want to see the entire plant kingdom. There are bound to be plants, and animals for that matter, that they have never seen of. That's a very real reason to come here.

"You're beginning to drift, Hansie dear. Let me put your feet back on the ground," she said almost condescendingly. "The people that are serious about studying UFOs have determined that there are at least four different kinds of ETs coming and going on this planet all the time. One of those groups, and quite possibly two of them, are living here on the planet in secret underground bases. They most likely land their spaceships out in the ocean and then enter their underground dwellings from caves hidden deep in the ocean.

Up until recently no one was able to coordinate the sighting data. In this century however, just over the last twenty years, there are several good databases that show patterns in UFO activity. The little town of Gulf Breeze, Florida, for instance, has had an unusual number of reported sightings. Gulf Breeze is right on the ocean. If there were an underwater cave somewhere nearby deep in the ocean, then that little town would be an ideal place to see UFOs coming and going."

"I'm open to the possibility that ETs with really advanced technology might come by now and then, but telling me that at least one kind of ET is living here underground is a rather different story. How on earth could such a thing be kept a secret?"

"Well, that's just it." She said. "If I know it, then it's not a secret anymore."

"But you really don't know. Do you know where the base is located?"

"No, but there are people that I do know who know the people that know where it is."

"But you don't know where it is. You and your UFO buddies have just convinced each other that it's a good possibility. Have you or any of your friends been there and talked to the ETs?"

"There are two different men that claim to have been there. I haven't yet been able to talk to either one of them. As the story goes, the government has contacted them and told them they know what's going on and it would be good for their health if they'd keep their mouths shut."

"This is getting ridiculous," he grumbled. "You said you were going to put my feet back on the ground after I said an ET might like to come by and look at the plants and animals; but with your feet on the ground, you're telling me ETs live here underground, but never come up and talk to us. If they are effectively hiding from us, and never interfere with what we are doing, then they are of no concern. Ultimately, if they don't talk to us or make their presence known, we are better off assuming they are not even there."

"They are here Hans, believe me, they are here. The government knows a lot more than they are admitting. It's because of the government that the people that tell me things must stay anonymous."

"Oh, right. You know, I've gotten the impression there is an ever-increasing number of anonymous insiders willing to tell you almost anything under the sun. This, too, seems to be becoming a national pastime."

"There is an increasing number, Hans. Please don't get cynical with me. The people that talk to me are very credible. The twentieth century is dead and gone and buried in history books. Things are about to change. You need to open your eyes, dearie. This is a very strange time."

Hans-Peter looked at her seriously. "Do you think you're physically up for the next flight aboard the Rebel?"

"Yes, I do. My last physical was just fine. I'm probably not as strong as Cathy Bear, but I'm no weakling either. Besides that, your maiden flight didn't look any more demanding than a ride in a jet liner."

"Well, actually, it wasn't. You look about the same size as Cathy Bear. Would you mind being fitted into her space suit?"

"Of course not. I like what little I know about her. It would be an honor to wear her space suit. I like knowing she's got it all broken in."

Hans-Peter and Ruthiebell talked late into the night reviewing what he had accomplished with rocket propellants and what she had learned about UFOs and the unexplainable events that accompany the best sightings. When Mr. and Mrs. Maltby brought the fine brandy, Mrs. Maltby offered a guest room to Ruthiebell for the night. Ruthiebell graciously accepted, acting as though she had lost track of the time. She then said she had a few things in her car. Only Mrs. Maltby wasn't surprised when Ruthiebell unloaded two large suitcases and said she could move in for a few days.

Just before that fine old bottle of brandy appeared, Ruthiebell had secured the observer's seat on the next flight. Hans-Peter hadn't bought into most of the UFO stuff she told him, but the chance to have the science editor of a major newspaper on board was much too advantageous to miss. Besides all that, just being with her again made him remember how much he really liked Ruthiebell.

Out at Cactus Patch the following day, Major Hayes saw Lieutenant Raymo Woodburn sitting in the shade away from the others, reading a book. The major walked over and took another place in the shade near enough to converse with the lieutenant. Suddenly the lieutenant realized the major was there, and started to stand up. "As you were, RAINDROP, as you were. You've found a nice spot here. We're both in the shade and outside at the same time, and that's just fine. May I ask what you're reading?"

Oh man, this guy's up to no good, thought the lieutenant. He's not going to trick me into something. "Yes sir. I'm reading Caruso Phillip's book, *In the Shadows of Roswell*."

"Does it have any pictures?"

The lieutenant smiled; he remembered his eight year-old nephew asking him the very same question. Raymo turned to the several black and white photos and handed the open book to the major. "The people look real enough, but I don't think that UFO, supposedly in flight, is very convincing."

"Isn't it remarkable how all the UFO photographs are slightly out of focus?"

"Yes sir, I've thought that myself," answered Raymo cautiously.

The major looked at each photo then handed the book back to Raymo. "I'd heard of this book, but I've never seen a copy. Lieutenant, please think of this conversation as totally off the record. As I'm sure you know, UFOs seem to be becoming a major national topic. You probably recall how the photographer who came out here with that reporter from the *Herald Express* brought up the topic?"

"Yes sir, I do," answered Raymo. "As I recall, he said that if we ever see any little green men in a UFO, the A-10 gun would be the right weapon to nail them."

"That's the way I remember it. I also recall your request to carry ammunition for the rotary cannon when we fly the recon sorties. Is there any connection?"

"No sir. I wasn't thinking of little green men at the time," said Raymo as cool as a cucumber. He could feel his heart pounding. He had his own very real reasons to take UFOs seriously, and from experience he knew the topic would only get him in trouble. Over the years he had perfected many ways to change the topic. "The enemies of our nation are becoming ever more sophisticated. I don't want to be flying my Hog and see a problem developing and have an empty magazine."

"Well, none of us do, lieutenant, but the sheriff deputies, or the park rangers, or even the highway patrol never really need the kind of help an A-10 can give them. You know, in all my years with the A-10s, I've never needed any ammo while flying here in California. You know that photographer looked like a burned-out hippie to me."

They both laughed. "Yes sir. He has definitely seen better days, but then I got the impression he may have seen a UFO."

"You know good and well that our own government is flying aircraft no one can recognize," said the major. "Now, don't ever repeat this, but

I know for a fact that the UFO fad is part of the way our government is hiding our best technology. He probably did see something he couldn't recognize, but it was made here on earth and the USAF was flying it. And just one other thought, if you really did encounter a spacecraft from another star system, do you think an A-10 would even have a chance against it?"

"No sir. We can't even get back to the moon, so we're pretty far behind the curve on that one." Raymo had just given his commanding officer another one of his canned answers. His thinking was more like, just let me get one of those ET jerks in my sights and I'll give 'em something they'll regret. What should he say next? "Sir, would you like to read my copy of Caruso Phillip's book?"

"Not right now, but thank you. When you've read through it, bring it by and I'll take another look at it." The major sat for a moment wondering what the lieutenant might say next. The lieutenant had mastered the art of being attentively quiet and said nothing. "You know, not long ago I saw an amazing YouTube post, shot with a smartphone," said the major, "from someone who thought they caught a UFO on video. It really looked like a flying saucer until it turned and was unmistakably an F-117 Nighthawk."

The lieutenant nodded his head in agreement. "I believe I saw that same post. I think it was shot near sunset and in that light, and when it's flying straight at you, the F-117 looks just like a UFO. In fact it looked so real to me, that I actually thought it was a UFO until it turned and I could see what it was."

"I was also surprised," said the major in full agreement. "It was sure a good thing the guy with the smartphone didn't have a significant weapon." With that, the major made eye contact with the lieutenant expressing things he didn't need to say.

"Corporal Tabby has told me that Hans-Peter has announced the next flight for his Rebel will be in just three days," said the major. "I took some heat from the FAA for the last flight you and your buddies flew. Seems you were flying much too low again. Next time, I'm going to fly the same recon sortie with just one other plane to show them we can do it right. I want you to fly on my wing. I think you and I can get it right this time and turn down the heat from the FAA."

The major then stood. "I enjoyed the chat, lieutenant. I'll leave you now to your book. I hope the good guys win in the last chapter." The major walked away as though nothing more important than a ball game had been discussed.

The next day I was welcomed through the gate at Titanium Composites and was taken out to the shop floor to where Hans-Peter was working.

"Traypart, so good to see you. I was hoping you'd come out a day early. Are you here only to take notes, or can I put you to work?"

"I'd love to help out. I'll take the notes while you're in the air. What would you like me to do?"

"You probably know Ruthiebell from the *Herald Express*. She has asked me for the observer's seat on the next flight. She wants to try and hail a UFO when we get to the higher altitudes."

"Really," I said, not letting on that I had already had this conversation with Ruthiebell a few days ago. "Doesn't she realize the flight is so short, it will be very unlikely for any UFO's to see her go by?"

"Oh, I know. That's what I told her. It was very decent of you not to laugh at me when I said UFO. There's a growing consensus that UFOs really are out there. I personally haven't seen one, but there's a lot more talk than ever before. So I thought it would be great PR if we flew an editor from a big newspaper and helped her look around."

"That's a very nice way to put it, Hans-Peter. Having a look around for UFOs at altitude will certainly add some human interest to your flight. What would you like me to do?"

"I'd like you to help my communications people. Ruthiebell wants to broadcast out to the 'likely' UFO on several frequencies at the same time. She thinks if she initiates communication before they do, then they'll talk to her. What I'd like you to do is help my guys figure out the best frequencies to set up for Ruthiebell."

"No problem," I said. "We need the highest microwave frequencies."

"How could you possibly know that, Traypart?" said Hans-Peter. "You sound like you think you know what you're talking about. Do you talk to UFOs often?" Hans-Peter's tone was both disbelieving and a humorously condescending.

"Well, of course I don't know. I just got carried away with the spirit of the undertaking. It's very good of you to be so open-minded."

"Right," said Hans-Peter. He then asked the driver of the small electric truck to take me over to communications.

In the mean time, Ruthiebell was upstairs with the two women that had helped Cathy Bear with her space suit. The space suit turned out to be just a little two large, which was easy to pull in and fix. The challenge for Ruthiebell was to learn everything she needed to know to use the suit safely. It wasn't a game. If she didn't learn to use the pressurization controls correctly, it could lead to a life-threating situation. Needless to say, she was a very attentive student.

Back down in the shop, the technician I was working with had no preconceived notions about what frequencies he thought UFOs would use. I could tell he thought we were all nuts. He knew that, if the one in a billion chance for an alien encounter happened and we had the wrong frequency, it would be better if it was my mistake rather than his.

The young man was very conscientious. Together we set up the equipment to scan many frequencies at once, but I made it a point to be able to scan the microwaves way up to the high end. We went back and forth between the shop and the airplane several times and each time I was impressed with the very high standards every one was working toward. This was a very good airplane. I was sure Ruthiebell and the entire crew would be safe as they raced for the edge of space.

Chapter Seven
The Edge of Space

Tuesday morning came, and the city of San Bernardino was more alive than anyone could ever remember. The Rebel had caught the imagination of everyone. The very thought that Hans-Peter and his upstart company were going to try and fly all the way up to Low Earth Orbit was nothing short of a rebellion that no one else had the guts to try. His sheer daring became the number one Internet topic. Titanium Composites posted the objectives for today's flight on its company web site, and that posting had attracted more than five hundred thousand hits.

Today the Rebel would defy the limits of rocket engineering and touch orbital space, or it would explode while trying.

The Rebel was pulled out of its hangar and parked in plain view. The sleek aircraft looked fit for space flight. Its buffed titanium skin was unlike anything else that was flying. While being similar to the Space Shuttle Orbiter in size, its profile was dramatically different. The Rebel was no legacy of the past; it was stolen from the future.

The crowd along the south side of the runway was steadily increasing and already much bigger than the attendance for the first flight. The county had cut a deal with the Army Reserve. Seventy men and women, reserve solders in uniform, came over for the day and brought along three army-issue fire trucks. The army personnel and their trucks were stationed along the south side of the runway to assist two dozen sheriff's deputies in containing the crowd. City police and company security were looking after the rest of the company grounds, while the Highway Patrol maintained order on the streets.

Unlike the rollout and the first flight, the time for today's flight was scheduled for a much more civilized hour. Titanium Composites invited the four other journalists who came out for the first rollout to a 9:30 a.m. briefing. Today's flight was scheduled for 11:00 a.m. and today each of the journalists brought along a camera crew. The company set up a tent again the way they had for the rollout. The same marshal had driven Claudius Thud of the FAA out from LA. Claudius was sitting in the tent with Eleanor Scribble. The marshal was standing by the door as before. There were also a number of county officials in the audience, which made the number attending more than four dozen. The side of the tent behind the podium was left open allowing the audience to see the Rebel behind the speaker.

When Hans-Peter stepped up to the podium, he was greeted with enthusiastic applause. "Welcome, welcome everyone. Titanium Composites is proud to be located here in the Inland Empire, and we are pleased that so many of you could be with us for our second flight. Again today, we will fly the same course that Claudius Thud and Eleanor Scribble gave us for the first flight. Today, however, we have a flight plan that calls for an assault on the altitude of Low Earth Orbit." He had hardly finished his sentence when another round of applause interrupted him. "Today we will have a much longer rocket engine burn than we had before and it should take us up to 100 miles. We should be at max altitude somewhere over Arizona, and that's about it. We've set up telemetry monitors here in the tent and we have set out food and drink if you're so inclined."

Keith Wiley immediately asked, "How much speed will you have at maximum altitude?"

"Zero. Our rocket engine will have burned out and when we stop coasting up, we will start to fall back. Today's objective is altitude and not speed."

"On the maiden flight I recall a max altitude of about 15.8 miles," said Claudius. "Does that mean todays rocket is six times better than last time?"

"No, but that's a good guess," answered Hans-Peter. "The relationship between rocket performance and vehicle altitude is not linear, it's more of a logarithmic function. So by, say, doubling rocket engine performance, you can more than quadruple the altitude."

"Yeah, but as Mr. Thud just said, you're going for six times the altitude not just four. So are you throwing some tri-propellant stuff into the burn?" asked Keith.

"Yes, we're adding just a pinch of lithium."

"Lithium!" exclaimed Keith. "You're going to burn lithium? That will surely explode and take us all to the big airport in the sky."

Most everyone laughed at Keith's observation. Even Hans-Peter started to smile. "Mr. Wiley, all rocket engines are more or less controlled explosions and the more violent the explosion, the better the performance. Tell me, do you think I'd actually fly in an airplane with an unproven engine?"

"Okay, so you've tested it a couple of times. I looked up tri-propellant engines and found that the good ones used liquid fluorine as an oxidizer. Do you have a tank of liquid fluorine inside your airplane?" As soon as he said 'fluorine,' both Claudius and Eleanor became visibly concerned.

"No, we are not using liquid fluorine. Fluorine would create hydrofluoric acid in the exhaust and that stuff is very poisonous." Hans-Peter shook his head slightly. "I'm sure Cathy Bear of the U.S. Forest Service wouldn't allow anything like that near a national forest." Claudius and Eleanor relaxed a bit, but seemed much more attentive.

One of the other reporters interrupted Keith's line of questioning. "I for one am glad to hear you're not carrying any liquid fluorine. At this time are you willing to tell us how much specific impulse your engine can deliver?"

"I'm sure my competitors would like to hear that."

"Most everyone in the aerospace community would like to hear what you've achieved," continued the reporter. "I'm guessing you're actually getting better performance than the Space Shuttle Main Engine. Yes! Please make that my question. Are you getting better performance than the SSME?"

"We are, but let's make sure we're on the same page. The open literature reports that the SSME gets 366 seconds of impulse at sea level and 452 seconds in the vacuum of space. The engine we are flying today does a little better at sea level than the SSME did in space."

"That's impossible," blurted Keith Wiley. "You shouldn't go outside without your hat." Several of us chuckled at Keith's remark. We all thought Keith was sounding more like the fool than a technology reporter. "So, give us some numbers," continued Keith. "Please tell us what specific impulse you are expecting at the altitude where you're going to light off your rocket engine?"

"I'd rather not say. For now, we're keeping the performance numbers under wraps. Of course, you can derive the numbers from the flight performance. Let me give you a few numbers to play with. Today our takeoff weight will be 283,334 pounds. We will be carrying 20,000 pounds of JP-4 and a total of 93,334 pounds of rocket propellants."

Yesterday I had learned those numbers when I was inside the hangar. By then I already knew he was going for the LEO altitude. So I did a few of my own calculations. What Hans-Peter had just told us was that he had a rocket engine that could deliver what would be an average of about 800 seconds of specific impulse. And you know as well as I do, that 800 seconds is very high. That's a number that is generally thought to be impossible with chemical propellants. It's a number that neither NASA nor the Air Force or even DARPA or anyone else has ever achieved, or at least it's a number that no one has ever admitted in the open literature. Heaven only knows what's going on in the black world.

"You make the Rebel sound more like a rocket ship that an airplane," scoffed Keith.

"In a way that's true," answered Hans-Peter. "The Rebel is about the weight of a Boeing 767 and most of its cargo is rocket propellant."

"Yeah, but last time you told us that you wanted to explore Mach 7 at 120,000 feet. Today you're telling us you're going clear up to 100 miles of altitude and when you get there, you'll have no velocity at all! So, are you going to research hypersonic flight like you said, or are you going to research high altitude flight?"

"Today, Mr. Wiley, we are going to explore high altitude flight." Hans-Peter then looked directly at Mr. Thud and Eleanor. "My flight plan shows that with rocket propulsion, we expect to fly near Mach 3 in almost vertical flight somewhere east of the Colorado River. We will not reach the hypersonic speed of Mach 5, and somewhere over Arizona we should reach an altitude of 100 miles. My flight plan, as you know, has been approved and is on file. Now if you'll excuse me, I need to suit up. Please make yourselves at home."

"No! Don't go! I got one more question," protested Keith frantically and to no avail. As Hans-Peter walked away, a man stepped into Keith's way and asked if he could help him with something.

"So, who are you?" demanded Keith.

"My name is Eustace Gray. I'm senior counsel for Titanium Composites. Hans-Peter is now suiting up for the flight. May I help you?" As Mr. Gray spoke, two security men came and stood on either side of him. The three of them seemed politely disinterested in Keith and more than able to restrain him.

"Okay, Mr. Gray, Hans-Peter didn't tell us who is going to fly with him today."

With that question, all other sound in the tent vanished. No one liked Keith's rude approach to questions, but everyone wanted to hear the answer to that question.

"Again today Hans-Peter will fly as the commander and flight engineer. Like last time, Angelo will be the pilot; but for today we have a new copilot. Colonel Stevens, now retired from the Air Force, will be our copilot."

"Does Colonel Stevens have a first name?"

"Yes, of course. His name is Larry and I might add that we feel fortunate that he has joined our organization."

"And the observer," asked Keith, "We saw a fourth person. Is the observer again Cathy Bear from the Forest Service?"

"No. Today's observer will be Ruthiebell, the Science and Technology Editor for the *Herald Express*."

"Ruthiebell!" blurted Keith Wiley. "You mean our lady of the UFO and other extraterrestrial nonsense? Are you taking her up to the edge of space so she can interview the next flying saucer to go by?"

"Many of us here at Titanium Composites have enjoyed reading the even handed way Ruthiebell has presented UFO folklore in her books. Keep in mind that she is the science and technology editor of a major newspaper. We are pleased to have her flying with us today. I personally was hoping she would interview Has-Peter, but you never know what may happen."

Mr. Gray's words ignited a dozen conversations. No one ever admitted to reading her stuff, but everyone seemed to know who she was. Sandy and her photographers seemed very surprised to hear Ruthiebell's name.

Apparently, no one at the newspaper knew what Ruthiebell was up to. The time passed quickly until someone announced the crew was boarding. Sandy's camera team was already outside shooting the flight crew as they boarded. They tried their best to focus on Ruthiebell with their telephoto equipment. Sandy scrambled outside to join them.

Claudius and Eleanor and the federal marshal were all up in the control tower. There wasn't enough room in the tower for any of the county officials, so they were all still on the ground with me, outside the tent watching the Rebel getting ready to taxi.

Looking across the runway, there was a much larger crowd of spectators on the south side of the field. There were also many people out on the Santa Ana Wash with expensive telephoto equipment set up on scaffolds or on truck beds that let them look over the crowd and follow the Rebel unobstructed. As the engines spun up, everyone cheered and the Rebel began to roll.

No one was disappointed. The Rebel gave them another beautiful takeoff, but I could tell she wasn't climbing as fast as last time. As the Rebel ascended into the eastern sky, two A-10s streaked overhead and followed it. This time they were quite a bit higher and slower than they had been for the maiden flight. I had actually forgotten about the A-10s.

With the three aircraft disappearing into the eastern sky, everyone came back into the tent and crowded around the telemetry displays.

"Affirmative, San Bernardino." The radio reception was very clear and Hans-Peter's voice was recognizable. "We are holding a constant speed of 370 knots and we are climbing at 2,000 feet per minute."

Claudius radioed back, "Rebel, your speed and rate of climb are slower than on your first flight. Is there a problem?"

"Negative. We are heavier today and I am taking the optimum speed and rate of climb for fuel consumption. We plan to maintain this level of performance for the first twenty minutes."

The two A-10s had maneuvered into positions on either side of the Rebel and were far enough forward to be seen. "A-10 aircraft, this is the Rebel, do you copy?"

"Loud and clear, Rebel. This is Major Hayes flying lead. May we fly along with you?"

"Yes, Major Hayes. Your company is appreciated. My office has been having trouble contacting you. It's so very nice to be able to talk to you directly. On our maiden flight, three of your A-10s escorted us with recon pods on their rails. So far we have not been able see any of the reconnaissance that your people recorded? When can we see your images?"

"Well, of course all reconnaissance is released 'on a need to know' basis. I myself have not seen any of it. I have a very fine corporal back at our airstrip that handles most of our administrative work. When you call back, ask for Corporal Tabby. I'm sure he will be able to help you."

"Thank you, Major Hayes, we have noted your instructions. We are now turning to a north-northeast heading over the Big Morongo Canyon. Can you stay with us for a while?"

"That's affirmative, Rebel, we will stay with you as long as we can keep up."

"Very good, A-10s. Would you mind falling back and looking at the jet engine exhaust nozzles?"

"We are falling back now. What are we looking for?"

"What can you tell me about the color around the exhaust nozzles? Do they all look about the same?"

"Yes, that's affirmative, Rebel," replied the major. "There is no color on the nozzles. The exhaust plumes for the four wing engines all look the same. I understand your central engine is a rocket and it looks cold."

"That's correct, major. The central engine has not yet been lit."

Corporal Tabby, back at the A-10 airstrip, had managed to patch into the Rebel's telemetry. He was following it and the radio transmissions in real time. Both of the captains and several of the lieutenants were standing behind him in the operations tent. Hearing Major Hayes pass off Hans-Peter's request for information to the corporal made them all groan with sympathy.

Lieutenant Martinelli gave Corporal Tabby a pat on the shoulder and said, "Sure glad I don't know how to do any of that operations stuff."

"Did you hear the major?" said Lieutenant Potash, "he actually asked them if he could fly along with them. That's not military protocol."

"The Rebel isn't a military plane," answered one of the captains. "The major's just trying to talk their language."

"That Hans-Peter guy has been around for a while," said Tabby. "You'd think he'd know better than to ask for military recon data."

"So are you going to give it to him?" asked Martinelli.

"That's not up to me," said Tabby, "But if the major asks me to, I'll try and find a way to get it released." Tabby's voice fell off as he said his last word. Both he and Martinelli became transfixed looking at the large radar display. "Who's that guy?" said Tabby.

"That's not a real image," said Martinelli sounding like he actually knew what he was talking about.

"That's a third A-10," said Tabby. "Look at it. It has the same signature as the major and Raymo, but that guy's not one of us."

"There's nothing there, corporal." Lieutenant Martinelli was no longer sounding friendly. He was giving Corporal Tabby a direct order.

"Yes sir. How should I write up the image?"

"It's an electronic shadow of the major's A-10. You may say it was remarkably clear and indicated a need for our equipment to be rebuilt."

"San Bernardino, this is the Rebel and we're now making our turn to Joshua Tree and heading due east. Major Hayes, are you going to turn with us?"

"That's affirmative, Rebel. We are turning with you now. So far, keeping up with you is no problem. Have you started the count-down for your rocket burn?"

"Not yet. We will fire the rocket when we reach an altitude of 40K. Are you carrying reconnaissance pods?"

"That's affirmative, Rebel. Today's flight is a recon drill. We are both carrying reconnaissance equipment."

"So are you taking some more pictures I can never see?"

"I don't control military reconnaissance. My Corporal Tabby is qualified to answer your questions. I am, however, tracking you as we speak."

The pilot spoke to Hans-Peter. "We have just crossed 32,000 feet. We are now four minutes to 40K. Are we still 'Go' for the rocket burn?"

"Yes. The lithium is very hot and the pressurizing sequence for the LOX and the fuel is almost complete. If the tanks pressurize correctly, then we'll fire the rocket as planned."

"Very good," answered the pilot. "I'm ready when you are."

"Tank pressure is good. It came up fast. I'm now starting the ignition sequence. Bring up the jets to full power now! Hold the rate of climb. We want to be at 40K or a little better and going as fast as we can," said Hans-Peter.

"Understood," said the pilot, "and the jets are coming up to 100%."

"We just crossed 37.5K," said the copilot, "and the speed is increasing."

Back down in the airfield control tower, Claudius broke the intense silence. "I was hoping the lithium was blended with his fuel. I don't recall anyone ever injecting hot lithium. He's messing with the devil. I sure hope he's tested that thing more than a couple of times."

Eleanor had a copy of the Rebel's flight plan open to the second page. "Hans-Peter will light his rocket at 40K for a planned 248 second burn. His flight time is at 19 minutes even," she said with total cool. "Our instruments show his altitude at 39,400 feet. He's 400 feet higher than planned. Let's be ready to mark the rocket ignition time."

Hans-Peter uncovered his ignition switch. "Okay, here we go. I will light in 40 seconds."

"At mark 40 seconds we were just over 39,500 feet," said the copilot. "We will be over 40K at rocket ignition."

"Excellent," answered Hans-peter. "I'll take every foot you can get from the jets. Mark 18 seconds to ignition, 16 seconds, 14, 12, 8 seconds, 6 seconds, 5, 4, 3, 2, Fire. I show ignition. We have fire and 1, 2, 3, 4, 5, 6, 7, 8 and now maximum thrust."

As he counted off the eight seconds the engine needed to come up to full thrust, they could hear it finding its own thunderous voice. Fortunately the crew was sheltered from its tremendous power by four bulkheads. Even so, its great voice could be heard as though coming from far offstage.

"Very smooth," said the pilot. "No boot in the butt this time either, but I feel a lot more thrust. How much are we getting?"

"300,000 pounds, just as planned. Take a steeper rate of climb."

"Major Hayes, do you copy? I have significant static over our frequency. Before I lose you, what does the flame look like?"

"Rebel, your flame is spectacular. I've never seen anything like it. It's alive with a deep purplish red color. Away from the nozzle the flame becomes almost clear. There's no black smoke at all. I can also see four very distinctive Mach diamonds and a trail of smaller ones fading away in the flame. Our signal is breaking up. Do you copy?"

The Rebel heard nothing from the A-10s but static.

"We just passed 548 knots," reported the copilot, "and we are accelerating. Correct that. We just went supersonic."

By now, we're probably over Arizona," said Hans-Peer. "I think we lost our friendly A-10s. The rocket blast is giving off way too much radio static to hear them."

At maximum speed and altitude, one A-10 called to the other. "RAINDROP, let's split up. Move over fifty miles south of them. I'll move fifty miles north. Let's try to reestablish radio contact off to the sides of their rocket plum."

The lieutenant turned southeast and the major headed northeast.

Onboard the Rebel, Hans-Peter said, "Okay, we're holding at the planned thrust level. The rocket looks good, but I'm seeing a little more heat in the lithium injector than I'd like. I've taken full control. Hands off."

"Understood," replied the pilot.

"We're climbing faster," said the copilot. "We just crossed 170K."

"A-10 group, this is the Rebel. Do you copy?"

There was no reply.

"We have 84 seconds of rocket burn left," said Hans-Peter. "At flameout I'll try to raise Major Hayes."

As the Rebel accelerated in its climb, the A-10s flew further apart.

"RAINDOP, do you copy?"

"Major Hayes, that's affirmative. I'm still heading southeast. So far, no Rebel radio contact."

"Very good RAINDROP. Let us just listen for Hans-Peter."

When the last seconds of rocket burn were finally accomplished, the Rebel continued racing to higher altitudes. Hans-Peter called out, "A-10s, this is the Rebel. Do you copy?"

"Affirmative, Rebel. This is the A-10 lead, your transmission is now clear."

"A-10s, can you still see us?"

"That's a negative, Rebel. My recon pod is still tracking you. We lost your signal during your rocket burn. I'm showing your altitude at 210K and climbing."

"A-10s, your altitude number is good. It's what I'm showing here. Thank you for the confirmation."

"Rebel, we saw flameout at about 70 miles of altitude. How much longer will you continue to coast up?"

"A-10s, it will be about 100 seconds longer."

"We're in space!" said Ruthiebell. "The sky is black. I can see the stars. When can I start? My independent radio is on, but not transmitting,"

Apprehension began to spread among the four crew embers of rebel as they realized they might actually contact an alien. Could there really be a stealthy UFO following along with them?

They were weightless. They had all become accustomed to the rocket's great voice and with it now gone, the absolute silence of space filled the aircraft.

"Okay," said Hans-Peter. "The cabin pressure is good. You may open up your helmets or take them off if you like." Hans-Peter and Angelo took off their helmets. Ruthiebell and Larry Stevens opened their visors, but kept them on. "Okay, Ruthiebell, you may start your transmissions."

"This is the Rebel aircraft hailing our unseen spacecraft companion. Do you copy?" Ruthiebell had transmitted her message over the first 14 frequencies simultaneously. Nothing came back. She shifted to the next 14 frequencies. "This is the Rebel aircraft hailing our unseen spacecraft companion. Do you copy?" Nothing. Nothing came back. "What's on the radar? Do you see something flying along with us?"

"No ma'am," answered Colonel Stevens. "I see nothing in our proximity."

"Well, how about behind us? What's back there?"

"Nothing," answered the colonel. "Our aft-looking radar appears to be working correctly. There is nothing behind us that I can see."

Ruthiebell shifted to the next 14 frequencies. "This is the Rebel aircraft hailing our unseen spacecraft companion. Do you copy? We know you are there. May we see and admire your spacecraft?"

Nothing came back.

Angelo and the colonel and Hans-Peter began to relax. It was looking like this would not be the day for a close encounter. None of them had ever had a close encounter. Recalling the apprehension they had felt when Ruthiebell had radioed out the first time was now a bit embarrassing. They wouldn't ever admit that for just a minute they thought Ruthiebell might actually find an alien, in a UFO, and talk to them.

Ruthiebell shifted to the next 14 frequencies and called out again. Nothing came back. "Okay, I'm going to put this thing on automatic," she said. "I'll let it try as many frequencies as it can."

Hans-Peter focused his attention on the instruments monitoring the rocket engine. "The lithium injector is 300 degrees too hot," he said. "It hasn't taken the automatic shut down yet."

"Mark 108.8 seconds," said Angelo. "We are at zero velocity. San Bernardino, this is the Rebel. We mark maximum altitude at 562,700 feet or about 106 miles. Altitude accomplished. We are now falling back."

"Rebel, this is San Bernardino Flight Control. Congratulations on accomplishing your altitude objective. Your telemetry shows excessive heat in the lithium injector. Is this anomaly becoming critical?"

"The anomaly is not yet critical. I just shut it down manually," answered Hans-Peter.

"Very good Rebel, now bring that buggy home safely."

"Thank you, San Bernardino. What max altitude did you read?"

"We read 106.8 miles and we will affirm your objective accomplished."

"Hailing the Rebel aircraft. This is the International Space Station, do you copy?"

Hans-Peter was amazed. The voice had a slight Russian accent. His first thought was that someone on the ground was pulling his leg, but he wasn't sure who could fake a Russian accent. "This is Hans-Peter of the Rebel aircraft. We received your transmission, loud and clear. Can you actually see us?"

"Negative, Rebel, you are much too far away. We have been following your flight telemetry and extend our congratulations. Are you aware of an Indian Space Research Organization satellite in Low Earth Orbit closing on your position?"

"ISS, that's negative. What altitude is it at?"

"Rebel, we read 94.2 miles and on a near collision course with you. At the rate you are falling, it should pass over you by about a quarter mile. This will give you an opportunity to test your photo recon equipment. Do you see the satellite due west of your position?"

"Yes," said Larry Stevens. "I have it on radar and closing fast."

"Is there any chance of collision?" asked Hans-Peter.

"No," answered Larry. "The ISS prediction looks good. It will be about a quarter of a mile when it passes by us."

"LOOK!!" yelled Ruthiebell. "There it goes. It could be a UFO. It was going so fast, if you blinked you would miss it."

"It was fast. In fact I'd bet it was fast enough to be in Low Earth Orbit," said Hans-Peter. "Satellites in LEO are going about 17,500 miles per hour. If we weren't looking in just the right direction, at just the right time we wouldn't have seen it go by."

"How can we be sure what it was?" asked Ruthiebell.

"Rebel aircraft, your communication we are hearing. The object was Yamsat-3. It is of the Indian Space Research Organization. Its telemetry we monitor. Your path is now clear."

"Yeah, that's what they all say," grumbled Ruthiebell. "Next thing you know you'll be telling us it was swamp gas or a weather balloon."

"ISS, this is the Rebel. I thought that the Indian Space Research Organization liked 300 to 400 mile orbits."

"That is true comrade, but that one never made it. Yamsat-3 is in a decaying orbit. It will fall back to earth in a month. We have now passed over your position."

"This is the Rebel, we are falling back into the atmosphere and you are getting much farther away. Were you able to measure our maximum altitude?"

"Affirmative Rebel, we read 562,822 feet, or 106.59507 miles. There is no question, comrade, that you have accomplished your goal. May your trip home be safe and most likely pleasant."

"Thank you, my new friend. Before you leave, may I ask your name?"

"This is no problem. I am Cosmonaut Yuriy Brominkov and this is my seventy-fourth day in space. We are moving away from you at a rate of 4.76 miles per second."

"That sounds pretty fast. Was it something I said?"

Angelo still had his helmet off and started to laugh.

A different voice came from the space station with a thick Australian accent, "No, mate. Try to remember what you can about orbital mechanics. Is there any chance you can get your airplane to go about 18,000 miles an hour faster?"

"ISS, that would be quite an accomplishment. Do you think that's even possible?"

"Rebel, it's no secret your airplane can hold itself together in space," replied the Australian. "What you're lacking, my friend, is a better rocket. Have you given that a little thought?"

"I think about that all the time," said Hans-Peter, "but it can't be done with chemical propulsion. So you tell me, if I could get it going faster, what did you have in mind?"

"Rebel, you know our address. If you ever procure the right engine, then by all means stop by for tea and cakes next time you're up our way. All of us here in the space station want you to know that the welcome mat is out for the Rebel and her crew."

"Thank you, space station. I'll definitely look into that possibility. Space station, your contact was unanticipated and a pleasure to receive. As we fall away, let us wish you and your company our very best. This is the Rebel signing out."

"So it really was a satellite," said Ruthiebell, her voice drifting into despair.

"Angelo, I'd like you to modify our attitude by hand," said Hans-Peter. "Let's log some more experience with the Reaction Control System. I'd like some real-world data on the RCS rocket engine performance. Put us nose down 45 degrees. Line us up with what I just put on your display. Start the maneuver now. We're looking for the first signs of the atmosphere."

Each time Angelo moved the RCS stick, small RCS rocket thrusters nudged the aircraft into a slightly different orientation. He proceeded cautiously, building experience with every try.

"How much atmospheric heating will we get on reentry?" asked Ruthiebell.

"Nothing at all. I doubt our free fall will take us too much above Mach One. Atmospheric heating doesn't start until well above Mach Two."

"The craft is aligned with your request," reported Angelo.

"We are falling fast and just fell through 200,000 feet," reported the copilot. I'm also still showing a red light for the engine compartment. It just started flashing. Is it flashing on your panel?"

"Yes. I have it also. I've been watching it. My manual shut down must not have worked. I'm cutting all power to the engine. If it doesn't start cooling, I'll eject the whole rocket assembly out the tail. I don't like the heat, but it's not yet threatening the aft structure. Okay, we're not cooling, but we've not getting any hotter either."

"Rebel, this is San Bernardino. The red light for the lithium injector has stopped flashing but it's still on. Will you need to initiate an emergency procedure?"

"No, San Bernardino. We are hot, but stable. The temperature just dropped 5 degrees. We're cooling. We should be home in 28 minutes."

Chapter Eight
Talking to Tabby

Major Hayes and Lieutenant Raymo Woodburn banked their A-10 aircraft into the final approach to the Cactus Patch airfield. The lieutenant was only four seconds aft of the major and their landings were flawless. Knowing the Rebel was still in flight, they taxied quickly to the hangars, as they wanted to hear the telemetry coming in. Neither one hit the locker room. They went directly to the operations tent to see how much of the telemetry Corporal Tabby was getting.

Tabby was seated at the table with the displays and controls. Four of the lieutenants and the two captains were standing around behind him. When the major and Lieutenant Woodburn came in, no one was saying a word. None of them, including the two captains, had wanted to challenge Martinelli's certainty that the third A-10 radar profile was an electronic shadow. Martinelli hadn't sounded like himself when he had instructed Tabby how to write up the mysterious third aircraft. Lieutenant Martinelli's certainty had made everyone apprehensive. The quiet inside the tent had become eerie. Everyone was waiting to see what would happen next.

The major could feel the strange tension as he entered the room. "What's happened?" he asked.

"Nothing really," said Martinelli. "The Rebel developed a thermal problem in the rocket engine bay, but it sounds like they have it under control."

"Okay. We heard about that as we were landing," continued the major. "What else? I can feel enough apprehension in this room to sink a ship. What else went wrong?"

"Corporal Tabby saw an electronic shadow on the screen that looked a lot like another A-10," said Martinelli. "I was briefed on such phenomena when I was stationed at Wright Patterson. I passed along the correct procedure to the corporal, and we were all watching closely to see what would happen next." As Martinelli spoke, he removed what looked like a black credit card from his wallet and gave it to the major. "Major, may I ask if you saw a third A-10 flying with you?"

The major examined the plastic card carefully. "I have never seen one of these. This is no time for an elaborate joke. Is this real?"

"Yes sir, it is."

The major returned the card. "Was there anything wrong with the way Lieutenant Woodburn and I flew our sortie?"

"No sir. Your altitude and speed over Norton Field were correct. I doubt we will be hearing anything critical from the FAA."

"Okay, that's good," said the major, starting to relax. "Turn up the volume, corporal, let's listen in to Hans-Peter and see how he's doing."

The voice of Hans-Peter came over the speaker. "San Bernardino, we have passed the Big Morongo Canyon and are now turning to 315 degrees northwest. I estimate our touchdown in six minutes."

At the same moment in San Bernardino, Claudius had taken over Eleanor's desk and didn't like what he was seeing. "Rebel, this is San Bernardino, we see your position as reported. We are still seeing the red light from your engine bay. Your telemetry is no longer reporting a temperature. Are you still reading a problem?"

"Roger that, San Bernardino. We still have too much heat back there, but it's cooling slowly. I see no problem for our landing."

"Rebel, this is Claudius Thud, you have an emergency option. We can help you. If that thing looks too hot, eject it over the Santa Ana Wash before you touch down. We can tell you the safest time to eject that engine before it catches fire. We can tell you when you'll be over rocks and sand. Do you copy?"

"Yes San Bernardino, we copy," said Hans-Peter. "We understand. I am unlocking the rocket assembly for an eject. If we start to reheat, I will eject it. If it continues to cool, I'll bring it home. The unlock is accomplished. Please give me your countdown for the best eject time."

"Are you going to eject your rocket engine?" asked Claudius.

"So far no, but let me hear your countdown."

"Rebel, you needn't risk a fire on landing."

"Understood, San Bernardino. Please let me hear your countdown."

"Best eject time is 115 seconds. What is your temperature?"

"812 degrees make that 810 degrees."

"The best time is in 82 seconds. . . . 72 seconds. . . . 62 seconds."

"We will not eject. Repeat, we will not eject. The temperature is 785 and falling. We are now turning west to our final approach."

Claudius spoke directly to Eleanor. "Roll your fire equipment. Let's prepare for the worst. He then stood up for a better look out the windows.

"I'm turning onto 237 magnetic," said Angelo. "Gear is down and locked."

Many of the spectators were listening to the Rebel on their own radios. Everyone knew a fire was possible on landing. As the Rebel came in, the two airport fire trucks came into view with their sirens screaming as they rolled toward the runway. The soldiers manning the Army fire trucks were listening to the Rebel's frequency and had started their engines. They were holding their positions. If or more likely when they were called, they were ready to roll in a heartbeat. Eleanor was outside on the balcony watching the Rebel come in through her binoculars.

Angelo adjusted slightly for the small crosswind and touched the main gear down where they belonged. The sleek titanium bird came in fast and as it slowed, Angelo lowered the nose gear to the runway and then spun up the jet engines for reverse thrust. The Rebel rolled along for its second prefect landing. The crowd cheered and so did I. Hans-Peter was home and he had managed to bring his faulty rocket engine home with him.

Out at Cactus Patch, when the Rebel turned and started to taxi, the officers standing behind Tabby clapped and complemented pilot Angelo out loud.

Major Hayes didn't seem too surprised with the textbook landing and said, "That's really what I expected. Those people know what they're doing." The major then turned his attention to Tabby. "Have you uploaded any of that shadow data yet?"

"Yes sir. It uploaded at the ten-minute mark automatically. My transmission note stated that the shadow was remarkably clear and confirmed the need for our equipment to be rebuilt. Ten minutes later the system uploaded you and Lieutenant Woodburn along with that shadow breaking away from the rebel and starting back to our base. That second upload was also automatic, sir."

"How long did that shadow stay with us?"

"All the way back, sir."

"Did it land with us?" asked the major. "If it's a true shadow, it should have stayed with us all the way in to our parking place. Did you see it?"

"Only the radar image," said Tabby. "It came down with you to fifty feet and then flew over you staying at fifty feet. At the end of the runway it stopped for about seventy seconds and then it flew straight up."

"The radar can be anomalous. Did you actually see the physical object?"

"No sir. I was here inside, but I trained the video camera where the radar was pointing and there was nothing there."

"How about the airmen outside? Did anybody see it?"

"Not that I know of. No one has reported anything."

"Did you see it, Raymo?" asked Martinelli. "Did you see it as you taxied off the field?"

"No, but I wasn't looking for it. I was following the major off the field."

"So, what happened after the seventy seconds?" asked the major.

"The image flew straight up over 80,000 feet and disappeared. Would you like me to let the system upload your return and safe landing and whatever it saw of the shadow?"

The major looked at Martinelli without saying a word. Martinelli gave the major a subtle 'yes' nod. "Yes, Corporal Tabby," said the major, "let the system upload that last data set. Lieutenant Potash, given your qualifications, I'd like you to take Corporal Tabby's place until this shift changes."

"Yes, sir," snapped Potash and came forward.

Tabby had released the last data set, and stood up from the table. Potash took Tabby's place and turned off the telemetry patch. "The Rebel is no longer sending telemetry," said Potash. "I have turned off our patch."

"Corporal Tabby, I'd like you to join me, Martinelli, and the two captains in my office right now; and you too, Raymo. Come along, gentlemen."

The major's office was a canvas affair inside a larger tent. It was rather like a small tent inside a much larger tent and it was fairly quiet and secure. The major stayed by the entrance while his men came in. He told the sergeant standing outside his office that they were not to be interrupted. He directed the sergeant to stand about ten feet away and then he let the flap down. As he entered, he closed the door that was inside the flap. The major took his place at his desk and then thought for a minute. He didn't want to proceed, but he had no choice. "Gentlemen, Lieutenant Martinelli is holding a clearance I don't have and I had hoped I would never see.

Lieutenant, please give us the correct debriefing for this event."

"Thank you, major. What I'm about to tell you, you may never talk about outside of this meeting, and you may never confirm or even mention that this meeting ever happened. Over the last three years, the Air Force and the CIA have confirmed that extraterrestrials are operating small flying craft from a large mother craft somewhere out in the Pacific Ocean. The mother ship is hidden under water and can move at will. Our navy knows it's there, but they can't keep track of it. Its stealth is very good. They can also cloak their small aircraft optically, so we can't see them, but they can't cloak their radar image. What they can do, however, is disguise their radar signature, so it looks like an A-10 or a 737 or whatever they want." Martinelli now looked at Tabby. "Corporal Tabby, you were probably reading the radar signature of a real UFO flying with the major and Raymo."

Raymo's right hand became a fist as his adrenaline surged for a fight. He let his fist settle into his left hand. It was all he could do to appear calm and composed.

Tabby turned white and seemed unstable where he stood. The medical officer was at his side in an instant. "Steady there, Tabby," said the captain with genuine sympathy. "Come on over here, I'd like you to sit in my chair. It's okay, just sit right down here." The medical officer stood behind him and put a comforting hand on his shoulder. "Please continue lieutenant."

"A number of us were briefed on this alien presence and how to handle it. The good news is that they appear to be totally benign. The bad news is we don't know who they are or what they want. The last I heard, we have had no communication with them despite our best efforts. Okay, so now you know I'm your liaison. Don't talk about this. It never happened, but if you learn anything more, come and talk to me when we are away from everyone else. It's possible, and we are all hoping, that they'll just go away as they usually do."

"You're telling us this has happened before?" asked the major.

"Yes sir. The little craft that shadowed you today is about the size of the one that crashed at Roswell."

"That was supposed to be a weather balloon," said the medical officer. "You're now telling us it was a real UFO?"

"Yes sir. I saw some of the wreckage at Wright Patterson and believe me, that was no weather balloon and it sure wasn't anything the Soviets built, either."

The Rebel had now rolled to a stop in a fire control area away from the hangars. The fire trucks had followed it there and stood ready while ground personnel helped the crew with an emergency disembark. Hans-Peter was the last one out and talked to the ground crew. After giving some instructions to his ground crew chief, he took a ride to meet up with the rest of his crew.

Back inside the tent, the three crewmembers had taken seats on the speakers' platform and were waiting for Hans-Peter. The side of the tent behind the platform was still open, but the Rebel couldn't be seen. The fire control area was around behind the large hangar and out of view.

We all saw the jeep with Hans-Peter come around the side of that hangar and then over to the tent. It stopped near the platform and when he got out, everyone stood with enthusiastic applause. He came inside and took the podium.

"We're all home safe and sound," he said. "What more can I say?" Even before he finished his sentence we all applauded again. "As you all know, we flew an experimental tri-propellant engine and I had trouble shutting down the high-temp lithium injector. The engine, however, performed beautifully; and as you all know, we made our altitude objective. I appreciated the fire trucks coming out to help if needed, but it really was a lot more precaution than necessary."

Today we had a flight plan that called for an assault on the altitude of Low Earth Orbit." He had hardly finished his sentence when another round of applause interrupted him. "Aboard the Rebel we recorded 106 miles of altitude; and as you probably heard, the FAA also recorded 106 miles, but for the best accuracy, the International Space Station gave us an altitude of 106.59507 miles." Without being entirely sincere he continued with, "At the time, I wanted to ask the ISS if their altitude reading was plus or minus 2 inches, but I thought it best to maintain a grateful silence."

I always enjoyed his sense of humor, but often, like right now, no one else seemed to be getting it. He seemed to be waiting for a little laughter that wasn't coming, so I asked the first question. "Was the tri-propellant engine you flew today meant to be reusable?"

"Yes. It is designed for twenty flights," he answered. "As we speak, they're removing it. In the open air I'm sure it will cool down much faster. I'd like to thank Claudius Thud of the FAA for keeping us mindful of a safe place to eject the engine if it became a fire hazard. Thankfully, it didn't get that hot. Bringing it home in one piece will make it a lot easier to analyze." Hans-Peter looked directly at Claudius and Eleanor and said, "Again, thanks for your help."

"I think it's pretty clear to anyone who cares about safety," said Keith Wiley, "that you have no business flying an experimental rocket ship from Norton Field. I needn't make a hypothetical argument! Just look at what almost happened today."

Eleanor had stood and walked up to the platform as Keith was talking. She had a document in her hand. "Did you wish to challenge my competence or Mr. Thud's competence?" she asked Keith.

"I wouldn't dream of challenging the FAA," stammered Keith. "But today's flight gives us all some experience to consider very carefully."

"We now have had two flights for the Rebel without any problems," continued Eleanor. "Is that what you'd like us to consider?"

"Without any problems?" said Keith. "We need to consider the very reason why you rolled your fire trucks."

From his seat in the audience, Claudius called out, "I called for the fire trucks, not Hans-Peter. This airport belongs to Eleanor and I was very pleased how responsive her emergency vehicles were today. Hans-Peter made the right call for his airplane and Norton Field handled a possible problem correctly. Mr. Wiley, I think your concerns are unfounded."

Keith Wiley stood up at his seat. "Don't you people understand? Hans-Peter flew a tri-propellant rocket engine with a hot lithium injector in it. NASA never flew a tri-propellant engine on the Space Shuttle or on project Apollo or anywhere else. It wouldn't surprise me if right now we hear that thing blow up over on the other side of that big hangar."

Eleanor waved the document from where she was standing. "Mr. Wiley, I have the Rebel's flight plan right here. The rocket propellants the Rebel burned today are nothing out of the ordinary." Eleanor looked at the document. "It says right here that the rocket engine burned liquid oxygen with liquid methane, and a hot liquid lithium compound was injected into the combustion chamber. Mr. Wiley, you do understand that liquid methane is simply the cold version of the same natural gas that people burn in their kitchens?"

"Okay, okay," said Keith. "And next you're going to tell me that lithium is very much like sodium, and we all eat sodium in table salt."

Eleanor started to smile. "Why yes Mr. Wiley, you took the words right out of my mouth. It's time for you to sit down. This topic is closed.

Does anyone have a question on a different aspect of the flight?"

Sandy Koop from the *Herald Express* stood up and said, "We were all delighted to hear the Rebel communicate with the International Space Station. I gather the ISS flyby was a lucky coincidence?"

"Yes," said Angelo. "Remember the ISS orbits at about 250 miles of altitude and we were only at about 100 miles. So if they hadn't been looking down with some pretty good equipment, at just the right moment, they would have never seen us."

"We all heard that Australian astronaut, Rodney Ellis, ask if you could make the Rebel go faster," continued Sandy. "In fact he said 18,000 miles per hour faster. Is such a thing even possible, or was he just giving you a bad time?"

Ruthiebell and Angelo both sat back with the pleasant expressions of those who knew a great secret. Colonel Stevens, on the other hand, seemed clueless and looked at Hans-Peter with the same curiosity that Sandy had.

Hans-Peter couldn't help but smile as he answered. "We're not sure. I believe we've found something in chemical propulsion everyone else has missed. Over the next three flights we hope to reach 300 miles in altitude and get there with orbital velocity." No sooner had Hans-Peter said, 'orbital velocity' than the audience erupted with both the sounds of disbelief and amazement all at once.

"That's impossible, totally impossible!" said Keith Wiley over the general noise. "Today you just barely got up to a hundred miles, and when you got there, you had no velocity at all; and your engine almost caught fire. You can't just stand up there in front of us and tell us the Rebel can fly into orbit. Is this some sleazy way to overprice your stock for an imminent Initial Public Offering? Are you about to bring Titanium Composites public?"

Hans-Peter was beginning to tire of Keith Wiley and shifted his weight as he stood. "No, Mr. Wiley, there are no plans to make Titanium Composites a publicly held corporation." The audience fell quiet waiting for Mr. Wiley's reply.

"Keith you're a brain-dead disappointment," said Ruthiebell from her seat on the platform. "You're nothing but a tabloid hack looking for a sensational sound bite. You ought to be ashamed of yourself."

"Yeah, well those are pretty tall words for somebody who believes in little green men and that hollow moon nonsense," retorted Keith without letting a second go by. "We all heard your lovely voice hailing an 'unseen spacecraft companion.' Is an unseen spacecraft anything like a UFO?"

"Look on the Internet, Mr. Wiley," snapped Ruthiebell. "There are astronauts saying that every human space launch is accompanied by a UFO. I find that testimony, deeply troubling. It's something we can't ignore anymore."

"So what are we ignoring?" pressed Keith. "Did you actually talk to an 'unseen spacecraft companion.' Were there some little green men following you?"

People started laughing, but I wasn't sure if they were laughing at Keith or at Ruthiebell, maybe both of them.

"No, Mr. Wiley," Ruthiebell answered, showing some disappointment in her voice. "As you heard, I did call out on many different frequencies, but just because nobody answered, doesn't mean some ET wasn't right there with us. If there was a UFO flying along with us, it stayed hidden from view. We didn't see it."

At the moment, Hans-Peter seemed surprised and amused by the way Ruthiebell was handling Keith Wiley.

Hans-Peter and I had talked about how much he wanted to reveal. It was time for me to drop his rocket performance number into this briefing. I stood up and said, "I would like to congratulate you all on your second successful flight. What you have accomplished today is astonishing. My best guess is that to get the Rebel up to 106 miles in altitude, your rocket engine had to deliver about 800 seconds of specific impulse. Can you comment on my best guess?"

"That's a pretty good guess, Mr. Artamus," said Hans-Peter with just a hint of friendship. "It's apparent that Mr. Artamus here actually knows a few of the equations. The answer to your question is, 'Yes.' Our tri-propellant engine delivered very nearly 800 seconds of average performance today, and that's how we reached 106 miles of altitude."

"Nobody has ever gotten 800 seconds out of a chemical rocket before," protested Keith. "It can't be done."

"It was done today and I was there," said Ruthiebell. "Looking out the window of the Rebel was nothing like looking out the window of a jet liner. We were there. We were at the edge of space, but my testimony isn't so important. Mr. Wiley, are you saying that the FAA number of 106 miles and the ISS number of 106 miles are both wrong and fraudulent?"

"No, Ms. Ruthiebell, I'm not calling the FAA or the ISS wrong and fraudulent," said Keith rather hastily. "Listen, I happen to know, and I'll bet Mr. Artamus also knows, that even if you could get 100% of the chemical energy out of the propellants, you still couldn't get 800 seconds. It's just not there!"

"That's true for LOX and methane, Mr. Wiley, but are you quite sure that you used the correct coefficient for lithium?" asked Hans-Peter.

The other three reporters stood up and started firing questions at Hans-Peter. I continued to stand, but it was only to hear what the others were saying. At this point I knew Hans-Peter had built an aerospace plane. The hypersonic airplane story was just a cover. I listened carefully to see if any of my colleagues from the press even knew how to ask the right kind of questions.

The next day, Sandy was beaming with success as she typed her copy within her new office at the *Herald*. Her new office still didn't have a door, but she didn't care. She was the only one at the paper, other than Ruthiebell, that had access to Titanium Composites and the amazing Rebel aircraft, or was it the amazing Rebel rocket ship? The old fashioned telephone on her desk rang. "Yes sir," she said playfully, "I'll be right there."

When she entered Max's office, Milo Schotts was already there. "As you come in, please close the door behind you."

"You know, Max," she said, "some of us don't actually have a door."

"Yes, yes, of course. Please sit down. Milo here has something more interesting than anything I've ever heard. Just listen to this man."

"You're on your way to becoming a reporter," said Milo. "Can I trust you? What I mean is if I tell you what I know, will you promise to never divulge your source? And I mean it. This is no fooling around here."

"If you want to tell me about breaking the law or some kind of criminal activity, don't bother. I'm not going to do that kind of stuff. I'm out of here."

Max smiled. "I'd never do that to you, but sometimes a source doesn't need any credit and wants to remain anonymous. Can you respect that kind of a source?"

"If you're talking criminal activity, count me out."

"What Milo can tell you now, you might figure out in a couple weeks on your own. If you keep Milo's name anonymous, he'll give you a head start."

She looked at Milo, and he gave her the smile meant for a colleague, not a competitor. "Okay, that sounds okay. I will keep you anonymous, Milo. You can trust me. So what do you have?"

"Well, there's an old guy out at Cactus Patch that I've known for a long time and he knows how to hear things. So you remember that Corporal Tabby, the one who was so sweet on you?"

"What are you talking about? There was no time for anybody to be sweet on anybody out there."

"Think for a minute," said Milo. "He was the corporal in the new uniform who started to introduce you to the major and lost his voice just because he was near you."

Sandy stifled a smile, remembering full well what had happened. She remembered that moment with great clarity. Tabby was her age and not a bad looking man. "Oh, yes," she said. "He was about my age. I think he's been out in the sun too long."

"Yes!" said Max. "He'd walk over the hot rocks to talk to you."

"Oh, perhaps," she said indifferently. "Why do we care?"

"Corporal Tabby runs their operations desk," continued Milo. "He was the one back at the field keeping track of the A-10s when they escorted the Rebel yesterday. The Air Force has much better radar than the FAA does. He could see things they couldn't."

"So what did he see?" she said with increasing interest.

"The two A-10s were shadowed by a UFO about the same size as the Roswell UFO. The UFO was optically cloaked so nobody could see it; but Tabby, with his fancy radar, tracked it with precision. The Air Force uses the phrase 'radar shadow' as their code for UFOs. And get this, Tabby said he had a 'radar shadow' that stopped midair then flew straight up to 80,000 feet and then disappeared."

"Are you making this up? Max already told me he wanted a UFO angle, and I already told him he was nuts."

"It's not my story, it's Milo's," said Max. "I want you to have lunch or maybe a dinner with Tabby. You know, just be friendly and ask him some questions. Let him have the pure joy of your company."

"Do you want me to fly back out to Cactus Patch?"

"No. You need to get some time with him away from the other guys," said Max. "Call him up and ask him if he ever comes into one of airports with one of their cargo planes. Tell him you could meet him for lunch. Be creative Sandy. Now go figure it out. Get out of here, I got work to do."

Corporal Tabby was at the desk trying to figure out what exactly that black card was that Martinelli had shown the major.

Back at her desk, Sandy dialed the only number she had. "Hello, this is Sandy Koop of the *Herald Express*. Have I reached the A-10 field called Cactus Patch?"

Tabby recognized her voce even before she said her name. "Yes ma'am, you have reached the A-10 field often referred to as Cactus Patch. How may I help you?"

"Is that you, Corporal Tabby?" she said with a bit of enthusiasm.

"Yes ma'am," he said from rote while his blood pressure was going astronomical. "How may I help you?" His mind was on fire with pure joy. She remembers me, was his only thought.

"My photographer and I thoroughly enjoyed our visit to Cactus Patch, but I regretted not being able to hear about the Rebel flight from your point of view. Do you ever fly into LA on one of those transports to help with the supplies?"

Tabby knew the major owed him one for uncovering the Rebel story before anyone else even knew it existed. The major was a good man; in fact he was a bit fatherly toward his younger men, and he didn't mind letting Tabby fly into LAX the next day on a transport returning used equipment.

Sandy drove to the south side of Los Angeles International Airport to meet the C-130 from Cactus Patch. The south side of the airport was mostly freight. She didn't have to park. Tabby was waiting for her outside the hangar and as he stepped into her car, she asked, "How long do you have for lunch?"

"Today, I have at least four hours."

She left the terminal driving west along the south side of the huge airport. When the road ended at the beach, she turned south to a lavish restaurant she had always wanted to try. The place was expensive, but Max was paying. Inside, and at the best table with a view of the surf, she said, "It's my treat, or I should say it's on the paper; so please order anything you like."

Tabby felt good about wearing his newest uniform, but with lunch on the paper he realized this wasn't a date. He realized it might be a trap, but then she couldn't possibly know about the radar shadow. "Did old Milo Schotts get some good photos of our FOB?" he asked.

"FOB?" she said letting her tone of voice make it a question.

"Yes. Cactus Patch was built just like a Forward Operations Base and we run it that way. The tent where you had lunch was just like the ones they put up in a war zone. My job is an exact match to combat operations," said Tabby starting to feel more in control of the conversation. "What part of my day did you want to hear about?"

Sandy could tell he was feeling in control. She found that amusing, but didn't let it show. She knew how to let her eyes tell him she was interested in more than the A-10s. Tabby wouldn't be the first man whose thinking she had derailed with the hint of a more passionate encounter. "Now, it was my understanding that while they were off flying their airplanes, you were the one that kept track of what was going on back at the FOB?"

"Yes, I was the one on the operations desk for both of the Rebel flights," he said with great confidence.

"Does the Air Force have much better radar than the FAA?"

"Well, of course, I can say with pride that the Air Force has very good radar, but I can't compare them. I really don't know what the FAA has."

"On that first flight, three A-10s escorted the Rebel. If there was a biz-jet, that was about the same size as an A-10, that just happened to fly by, could you tell the difference?"

"Yes, of course, some of the guys couldn't tell the difference, but I can. I assure you that I know all the subtle differences. I can identify them all. To date I haven't made a mistake."

"Really," she said with a sigh of admiration. "I would guess those guys in the air depend on you for navigational support and other kinds of help I don't even know about."

"Yes ma'am, it's part of the job. It's all in a day's work." He returned her gaze with the best blend of affection and respect he could muster.

"Then you would know. On that second flight, were there really three A-10s chasing the Rebel?"

"No, that's nonsense. That third image was nothing more than a 'radar shadow.' It was a technical anomaly. It really wasn't there at all." Instantly, he realized he had just given away the very thing Lieutenant Martinelli had told them to never say. His mind went into high gear. What could he say? "You know the government is very sensitive about the quality of our equipment. Would you please not mention my name if you decide to write about the occasional anomaly that can happen on a radar screen?"

"Don't worry about that for a minute. My readers don't want to hear about problems. They want to hear about the important work you do supporting our troops in the field." My God, she thought, he said the phrase 'radar shadow,' and now he's trying to distract me and cover it over. He's proving to me that a 'radar shadow' must be important. I'm not going to quote this guy and get him in trouble, but I need to talk to Max and Milo. Old Milo might be onto something.

Chapter Nine
Seven or Eight Rocks

A couple of days after the Rebel's second flight, I had finished up three articles including an editorial for the Sunday Paper. I gave Hans-Peter a call and said I'd like to come out and let him read my copy before I submitted it. I wanted to include his flight objectives for the next flight.

Hans-Peter liked the idea, but told me that the FAA had just grounded the Rebel until they had a better technical description of his tri-propellant rocket engine. They had apparently decided that they needed to understand the thermal problem with the lithium injector. He therefore had no idea when he could schedule the next flight. He then asked me if I could possibly find out what exactly they were concerned about. He told me he was sure there was more to the grounding than concerns about a bad solenoid. We talked a bit further and he invited me to come out to his place for a few days when I knew what the FAA was looking for. I was pleased that he had asked me to help him deal with the federal bureaucracy, and I agreed to drive out when I knew something.

Needless to say, I called Claudius Thud over at the FAA as soon as Hans-Peter hung up the phone. After we were finally connected, I started by saying, "When I was writing up that second Rebel flight, I gave Hans-Peter a call and he told me that the FAA had grounded the Rebel." Then I asked him what he could tell me about the decision to ground the Rebel.

"The Rebel aircraft is not actually grounded," said Claudius. "We have grounded his tri-propellant rocket engine. If he wants to fly that thing with the JP-4/LOX engine that he used on his first flight, that's fine with us. If you may recall, he fired the JP-4/LOX engine twice. At the lower altitude his engine gave him an average of 287 seconds of impulse and at the higher altitude it averaged 315 seconds. We understand those numbers.

His tri-propellant, on the other hand, gave him a performance that is impossible. We have grounded the tri-propellant engine until we know what he's doing. That one may not fly again until we give it full certification."

"Isn't that more reactionary than needed? I was there and I heard the way he dealt with that thermal problem. At the time, we all thought it was just a solenoid problem. Now, I do understand that some components should be fail-safe, and I'm sure they do too. Even as we speak, I'm sure they're working out a better backup. Will the rework description for the faulty solenoid be enough to get that engine certification?"

"No, you're not hearing what I'm saying," said Claudius. "We all know he can fix the solenoid. The problem is Hans-Peter is not disclosing enough of the tri-propellant engineering to account for its extraordinary performance. We listen to all of you guys. Do you remember Keith Wiley standing up and saying that Hans-Peter was getting more chemical energy out of his propellants than is possible?"

"Well, I remember Hans-Peter saying they got about 800 seconds."

"That's right!" answered Claudius. "Thermal chemistry and rocket engineering are very well understood nowadays. We ran the problem by some rocket engineers we trust and they told us Keith was right. You can't get 800 seconds out of LOX and methane even if you inject hot lithium into the combustion chamber. They also said that the only way Hans-Peter could get the performance we all recorded was if he was actually getting 800 seconds. That means the 800 seconds are real. They made it clear that his rocket engine was more than twice as good as anything now flying."

"So did your trustworthy friends come up with a theory for how he was able to get 800 seconds of specific impulse?"

"The only thing they could come up with, and I mean this is really off the wall, is that old Hans-Peter has figured out how to release just a pinch of the nuclear energy in his fuel. They were also very quick to say that only one of Hans-Peter's patents dealt with a unique concept for cold fusion, and of course we all know that cold fusion is impossible."

"So the real objection is that you don't trust an engine that can deliver more energy than is possible with the chemistry of LOX and methane and a pinch of lithium?" I answered trying not to give away my own thoughts on the matter.

"Yes, that's exactly our position," said Claudius. "Now listen, Traypart, I've been very candid with you. You know, I've stepped over the line a time or two for Hans-Peter, and I would like to see him succeed; but I can only push the rules so far. He needs to tell us how he's getting all that performance. If he has learned how to control a small nuclear reaction and he's not telling us, he's both brilliant and in real trouble. Anyone using nuclear energy must disclose what they're doing, and comply with every detail of the law, or they get thrown in jail. That's the law."

"Now, you're a good writer, and I expect both intelligence and discretion from you. Think about this carefully. See if you can interview Hans-Peter and find out what he's doing. When you talk to him, encourage him to give us a full disclosure before he even files the flight plan for his next flight. You tell him to let us help him operate inside the law. Now, I look forward to reading how you make sense of all this. Do you think you can do this? Is that a reasonable request?"

"Yes sir," I answered. "I will try to encourage him to give you the kind of disclosure you need. You have given me much to think about. I will make my best effort. Please let me thank you for your time."

Each day in Low Earth Orbit is bounded by the ever-changing beauty of the earth below, and above, by the magic of infinite space. Residents of the Space Station never lose sight of how unearthly their experience is. It's likely that many of them would rather it never ended.

Yuriy Brominkov floated along the corridor to join his Australian friend Rodney Ellis. Australia was not one of the five nations, or in the case of Europe we should say agencies, that own and operate the ISS. For this expedition, Rodney was flying on behalf of the Canadians. Yuriy had finished his rather complicated housekeeping tasks and knew that Rodney was also near a break. "And are you finishing your task?" he called forward as he floated along.

"I have. Why not join me down at the pub for a cold one? My shout," answered Rodney.

The Russian had heard this question before and didn't think the impossibility of such a thing made it humorous. He had also thought about how to respond to the Aussie at times like this. "That sounds good, my friend, but not today. I would like to talk about what the American said when I told him the ISS was moving away from him at a rate of 4.76 miles per second."

"Refresh my memory," said the Aussie. "What was it he said?"

"He said, 'that sounds pretty fast. Was it something I said?' Why would he make that his question?"

Rodney smiled remembering the words. "He was just pulling your leg, mate. Sometimes a person will leave someone when they say something they don't like. Rather than argue with them, they just walk away."

Yuriy knew that 'pulling your leg,' meant you were being teased. "But I said nothing that was bad," he answered, "and no difference happens by the things I say. The speed of the ISS is not dependent on what I say. The speed is not changed by words."

"Yes, that's right. The humor is that Hans-Peter is pretending to not understand fully what is going on."

Yuriy narrowed his eyes as he considered what Rodney said. "You are telling me, that for the sake of a smile, this man Hans-Peter is not afraid to poke at himself some little fun."

The dull sound of a hammer hitting outside the space station was heard, then instantly the vibration of the impact was felt. Several monitoring displays lit up red recording the event. It was likely a small meteor strike, something like a pebble or a small rock. Both men went to display screens and started looking for a problem. The computer systems quickly determined there were no air leaks in any of the modules.

"We have not been penetrated," said Rodney. "The skin is intact, but we are being pushed."

"I cannot feel it, comrade," answered Yuriy. "My computer says the force is like one of the thrusters on a Soyuz spacecraft is firing nonstop." Yuriy was at a Russian computer and was scanning the propulsion systems on the two Soyuz spacecraft. "The thrusters are all cold, but the level of hydrazine in the outboard Soyuz is falling quickly."

"It must have taken the impact," said Rodney. "If it put a hole in the tank, the escaping fuel is acting like a small rocket engine, and it would push us just like a small RCS thruster."

Nancy, the American astronaut floated into the cabin. "That's what we saw on our computer. "Chris and I want to fire an opposing thruster to compensate until the tank is empty."

"Yes." Yuriy and Rod answered in unison. Rod then said, "If you know the vector, fire the thruster."

Chris fired the thruster as soon as he heard the confirming 'yes.' Fortunately the thrust from the leaking tank was very small and Chris was able to control the station's attitude with very little force.

"That's it, that's all we need," said Yuriy. "I'm showing the hydrazine tank is now empty."

Chris called down the corridor, "I can also see it, Yuriy." Chris shut down the thruster he was using. "It pushed us into a slow rotation. I can fix it, it will take me about a half an hour."

"Let me help you, mate," called out Rodney. "This is my speciality." Rod then pulled himself past Nancy and over to the computer where Chris was working.

"We now have a problem," said Nancy speaking more or less to everyone. "I'm going to say what everyone is thinking. If we need an emergency evacuation, that undamaged Soyuz can only take three of us home. Therefore, nothing is more important than patching up the damaged Soyuz tank and then filling it with fuel from the station's attitude control system. We must do this as quickly as possible."

"I have Moscow Mission Control," said Yuriy. "If they can fly another Soyuz without crew then the other three of us can go home in that one. Right now they are determining when they can launch the next Soyuz."

"We don't need to abandon the ISS," said Chris; "we have one perfectly good Soyuz and if we can fix the other one, we won't need another one."

"That's if we can fix it. Right now three of us have no way home," said Nancy.

"Comrades, let us learn quickly if we can fix the broken tank," said Yuriy. "If we can fix it, three of us can go home in it before it be broken again, and the other three of us can stay here uninterrupted on their expeditions. Moscow can take all the time they need and launch the next crew in a new Soyuz, when they are ready. Yes? This is what we must do. Nancy is right. Now is when we start!"

Chris agreed to stay with the ISS attitude controller. Yuriy was the best choice for the Extra Vehicular Activity and Rodney went with him to help with the space suit. Nancy stayed in contact with Mission Control as Aleksey and Valentina came in from their sleeping quarters. Learning of the problem, Aleksey went to help Yuriy and Rodney as Valentina started scanning the storage tanks for the best place to draw stored hydrazine to refill the Soyuz tank.

"That is not the best news," said Nancy to Mission Control in Moscow. She looked over to Chris and Valentina, "Moscow is saying they can't fly for at least five weeks. They want us to talk directly to Kazakhstan for the repair. They also don't agree with our plan. If we can get the damaged Soyuz repaired, they want us to wait for a new spacecraft without a crew. When the new Soyuz spacecraft docks, we can throw away the damaged one. The damaged Soyuz is to be thought of as only a last hope to be used only in a desperate situation."

"So you're telling me they don't trust the one we're trying to fix," answered Chris.

"That's the way I read it, but they want us to try and fix it anyway," said Nancy.

"It is to be fixed, yes of course," said Valentina. "Last hope is something, and no hope is nothing."

"Hey Chris," called Aleksey. "We are ready to put Yuriy in the airlock. Is the station stable, or are you still firing thrusters?"

No sooner had Aleksey spoken, than the ISS was hit again seven or eight times. The meteors were all small, but they did considerable damage. Two of the modules started leaking air. A perfect hit broke off part of one of the solar panels and sent it flying off into space. Another hit penetrated the descent module of the other Soyuz spacecraft and started an electrical fire.

Yuriy was now in an extravehicular spacesuit. It protected him, but it was very bulky and restrictive for use inside. Air loss in some modules was slower than in others. Chris worked a minor miracle with the attitude thrusters and reestablished overall stability while the others rushed to put on their pressure suits.

In only twenty-four minutes, everyone was in a pressure suit and four of the air leaks had been plugged. When there was enough cabin air to breathe they took off their helmets. No one took off their pressure suit.

Aleksey had taken over communications as they passed over California. The American mission control was now below them. "Houston, we have a problem."

My conversation with the FAA turned up a real surprise. In the past, I had learned a great deal about different approaches to using nuclear energy in rocket engines, but I had never guessed the FAA had a clue.

Now that I knew what limitations the FAA was putting on the Rebel test program, I gave Hans-Peter a call. He seemed pleased with how fast I had learned the problems the FAA had written up against his airplane, but rather than talk about it over the phone, he invited me out for the next several days.

I left home at 10:30 a.m. when the morning traffic had finally loosened up. As I drove, I wondered if Ruthiebell might still be his guest. Mr. Maltby met me at the door and took me upstairs to the same guest room I had before. He said he would let Hans-Peter know I was here, and said that lunch would be served in the small dining room in about twenty minutes. The room I had been given was much nicer and bigger than the room I had over at the River Blossom Motel last week. It had a good writing table and chair, and a bookcase that was half full. I made a mental note to check out those titles later on.

When I walked into the dining room, Ruthiebell was already seated.

"Hello there Ruthiebell." Instantly a panic came over her eyes. I knew she didn't want me to say anything that would reveal that I was actually working for her. Acting as though this was a great coincidence I said, "I was delighted to see you fly in the observer's seat on that last flight. Did you know that I was actually here that day?"

"No, I didn't," she lied through her teeth, and spoke loud enough that Hans-Peter could hear her fabrication if he was walking toward the room.

"I'm looking forward to reading your description of your experience onboard the rebel." I thought that sentence should make me sound clueless.

"What can I say? My life is an open book," said Ruthiebell. "Were you hoping to ride along on the next flight?"

Hans-Peter came in through the double doors as Mrs. Maltby came in from the kitchen. As he sat down, he said, "Please sit down. Mrs. Maltby would prefer we all sat down for lunch."

Mrs. Maltby was skillfully carrying three salad plates and giving no indication that she heard a word that Hans-Peter was saying. Sitting down, I saw bread and butter was already on the table.

Hans-Peter was always the perfect gentleman and said, "bon appétit" to both Ruthiebell and to me. He then addressed me. "So very good to see you Traypart. I hope you are in good appetite."

"I am, and thank you." I stopped speaking to consider what was appropriate to say in Ruthiebell's presence. I wanted to be candid about what I had learned from the FAA, but I didn't know how much of this he was telling her. Ruthiebell and I were sitting across from each other and Hans-Peter was at the head of the table. I looked across at Ruthiebell. "Was that flight a chance to gather data for a new book?"

She looked at Hans-Peter with an expression that asked him how much she could say to me.

"I gather you two have never traded notes concerning how much of my work you each know."

We hadn't, and we both shook our heads 'no.'

"That's interesting," he said, "but then, you're both competing journalists and you have both honored my requests to keep certain things secret. You two are the only ones outside my company who know what I'm trying to do with the Rebel." Then he looked directly at me. "Ruthiebell and I are both eager to hear what you've learned from the FAA."

That meant Ruthiebell was an insider and I could speak freely. "I had a very good conversation with Claudius Thud. He told me the problem was not with the control hardware for the lithium injector. He told me the performance of the tri-propellant engine was so good that they could only guess it must be part nuclear; and he said if you were flying a nuclear engine without letting them know about it, you're in big trouble."

"I have said nothing about nuclear energy," said Hans-Peter. "Where on earth did they get that idea?"

"The Lithium-Fluorine-Hydrogen tri-propellant engine is only reported to have a maximum specific impulse of about 540 seconds. That makes it the very best of the chemical rockets. My friend, with the propellant mass ratio you told us you had, the only way you could get that 106 mile altitude was if your rocket gave you about 800 seconds of specific impulse. When we all saw the altitude the FAA reported, a little math confirmed you were getting 800 seconds. Anything over 550 seconds has to be something more than chemical. So they guessed nuclear; what else is there? May I ask you how you pushed the performance up that far?"

"Deuterium," he said flatly. "As I said, I burned methane with LOX and a pinch of lithium. What I didn't say was that one of the hydrogen atoms in some of my methane was the deuterium isotope instead of protium. I call the methane with deuterium heavy methane and I found a way to fuse the burning deuterium into helium-4. The more heavy methane I blend with the regular methane, the higher the specific impulse I can generate."

Ruthiebell smiled with profound satisfaction. "Cold fusion is not a fiction," she said, "and there are several ways to do it; and I think Hans has found the best way of all."

I looked at him, "You're actually fusing deuterium in your rocket engine?"

"Yes, and it's highly controllable, and I might add that my combustion chamber is more than ten times stronger than anything NASA has ever built."

"I would imagine you have tested many different concentrations of heavy methane?"

"I have."

"May I ask what the highest specific impulse is that you have been able to demonstrate?"

"Of, course you can ask, Traypart. You're being much too polite." Hans-Peter fell silent and looked at Ruthiebell. He then looked back at me and said, "I've demonstrated over 20,000 seconds."

"Oh come on! That can't possibly be true," I said, not sure if it was or wasn't. "If you can really do that, you can fly the Rebel all the way to the moon and back. That means you're sitting on better technology than anything else in the white, unclassified world. Is that even possible? 800 seconds is very high, but probably attainable. The difference between 800 and 20,000 is absurd." In fact, I knew that 20,000 seconds was possible with nuclear energy, but I thought it best to act like I believed all the twentieth-century orthodoxies. As my dad had said, you really don't need to show your hand.

Hans-Peter didn't answer me immediately. Ruthiebell didn't say anything either, and then Mr. and Mrs. Maltby came in with the main course. They had prepared Italian sausage with polenta. It was attractive enough that it ended our conversation while we tried it. Then looking directly at me, Hans-Peter said, "You know good and well if you can tap nuclear energy 20,000 is possible. The engineering isn't the problem. I must think carefully about how much I want to reveal, and what the best way is to do it. I have every confidence in you. That's why I asked you to come here. Let's talk about how I should reveal that my airplane can actually fly into orbit and back safely."

"Congratulations," I said. "You've accomplished something the other guys can't even imagine; but, my friend, you have yourself a real problem. You flew a nuclear hybrid, without disclosure, and that's grounds for a prison sentence."

"Are they going to throw me in jail, too?" asked Ruthiebell.

"They will if they can show you were a knowing contributor."

"For starters," continued Ruthiebell, "we can distract them with how correctly Hans controlled the lithium heating problem. I've already written that up. It's on the wire and it'll be in tomorrow's newspapers."

"That will make great copy," I said, "but it won't mean a thing to the FAA."

"The tri-propellant engine can work without the nuclear fuel," offered Hans-Peter. "Let's introduce it to the FAA as basically chemical propulsion, and tell them I just experimented with a little heavy methane. Keep in mind that deuterium is not radioactive."

"We can do that," said Ruthiebell. "Traypart could write that one up in his sleep."

"Let me think about it," I said realizing Ruthiebell was treating me Like an employee. I wondered if Hans-Peter was noticing.

"Sure," said Hans-Peter, "Sleep on it. We'll work it out in the morning."

"When will you be ready to fly again?" I asked.

"In a few more hours," said Hans-Peter. "When we removed the engine assembly, it was only warm, not hot. We have fixed the thermal sensors and reloaded the tri-propellant rocket assembly." Hans-Peter looked at his watch. "In fact, even as we speak, they may have it fully loaded and outside for taxi tests."

"Are you getting ready to fly it tomorrow morning?" I asked trying to hide my astonishment.

"No," said Hans-Peter shaking his head. "Claudius and Eleanor have made a very real effort to help us fly out of Norton Filed, and I'm not going to do anything to jeopardize or offend their contributions. I could fly it this afternoon, but I'm not going to fly without an approved flight plan; and of course you're telling me they're ready to go ballistic if I tell them about the deuterium in the fuel."

"That's an astonishing turn-around time. May I ask why you are preparing it to fly if you're not going to fly it?"

"It's a dry run for several modifications. We want to double-check the main landing gear while taxying with a maximum load. We then plan to park it inside and offload the propellants. I'm not going to fly without approval."

"That's absolutely right whether for good reasons or bad," said Ruthiebell. "There's no point in getting Hans thrown in jail. I've read most of your stuff, Traypart, and I know that you know most of the underlying technology. Have you figured out how to get Hans totally off the hook?"

I turned to Hans-Peter. "Did you patent your engine?"

"No. Tri-propellants were patented back in the sixties. I'm not using the old work from those patents. My tri-propellant engine is fundamentally different. My work is unique and worthy of its own patent," said Hans-Peter. "I'm keeping it secret. As you know, many patented ideas have been stolen by groups who simply read the patents and then do what they want."

"How much heavy methane is in the fuel tank for the taxi runs they are about to do?" I asked.

"Enough to give it about 5,000 seconds of specific impulse."

"Good grief," I said, "that's more than enough to get into orbit and back. If you fly the Rebel into orbit, there will be no way to hide the fact that you are tapping nuclear energy. Were you planning to fly to orbit next time out?"

"I really hadn't decided, but the question is now academic. I don't want to fly without an approved flight plan." He looked at Ruthiebell and me thoughtfully and then said, "Lets start writing the documents that will earn the blessings, or should we say, the approval of the FAA."

As Hans-Peter finished speaking, Mr. Maltby came in the room with a large desktop computer. He put it on the table where we could all see it. He plugged it into a coaxial cable port that was out of sight under a vase of flowers. "There's just been a meteorite strike on the International Space Station," he said. "I knew you would all like to see the story as it is coming in."

"This is Lacy Skater reporting live from the Johnson Space Center in Houston, Texas. NASA has confirmed that seven or eight small meteors no bigger than pebble-sized rocks have hit the space station with tremendous velocity. The meteorites hit the ISS on several different orbits while over Arizona, indicating the Earth may be traveling through a stream of meteorites. Given the speed of the Earth's orbit around the sun, we may now be past that threat. At the present all six astronauts are safe, but both of the Soyuz 'life raft' space crafts docked at the ISS, have been damaged sufficiently to render them inoperable.

The Russians have reported that their spacecraft factory in Kazakhastan has gone 24/7. They're trying to get the next two up to the space station as soon as possible. They thought they could get the first one up in eight weeks, but working 24/7 they might be able to launch in five weeks. At this moment in time, the astronauts on the ISS are stranded. They have no way home; and as you all know, the American Space Shuttles are no longer flying."

"Did you see what happened?" said Max as he came crashing into Sandy's office. "The space station got hit by some rocks and it's falling apart and it's going to kill everybody. Are you trying to call Hans-Peter on the phone? We gotta know what he thinks."

"No, I didn't think of that. He's a smart man, but he's got his own problems with the FAA and that hot lithium injector."

"I'll get you a van and a driver and Milo the photographer. Milo's okay, isn't he? You worked with him before. Is he okay? Who do you want?"

Sandy started to laugh. "Slow down Max. The outbound rush hour has started. We can't get out to San Bernardino in any less than two and a half hours. Why do you want more pictures of Titanium Composites?"

"I want video of you interviewing Hans-Peter," said Max. "You're the only one around here that has a pass to get in there. Look, I know they only flew their airplane up to 100 miles last time, but the Rebel's the only thing flying. I'd like to see you interviewing Hans-Peter. If we can get time with him on the Internet, we'll be number one."

"But I heard the FAA grounded his airplane," answered Sandy.

"Yeah, yeah, yeah, I heard that, too." Max looked at his watch. "You make some phone calls. Do you have an email address for those guys? You have twenty minutes. I'll be back here in twenty minutes. Go get 'em kid. Good luck."

Max went directly to Mrs. Rumble's desk and asked her to assign the best van and a driver. Then he went to photography to find Milo.

It didn't really make any difference to Max what Sandy could learn, he knew anything she could get Hans-Peter to say would be very big on the Internet. He wanted at least 100,000 hits.

Hans-Peter, Ruthiebell and I were still at his dining room table watching the computer screen. Mr. and Mrs. Maltby had cleared our lunch from the table and brought Ruthiebell her computer from the library and they brought me some paper. After watching several iterations of the story we weren't learning anything new. Hans-Peter turned down the volume.

"Can the Rebel do it?" asked Ruthiebell. "Do you think your tri-propellant can really take the Rebel up to the space station?"

"Yes, the first two flights have proved its flightworthiness. On that second flight, the tri-propellant worked perfectly. There is no question in my mind that the Rebel can fly a successful rescue mission." Hans-Peter was thoughtful for a moment. "Should I cut the FAA in on this, or should I just do it? What do you think? Tell me what you think?"

"You've got them over a barrel," said Ruthiebell, "how can they possibly say no? We knew the Russians said they can't fly at least another five weeks, and then they can only rescue three of them. What can the FAA say, but 'YES' and good luck?"

"Ruthiebell's right," I said, "but what if they want to put one of their people on the Rebel to 'direct' the rescue?"

"They wouldn't pull a stunt like that, would they?" asked Hans-Peter.

"I hate to say it, but Traypart is right," said Ruthiebell. "There is no telling what the bureaucracy will do to cut themselves in on the action."

"There's nothing wrong with Claudius," said Hans-Peter. "I'm not afraid of working with him at all. I like the guy."

"That's true, Hans," said Ruthiebell, "he's a good man. This, however, will be a big deal. The first thing that will happen is somebody higher in the bureaucracy will push Claudius aside and take over. Some politician, who doesn't understand anything, will try to grab all the credit. They will tell the public that without their technical insights, the rescue could never have happened. And then the big shot will tell everyone that for your cooperation, he won't throw you in jail for flying an uncertified nuclear rocket engine."

"You make it sound like it's all a big game," said Hans-Peter.

"It is a big game!" she said. "Back in the twentieth century people took things seriously. Nowadays people act like everything's just a big game."

"What if I brought Claudius out here on a different pretext? After he gets here, I'll tell him what the Rebel can do and ask him to fly as the observer. He understands the need for the rescue and cares about the astronauts. I'd ask him to write the flight plan as we flew, and there'd be no time for anybody else to take his place."

"That's not a bad idea," I said. "And if we couldn't get him to fly with you, we could get Eleanor. It would be pretty hard to condemn a flight with a senior FAA officer on board. Especially if he or she wrote the flight plan." As I was speaking, Mr. Maltby brought in a fancy, office quality, landline telephone and plugged it into the table near the computer plug.

"You make the call, Traypart," said Hans-Peter. "You know how to talk to the man. I have every confidence in you. I'm sure you can pull it off."

Chapter Ten
The Third Ascent

My phone call to Claudius Thud was an agreeable affair. He consented to fly to San Bernardino from the Los Angeles International Airport on one of Hans-Peter's business aircraft. The FAA offices were near LAX, and getting to the south side terminal was easier for Mr. Thud than getting on the freeway. Angelo and one of the copilots flew a company turboprop twin into LA.

We had determined it would be best if none of us flew into Los Angeles to accompany Claudius back to San Bernardino. We knew that with just a few questions, Claudius would easily figure out what we were planning. We needed to get him to San Bernardino before he even guessed the Rebel was capable of a rescue flight.

Hans-Peter had left Ruthiebell and me at his dining room table when he went to arrange the flight to pick up Claudius. Ruthiebell was writing out possible press releases for Hans-Peter in the event either Claudius or Eleanor would fly with him. We kept the computer turned on to keep track of the ISS. It appeared their situation had become stable.

Ruthiebell looked up and said, "Shouldn't you be calling Eleanor?"

"Yes, but this is going to be tricky. I can't tell her what we're doing until Claudius gets here."

"We all know Eleanor is your friend," remarked Ruthiebell. "Give her a call and see if she's even in town. If she's here, ask her if you could stop by in an hour and hear some of her thoughts about the Rebel. If she says yes, you'll be with her when Claudius gets here. You can then tell her he's come out to discuss the Rebel and bring her to the meeting."

"I'll bet Claudius will call her," I said, "and tell her he's on his way to Norton Filed."

"We don't know that. He probably thinks Hans wants to hear his advice about getting his tri-propellant engine certified. He may see it as some sort of off-the-record, man-to-man, discussion. He may in fact, not want anybody else around."

"That's very possible, Ruthiebell, very possible indeed. As I said, Claudius and his people have already figured out there may be a nuclear component to the rocket engine. They don't know what it is for sure, and it's likely they don't even suspect the Rebel could reach the ISS; so Claudius won't be thinking about a rescue possibility."

"Why not?" demanded Ruthiebell. "If they could figure out that Hans must be using nuclear energy, why wouldn't they suspect the Rebel could get on up into orbit?"

"All they know is the engine can deliver 800 seconds. You need at least 1,500 seconds to put an airplane like the Rebel into orbit."

"For now," she said, "let's hope Claudius sees it that way; but you still have to talk to Eleanor. We need to know where she is. What if she's out of town? If she's out of town, and Claudius won't fly the rescue mission we'll need a plan 'B'. If we ask the FAA to help us, they'll take the whole thing away from us. I'm beginning to think if we don't fly tonight we're dead in the water."

"There is also a very good chance the ISS is out of danger. The six people on board, have got it stabilized and they're patching the air leaks. If they don't take another big hit, they might be just fine until the Russians get their next Soyuz up there."

"That all sounds fine," said Ruthiebell, "but if Hans can rescue the astronauts, nobody'd have the nerve to throw him in jail. Hans needs a heroic accomplishment to save his butt."

"If they throw Hans in jail they won't kill him, but if the ISS takes another hit, those astronauts may die. For them this isn't just some photo-op."

Max came back to Sandy's office with Milo in tow. "There's a driver downstairs with our best van. Did you get Hans-Peter on the phone?"

"No."

"How about an email?"

"The company sent me a copy of the tech report describing that there was no problem with their rocket engine on the second flight. They said the problem was with the thermal sensor, and it's been fixed."

"Oh, put me to sleep on the floor. I can't imagine a more boring story."

"It gets better," she taunted.

"Really?" Max was instantly hooked. "Okay, so what's better?"

"They said they were putting the engine back in the Rebel because it was 'A-OK.' They also said they were going to taxi test the whole thing when they get it back together."

"Yes! I knew it. They're going to rescue the astronauts."

"Slow down, Max," said Milo with a measure of authority that Max had never heard him use before. In fact, the remark was so out of character, that it silenced Max altogether. Milo continued by saying, "The ISS is in a 250 mile orbit at more than 17,500 miles per hour. The best we've seen from the Rebel is only 100 miles in altitude with no speed at all. It's likely, not just possible but likely, that the Rebel can't fly high enough or fast enough to rescue the astronauts."

Max narrowed his eyes, "We don't know that. Maybe they're going to fly up as high as they can and release some kind of rescue package that can go on up and dock with the space station. What do you think of that, Mr. Photographer? Is that a possibility?"

Milo smiled, "Yes, it is. I like it. It's actually not a bad idea at all."

"Okay, okay, okay, we don't know what's going to happen. I want you both out there ASAP. Sandy can get us through the gate. Whatever they do, I want copy and pictures. Get me close-ups. Take telephoto lenses. If they taxi it, get me close-ups. If something starts to develop, I'll send more people out to back you up. Grab your bags and get downstairs." Max stopped and extended his hands to both of them, "I love you people; make me proud."

Out on the high desert at Cactus Patch, Lieutenant Raymo Woodburn was sitting outside in his favorite place in the shade. Today he had a laptop computer. Lieutenants Potash and Collins were seated on either side of him. They were watching the reports stream in from the International Space Station.

"I'll give them a fifty/fifty chance of making it," said Collins. "When they get back over Arizona, if the meteorite stream is still coming in, they're toast."

"I don't remember the number," said Potash, "but the Earth is moving pretty fast along its orbit around the sun. Each time the ISS makes it around the Earth, the Earth is much further along its own orbit. I think it's very likely that the Earth has moved far enough along to be past the meteorite stream all together."

"Yeah," said Raymo sarcastically. "That's only if you believe that crap about meteorite streams. The space station has been in orbit for years and this has never happened before. I say some damn UFO decided to make some trouble, just to see what we earthlings will do. Right now they're up there laughing at us."

Both Potash and Collins were startled by Raymo's intensity. Potash actually scooted a little further away from Raymo before he spoke. "Don't get too carried away, bro. Any night of the week you can watch the sky and see a meteorite or two come burning in from outer space. It happens all the time."

"Besides that," said Collins, "the crew knows how to deal with meteorites. They have pressure suits and repair kits. Just look at your screen. That one named Chris has stabilized their orbit and the others are patching the leaks." They could both tell Raymo wasn't buying anything they were saying, so they left him to his own thoughts.

Eleanor was in town. Ruthiebell's suggestion worked like a charm. Eleanor invited me up to the tower and perhaps thirty minutes later we saw the Titanium Composites turboprop come in and taxi over to the large hangar. I hadn't said a word about Claudius and she hadn't told me she knew Claudius was on the plane; but as it taxied she said, "Let's go meet Mr. Thud."

I didn't say a word. I thought it best to let this develop on its own. "May I give you a lift to the hangar?"

"Thank you, Traypart, but I'd rather drive over myself. This should be interesting," and then she said; "did Hans want you to be part of this?"

"I believe so. I'll meet you there and we'll see."

Hans-Peter took everyone to a second floor conference room built inside the hangar. There was a large flat screen on one wall that was turned to the developments on the ISS. At the moment the volume was turned off. Ruthiebell and I sat along the wall. Claudius and Eleanor sat at the table with Angelo and the copilot Larry Stevens. There were two other men and a woman at the table that I took to be from Hans-Peter's technical staff; and his senior counsel, Eustace Gray, was also there. Mr.

Gray sat at the other end of the table.

Hans-Peter was standing at the head of the table. He had already greeted Claudius and Eleanor. Everyone in the room knew the stakes were very high for Hans-Peter. No one wanted to slip into the noncommittal, decision postponing, rhetoric of politicians.

Hans-Peter addressed the group. "The FAA has grounded our tri-propellant rocket engine that powered the major part of the Rebel's climb on our second flight. While I doubt that Mr. Thud has sole control over that decision, I trust his insight concerning the grounding decision. Today we want to hear his thoughts on how to remove the grounding order."

Not waiting to be recognized, Claudius spoke, "That's a good concise opening. Let us not waste time. 800 seconds of specific impulse is impossible with chemical propellants. Is there a small release of nuclear energy in your engine?"

"Yes sir, there is."

Claudius seemed pleased with that answer; not so much as a cross-examining attorney winning a case, but as an engineer delighted with new technology. "Really! You didn't report any nuclear fuel in your flight plan. What kind of a nuclear reaction are you creating?"

"It's a fusion reaction. Some of the hydrogen in the methane is deuterium. The engine is able to fuse the deuterium into helium-4 in the combustion chamber. I found a way to get the lithium to catalyze the deuterium fusion. The LOX and ordinary methane are there to create the right environment for the nuclear reaction. They also act as a working fluid to convey part of the thrust."

"That's amazing. If I hadn't been in the tower with Eleanor tracking your altitude, I wouldn't believe you; but I was there." Claudius couldn't help but smile. "Congratulations, Hans-Peter, many of us have thought about that possibility, but no one has ever done it. Deuterium, however, is a fusible isotope and since you didn't call it out in your flight plan; you have committed a serious breach in the law."

"The law is focused on dangerous, radioactive materials," answered Hans-Peter. "Everything lighter than iron is fusible. Deuterium isn't radioactive. There is in fact a little deuterium in our drinking water."

"Precious little," objected Claudius.

"It's there, Mr. Thud, and our methane is a little heaver than ordinary methane, but it is no more radioactive than the methane that fills the municipal gas lines. Therefore we had nothing to report."

"That sounds more like a loophole than an answer. Tell me about all the products you're getting in your exhaust? No, better yet, tell me, are you getting any radioactive isotopes in your exhaust?"

"No sir. The product of the nuclear reaction is helium-4 and that stuff is as clean as the air."

"Well, let us hope it's a little cleaner," answered Claudius lightly. Most of us gave him a smile. "How much of your methane is 'heavy'?"

"Not much," said Hans-Peter. "The interesting question you're about to pose is, can we control the specific impulse by varying the amount of 'heavy' methane; and the answer is yes. We have hundreds of hours of ground testing with different concentrations."

"Really." Claudius was sounding like a kid with a new toy. "That's amazing. You guys are brilliant. What's the biggest impulse you've ever demonstrated?"

"We have over forty hours demonstrating a constant 5,000 seconds. The fuel concentration we loaded for today's taxi tests is that fuel. If we were to fly today, it would deliver 5,000 seconds of specific impulse."

"I remember the hypersonic proposals of the late nineteen-eighties," said Claudius. "In fact, I remember the work at UC Irvine that looked at hypersonic technologies for what they then called the National Aerospace

Plane. Back in those days they talked about 'Propulsion Alternatives' and if my memory is correct, they determined 1,500 seconds would put you in orbit with plenty of spare propellant to get home. Do you understand that you are telling me that your airplane can fly into any orbit you would like?"

"Yes sir. That's exactly what I'm telling you and I'd like you to know that we will be ready to fly in two or three hours."

"Do you think you can rescue the people on the space station?"

"Yes, and that's why we brought you here."

Hans-Peter turned up the volume on the large flat screen. "The electrical fire on the most significantly damaged Soyuz spacecraft has necessitated its release from its docking position before it can threaten the ISS. The Soyuz is not responding to external control. Unfortunately, it is not moving away as fast as planned. No one is sure what the spacecraft will do. This new development darkens the prospects for the six astronauts; and this just in, the ISS has lost its ability to hold air pressure. All six crew members are confined to their pressure suits." The volume for the flat screen was turned back down and everyone looked back at Hans-Peter.

"Mr. Thud, we can rescue those six people. Would you fly with us? We will call you our Director of Rescue Operations. We would like you to ride up front with us in the observer's seat, and we would also like you to write up our flight plan. We think that if you write the flight plan, and you're onboard, we won't get into any more trouble with the FAA."

"I'd love to. So help me God, I'd love to, but if I did, and survived the flight, my dear wife would kill me when I got home. Your question implies the Rebel can dock with the ISS. Do you have a docking port on your airplane?"

"Yes, we do, but it doesn't need to hold pressure. The ISS no longer has an atmosphere. When we come alongside, they can just float on over through the total vacuum of space."

Claudius gave his attention to Eleanor. "I think they're right about how important it is for one of us to fly with them. Do you feel up to a rescue assignment? Would you like to be the Director of Rescue Operations?"

"Tell you what, Claudius," she said, "I'll fly with them if you'll write up the flight plan and stay with their mission control people every minute we're aloft."

"You got a deal." They both smiled. When they shook hands, we all applauded.

Ruthiebell stood up behind Eleanor and put her hands on her shoulders. "Come along with me, dearie, I'll show you where to get a space suit. I've done this before, and there are some questions you may want to ask me."

Outside, Sandy and her colleagues from the *Herald Express* pulled up to the main gate of Titanium Composites. The guard received her warmly and asked her to have the van parked in the same place she had before. He went on to say that they were in time to film the last taxi runs for the day, and that the company was pleased to have them cover the tests. Milo was able to get some great video before the Rebel was put back inside its hangar. As the airplane was pulled inside, they packed up their stuff and drove over to the hangar.

We knew that Sandy and her people were outside. I was asked to go downstairs and talk to her. "Sandy, it's good to see you."

"We'd like to go inside and get some stills of them servicing the Rebel," she said.

"Not today, I'm afraid. At least not right now. Tell me, how did you know about the taxi tests?"

"We didn't. Max wanted us to come out here and see what's going on. Max asked me to try and get an interview with Hans-Peter. The *Herald* wants to know what Hans-Peter thinks about the space station situation."

When Titanium Composites learned that Sandy was coming, both Claudius and Hans-Peter thought she would be the best way to let the story trickle out to the public, but they couldn't reveal the rescue until the rebel was in the air.

"Really. There's no way you can talk to Hans-Peter right now," I said to Sandy and Milo, "but I got a tip for you. Can you keep this under your hat?"

"Of course, what do you know?"

"I happen to know that sometime after sunset, they're going to taxi test it again in the dark, and this time they're going to test fire the rocket engine while they are on the ground." I then looked at Milo. "If you can handle color against the night sky, you can get some great video."

"That sounds too good to be true," said Milo. "Why are you telling me that?"

"I'm not here with a camera. When you photograph what I'm telling you about, you'll owe me one big time. I want my pick of the best stills. When I write up my copy I'll need a good picture or two. Look, it's your call. Go get a nice dinner somewhere and be back here after sunset. I need to go now, but you don't want to miss what is going to happen, and I need a good photo."

Milo didn't say a word. He simply shook my hand. I knew he would be back.

As soon as the van was outside the gate, Sandy called Max. "You're not going to believe this, but when we got here they had the Rebel outside running taxi tests. Milo got some great video." She became silent listening to Max. "No, it's better than that. We got a tip that they're going to run a taxi test after sunset and actually fire their rocket engine; but don't tell anyone. I promised to keep it under my hat." When Sandy's call was over,

Max called his friends in Redlands and Riverside with the story and asked them not to tell anyone else. Of course, they only told their closest friends who they knew could keep the secret.

The aft-cabin of the Rebel was designed to accommodate twelve passengers. Installing six seats only took an hour. The Rebel was ready to fly at 8:40 p.m., but the next best time for an ISS rendezvous was 10:10 p.m. I was asked to stay with Claudius and assist him in any way that I could. Claudius and Eleanor agreed that the best time to file the flight plan was as the Rebel taxied to take off. It was also agreed not to contact the ISS until the Rebel was safely on its way.

Hans-Peter had accumulated so much respect over the years that none of us doubted his confidence in the Rebel. The fact that the Rebel had flown twice without any real problems didn't hurt our confidence, either. Our only focus now was the rescue mission.

Before sunset, Sandy called me for the best time to come back. I told her to come back at 9:30 p.m. She and her crew returned on time and set up their equipment. Their driver had a sophisticated radio that he had tuned to the Rebel's frequency. Milo had set up a much better camera than he had used for the daylight taxi tests. At just after 10:20 p.m. the Rebel rolled out of the hangar.

Claudius and I were up in the tower when we first heard from the Rebel. "San Bernardino, this is the Rebel." It was Eleanor's voice. "We are on taxiway 'A' proceeding to the west end of the runway. Are we cleared for takeoff heading 57 magnetic, 070 true?"

"Roger that, Rebel. You are cleared for takeoff on heading 070 true. Good luck."

"Did you hear that?" yelled the driver to Milo.

"I did," Milo yelled back. "I got my camera on that bird."

"They're going to fly," said Sandy. "This is their third flight. We've got to find out why they're going to fly out of here at night."

From the tower I could see several professional photo set-ups out on the Santa Ana wash. As I had hoped, Sandy wasn't too good at keeping the secret. The Rebel taxied fast and turned onto the strip. Its four jet engines went full throttle. We could hear it clearly. The sleek titanium beast accelerated down the runway and into the night sky. This was a third takeoff for Angelo, and he did it without a hitch.

Eleanor had turned the flat screen in front of her seat to the Rebel's flight instruments. She could read everything the flight crew was seeing. "San Bernardino we are over Oak Glen and starting our turn to 090 true," she said and then looked over at Hans-Peter. He gave her an approving nod. "We are climbing at 2,200 feet per minute, our speed is 390 knots, and all systems are 'GO.'

"Roger that, Rebel. We read your speed and rate of climb as reported."

The flight continued along the same course as the first two flights. Claudius left the controller's station to the other officer in the tower. "Come along, Traypart, let's get over to the company flight control center." It took a few minutes to get back down to my car and over there. As I drove, I imagined the Rebel turning north toward Joshua Tree and then due east again. We were greeted at the door and hurried to the control center.

Titanium Composites were calling themselves TC-Control and the room had several large flat screens. As we entered, Claudius took the place waiting for him next to the mission controller and we heard Eleanor's voice from overhead, "TC-Control, we are holding at 42,000 feet and heading due east."

Next we heard Hans-Peter's voice. "TC-Control, please give me the time for ISS rendezvous."

"Rebel," said their mission controller, a man I had seen in the conference room meeting. "Please come to a heading of 109 true. Your ignition time, for rendezvous, is four minutes and nineteen seconds and counting. Please call your course change."

Down on the field, Sandy's team was back in the van. Milo was driving and the driver was in the back seat with his fancy radio. "Did you hear that!" he said. "Max was right. They can fly that thing all the way up to the space station."

"TC-Control, our course change is complete. We are holding at 42,000 feet and 109 true. Please countdown the time to rocket fire."

"Roger, that Rebel. You are at three minutes and four seconds and counting."

Ruthiebell was at the engineering station she had been assigned and she stood up and waved me over. She was pointing at the monitor for her station and when I got there she said, "What the hell is that?"

The image was not clear. "What are you looking at?" I asked.

"That's what the aft looking radar from the Rebel can see. Did those A-10 guys fly out to see Hans off?"

I sat down next to her. "Very unlikely," I said. "No one was supposed to know the Rebel would take off tonight. Try to sharpen the image."

Then over the open frequency we heard, "Rebel, this your final count. Do you copy?"

"Roger, that TC-Control, we copy. Our engine injector is hot."

"Fire in 30 seconds, , , 20 seconds, , , mark 10, 9, 8, 7, 6, 5, 4, 3, 2, Fire. Rebel, I'm showing ignition. Do you copy?"

Nothing came back but static. The static on the overhead speakers was cut and the same voice that gave the countdown said, "We show a successful ignition. The rocket plume is too energetic to penetrate. Rebel transmissions are now blacked out."

Claudius had opened his workstation and tied it back to the control tower. "FAA tracking is showing the Rebel climbing along 109 true and accelerating now past Mach 1.4," he said.

The mission controller then spoke. "The Rebel's flight appears correct for an ISS rendezvous." There was applause and some cheering as everyone began to relax.

The Titanium Composites mission controller then spoke to Claudius. "Mr. Thud, I believe it's time for you to inform the ISS of our intentions."

Downstairs, Sandy and Milo and their driver were knocking at the door. Three company reps went down to meet them. The oldest man spoke. "We have very good news. The Rebel takeoff was a perfect success, and with a new fuel mixture we feel that the Rebel can rendezvous with the ISS."

Sandy and the other two were thrilled with the news.

"Excellent," said Milo, "That's great news. I didn't think it was possible."

Good grief, thought Sandy. Max called it right after all. He actually called the biggest story we've got; and he just pulled it out of thin air.

"Pay attention," said the older man. "We are going to take you three up to mission control. We want you to break this story as it's happening. You can bring your cameras and recorders. Don't say anything to people who are working. If someone has stepped back from their station you may ask questions. Come on up and we'll help you capture the story. Am I clear or is there a question?"

"No sir," said Milo. "We are honored to be here and will give you our best."

Back upstairs, the central large screen was showing the ever-changing position of the ISS. At the moment, the Rebel was ahead of the ISS but it wasn't moving as fast. Claudius's voice came back overhead, "FAA tracking is showing the Rebel altitude at 92 miles and her speed just passing 7,780 miles per hour."

I used the landline at Ruthiebell's station and called out to Cactus Patch. Corporal Tabby took my call. I asked him if any of his A-10s were flying as we spoke. He said no, and I could tell his curiosity was growing by the minute. I told him the Rebel was airborne and he could follow the story on the *Herald Express* website. I then wished him a pleasant evening.

Ruthiebell was listening to me, and when I hung up she said, "His A-10s are on the ground aren't? He didn't even know the Rebel was up. We're not going to get anymore aft-looking radar until they turn off the engine. Let's play back what we have slowly."

Then I told her I thought she had caught a 'classic radar shadow.'

As the Rebel was accelerating into orbit, the crew could see an object flying their exact course and staying eighty feet in front of them. Angelo spoke, "We've got some company."

"I see it," said Hans-Peter. "We're accelerating and it's holding a non-threatening position ahead of us."

"Can we talk to mission control yet?" asked Eleanor.

"No, there's too much energy in our plume. I'm going to throw a signal forward to the object. There's no static up front."

"This is the Rebel aerospace plane, do you copy?"

"You got to be kidding, Hans," said Eleanor. "UFOs don't talk to flight crews."

"As our ranking FAA officer, are you telling us the FAA knows about UFOs?"

"I'm your only FAA officer, and I don't know what that thing is; therefore it's an Unidentified Flying Object. Try to raise it again."

"Escorting spacecraft, this is the Rebel aerospace plane, do you copy?"

"Yes Rebel, we copy. Your transmission, as you like to say, is loud and clear," answered a man's voice that was clear and rather ordinary.

"Escorting spacecraft, your reply is appreciated," said Hans-Peter. "Are you a classified spacecraft we have no knowledge of? And how would you like to be addressed?"

"Rebel, those questions I'd rather not answer. The fusion reaction powering your airplane is beautifully balanced. May we congratulate you?"

"You may and thank you. May I ask with whom I'm talking?" pressed Hans-Peter.

"We are friends and visitors from another world. We see a very high probability for the success for your rescue mission. We wish to follow your progress and we will help you if problems arise."

"Escorting spacecraft, thank you. That's very thoughtful," answered Hans-Peter. "I will hail you as 'Visiting Friends.' Your English is remarkably good for a visitor from another world. I find it fascinating that you know how to use the human phrase, 'loud and clear.' Is your idea of another world, Groom Lake?"

"No, I've never been to Groom Lake. What makes you think we are speaking English?"

"English is the only language I know how to speak," said Hans-Peter, "and I suspect there is no problem with our communication. You sound like a native speaker to me."

"I am a native speaker, but you can't possibly understand what that means. We really are speaking the same language, but you don't know your own history. You are speaking the local form of Galactic. Others of my race have been helping Galactic develop on your planet for thousands of years."

"English isn't that old."

"The roots of human language are even older than that. We have been helping the language develop on Earth for a very long time."

"Visiting Friends, forgive me," said Hans-Peter, "but telling me English is really Galactic sounds like more Anglo-Saxon elitist propaganda. Are you sure you're not human like me and flying something that Lockheed built for the CIA?"

"Rebel, that's affirmative, as you say, I'm quite sure. Hans-Peter, do you realize that your vocabulary gives away your age? One scarcely hears the phrase 'Anglo-Saxon' anymore. The current minimalist generation will say 'white' instead. Be that as it may, if you terminate your rocket burn in twenty-two seconds, you will have the correct velocity for a space station rendezvous. You will also need to correct your course five degrees for the rendezvous. Best of luck."

"Hey, wait. Don't go away. You didn't give me your name."

"Oh come on, Hans" said Eleanor, "what did you expect? In all the close encounter stories, the UFOs always vanish just when you think you might actually be making contact. He was no alien anyway, and I don't buy that BS about speaking Galactic. He was speaking what I would call the American form of English."

Hans-Peter had been keeping track of his instruments. Looking back over to Eleanor he said, "Our new friend from Groom Lake came up with the same shutdown time that I did." Hans-Peter watched the last seconds tick off on his preset controller. The rocket started shutting down slowly and ran down to nothing. "That's it. Mark orbit insertion at 10:32 p.m. California time."

Silence. Without the rocket burning there was perfect silence; perfect weightless silence.

"I have visual contact," said Angelo. "I can see the ISS off five degrees to our portside. Our closing speed is 10 feet per second. I've completed an RCS retro program to correct that five degrees and accomplish a forty-foot rendezvous. Please check my numbers."

The RCS retro program Angelo had completed was present on Hans-Peter's engineering screen. "You have entered the data correctly, Angelo, please initiate it from your station." Hans-Peter carefully watched his display and was pleased as it depicted each RCS rocket firing in its correct order. "Okay, my friends, we must not talk about our visitor again until we're back on the ground. For now, let us pay close attention to the rendezvous. We have work to do."

Chapter Eleven
Rendezvous

From the outside, the International Space Station looked undamaged. The meteorite that had hit a solar panel broke it off clean and imparted enough energy to carry it far away. If one did not look very closely at the solar arrays, one would not know anything was missing.

Only one of the Soyuz spacecraft was docked to the ISS; the other was smoking slightly from impact damage and was moving away very slowly. It looked like a hazard. Hans-Peter scanned it and determined it was moving away at four inches a second.

Hans-Peter addressed his crew. "Now that we can see the ISS, let's prepare for our rendezvous. Disconnect your pressure suits from the ship and make yourselves autonomous. Larry, I'd like you to go back to the hatch."

After Larry left the cockpit, Hans-Peter scanned his instruments. "I see we are all autonomous. I'm now compressing our atmosphere. We'll be at full vacuum when we get there."

Eleanor had her radio tuned to the open frequency for the ISS and so far had heard nothing. She tried again. "This is the Rebel spacecraft trying to raise the International Space Station, do you copy?"

"Affirmative, Rebel. Of course we copy. We have been trying to raise you the last fifteen minutes. The FAA controller in San Bernardino informed us you were coming, and we have been following your progress with our own radar. We have also been preparing to evacuate since the first notice came from San Bernardino. Have you not heard any of our transmissions until now?"

"We have heard nothing from you, ISS," said Eleanor. "Oh, and by the way, my name is Eleanor Scribble and I am the FAA controller for San Bernardino. In my absence, Claudius Thud, a regional FAA controller, is covering my position. I have had this frequency open from the start, but this is the first that I have heard from you. How urgent is your situation?"

"Rebel, our situation is urgent. We need to get off this thing as soon as possible. It's very good to see your craft approaching. We are running out of time."

"ISS, Hans-Peter is our flight engineer and he is handling our approach. Please continue with him."

"Hans-Peter, this is Chris, speaking from the space station's stability control panel. "Your approach is very good, but just a touch fast. Please cut your approaching speed in half."

"Roger that, ISS. Our approach speed is slowing. Larry, please open and secure the outer hatch."

"Rebel spacecraft," called Chris, "may I make a request?"

"Yes ISS, what is your request?"

"We have no internal pressure. The interior of the ISS matches the vacuum of space. If you can, please take the interior pressure of your spacecraft down to zero. We can evacuate much more quickly through the vacuum."

"ISS, we anticipated that possibility. We are already at full vacuum. Is there someone at your docking port?"

" Yes, Yuriy Brominkov is at the docking port. He is actually wearing one of our extravehicular spacesuits. Please continue with Yuriy."

"Comrades," said Yuriy with his thick Russian accent, "your approach vector is correctly aligned with our docking port. Your port looks correctly built to match with our port. Let us not worry about pressure. Our mechanical grips are ready to receive your mechanical grips, and please be doing nothing. Are you prepared for me to make the attachment?"

"Yes Yuriy, please proceed. The Rebel is capable of making a ve, small RCS retro fire, would that be helpful?"

"No, comrade. Do not fire any of your RCS rockets. My attachmeı is designed to absorb your kinetic energy. Please stand by." Yuriy guide two of his mechanical grips to simultaneously capture the Rebel's grips "We have you. I'm absorbing your kinetic energy as you come in. There is here no problem. You had very little kinetic energy to absorb. Do your gauges show a successful docking?"

"That's affirmative, ISS; the docking is secure. Larry, do you copy?"

"Yes sir, and I am at the hatch."

"Please bring in our first guest." Hans-Peter looked over to Eleanor. "Do you feel able to assist Larry?"

Unbuckling her seatbelt and shoulder straps, Eleanor said, "Yes, of course; that's why I'm here. I'm on my way back now."

The first thing the ISS passed through the port was a cargo container about the size of a footlocker. Eleanor called to Hans-Peter; "These guys just passed a container through the port. Can this bird carry some freight back as well as six more people?"

"Yes, but not very much. I'm on my way back. Larry, move that thing to the back of the cabin and tie it down." As Hans-Peter moved back he radioed, "ISS this is the flight engineer, how much cargo were you planning to bring?"

"We have five more containers with our most valuable scientific material."

"ISS, that's not acceptable, we're here to rescue people, not experiments."

"Rebel, your people at TC-Control told us you could carry some freight."

"That's true," snapped Hans-Peter. "We can, but you said your situation s urgent. Let's get your people aboard first. Don't send any more containers. Send an astronaut through next."

As Hans-Peter entered the port area, a second container came through. "That's it, ISS, I want to see an astronaut next. Do you understand me?" Hans-Peter grabbed the handles on the container and passed it to Eleanor. "Help Larry with this one also. Tie them down together."

The American named Nancy came through next. She pushed a small package in front of her as she came onboard the Rebel. "These are the most important samples of my work," she said. "I can hold them in my lap. I've already sent my data to Mission Control. This is the physical stuff I need to take home."

"Sure, that's fine," said Hans-Peter. "Let Eleanor show you how to buckle up. We also have a second belt we can put over your small package."

Valentina came through next, pushing a small package like the one Nancy had. "For me," she said, "These are my most important ones. Also, I can hold them."

"Yes, that's fine. We have a place for you across from Nancy."

Rodney Ellis, the Australian came through next. He was also pushing his own small package. "G'day mate, good to meet ya. Bonza cabin you have ere, room for another container?"

"No, Rodney!" snapped Chris urgently over the frequency. "There's no time for that, just get aboard. My instruments are showing the Soyuz we cut free is changing course. The damaged circuits appear to be randomly firing its RCS thrusters. It's starting to move erratically. There is no telling where it may go. It may circle back. Leave the containers, Aleksey; get yourself through the port. Aleksey, evacuate! Evacuate quickly!"

Eleanor helped Rodney to one of the middle seats. Then Aleksey came through pushing his small package. Eleanor took his package and helped him to the other middle seat.

"Yuriy! Go now," called Chris. "Don't try to take anything with you Yuriy, you're much too big in that spacesuit. Please help Yuriy get through your port. This is Chris at ISS attitude control; I'm calling to the Rebel pilot. Do you have radar contact with the drifting Soyuz?"

"ISS, that's affirmative. The Rebel is tracing the drifting Soyuz. It is circling back toward us and gaining velocity. Please leave your control panel and join us as quickly as you can. We see an imminent collision. Come aboard as fast as you can."

"I'm coming. I'm coming as fast as I can. I've shut down all station keeping equipment and I'm on my way. Did Yuriy get through the port yet?"

"Yes," said Hans-Peter. "His extravehicular spacesuit came through without a hitch.

"Eleanor, this is Angelo. If your passengers are buckled in, please come forward and take your place. Larry, make sure the cargo is tied down. If that damaged Soyuz hits us and those containers break free; somebody could get hurt."

"I strapped them down tight," answered Larry. "They're not going anywhere."

"Did that guy in the spacesuit fit in one of our seats?"

"Just barely, we're working on it."

"Chris is the last man. Is he on board yet?"

The drifting Soyuz is closing on our position," called Angelo. "Our time is running out. Is their last man on board yet?"

Chris was still inside the space station and called forward, "Not yet, I'm coming. The attitude control panel is not close to the docking port. Give me just another minute, I'm coming as fast as I can."

Hans-Peter moved into the airlock port of the ISS entrance. He saw Chris at a distance pushing his small package and coming as fast as he could. Hans-Peter moved back into the Rebel and made way for the sixth ISS astronaut. As Chris came through, Larry helped him to the last seat. Hans-Peter went back into the port and simultaneously uncoupled the grips. The grips were still holding the stored mechanical energy they had accumulated during docking. Uncoupled, the grips were now releasing their stored energy and slowly pushing the Rebel away from the ISS.

"We're inside, Angelo. Get us out of here," said Hans-Peter. Then he closed the outer hatch.

"Prepare for impact," said Angelo, and even as his words were still in the air, the Soyuz crashed into the space station and the Rebel at the same time. The impact was not very hard, but it shook the Rebel and threw Larry and Hans-Peter down on the floor. "Be secure," called out Angelo. "I'm firing the large RCS engines to get us out of here."

As they moved away, debris from the collision dragged along the bottom skin of the Rebel. A scraping sound could be heard inside. Nancy cringed, knowing full well the Rebel's heat shield had just been damaged.

The two larger RCS rockets firing in the tail pushed the Rebel away much faster. Larry and Hans-Peter were still on the floor. "This is your captain speaking," said Angelo. "Please bring your seats and tray tables to their full upright and locked position." Eleanor and Rodney and even Valentina started to laugh quietly.

Nancy had been a new hire at the Johnson Space Center back in 2003 the day the Space Shuttle Columbia disintegrated during atmospheric reentry. As you may recall, it was a piece of foam insulation that was frozen solid like a slab of ice that damaged the heat shield under the shuttle's wing.

Nancy and her fellow astronauts had just escaped the ISS because it could no longer hold an atmosphere and now they were aboard a sleek new version of the space shuttle that had endured an unknown amount of damage to its heat shield. Nancy knew this kind of damage had signed the death warrant for the Columbia.

When she was scrambling to help repair the space station, she hadn't any time to think about death. Now aboard with nothing else to do, thinking about the Columbia's heat shield made her want to scream. She didn't scream. She choked that scream down her throat and began to tremble.

"The locks look good on our hatch," said Hans-Peter. "All the sensors are green, and now for your comfort, I'm recompressing the cabin. Breathable air will be available in two minutes."

Larry was still by the hatch. The coldness of the shadowy side of the space station was something that no one had noticed. The coldness began to disappear as the warm air filled the interior.

"TC-Control, this is the Rebel. We have all six astronauts on board. Do you copy?"

A cheer when up in San Bernardino, in Houston, and around the world. The secret rescue was now known and being followed everywhere.

"Affirmative, Rebel. Congratulations. We lost contact when you fired your main engine. We have, however, followed your flight on the FAA radar. We have been informed by the Johnson Space Center that there has been a collision and fire at the ISS. Have you been damaged in any way?"

"TC-Control, that's affirmative. The Rebel was hit by debris. This is Angelo, we are now clear of the ISS and moving farther away. Hans-Peter is now back to his engineering station. He can give you a better analysis of our condition."

The air inside Yuriy's spacesuit hadn't been completely refreshed and it started to go toxic. The air quality indicators, both on the inside and outside of the suit, lit up red. Chris saw it and left his seat in an instant.

The cabin air pressure was coming up fast. Yuriy seemed to be dazed and only semiconscious. Chris broke the seal of Yuriy's helmet and removed it. Yuriy's eyes snapped open and he took a breath. "Yes, comrade," he said, "did I not get my seat in the right position?"

"You did fine Yuriy, just fine. Now take a deep breath for me." Chris put Yuriy's helmet under his seat. The cabin air was fresh and warm. "Your seat is just fine, Yuriy. Now take another deep breath for me. That's it, now another. Mr. Flight Engineer, this is Chris in the aft-cabin. Yuriy has his helmet off. What do your instruments show? Is the cabin air now fit to breath?"

"That's affirmative, Chris. The atmosphere looks good. I'm removing my helmet. Attention, passengers and crew, you may all remove your helmets and shut down your pressure suits. I'm sending Eleanor and Angelo back to assist you. Larry and I will fly this thing. By the way, we are breaking a record. Back in 1985 the Space Shuttle Challenger set the record for landing with a company of 8. When we get home, we will be landing with a company of 10."

The RCS burn was finished and Angelo and Eleanor floated back into the aft-cabin. The Rebel was now far from the ISS and moving farther away in its own orbit. The Rebel floated freely and those onboard began to experience the infinite silence of space. The interior of the Rebel was as roomy as the Space Shuttle had been. The prolonged zero-g however, was something new for the Rebel's crew.

"TC-Control, this Hans-Peter. Do you copy?"

"Loud and clear, Rebel. Your internal pressure looks good on our instruments. How is it holding?"

"It feels right and it looks good on my instruments. The debris impact apparently has not damaged our pressure hull. We are breathing warm, pleasant air. Have you been receiving our full automated telemetry stream?"

"Affirmative, Rebel. Shortly after main engine shut down we started receiving full telemetry. We saw the collision at the ISS with the Soyuz and we are looking for damage. Do your instruments show any damage?"

"No, but there's all kinds of damage that these instruments can't read. I want to get outside and look at the skin before we start home."

Down on the high desert, the night air had turned cold. Tabby had pulled the night shift again and after taking the call from Traypart, he had his monitor tuned to the *Herald Express* webpage. It was approaching Zero One Hundred Hours and he had called Lieutenant Martinelli and the major. They were just now coming in. "Major Hayes, did you know that Hans-Peter has the Rebel in orbit and is trying to rescue the crew of the International Space Station?"

"No," answered the major. "I was asleep. You gave me the impression over the phone there was something pressing, something more to the story."

"Yes sir, there is, and I may have it wrong, but it might be something that Lieutenant Martinelli can help us with."

Tabby had also awakened Martinelli. The lieutenant came in just after the major. Martinelli was sleepy and wearing his bathrobe over his uniform against the cold night air. "Are you going to show us another electronic shadow?" asked the lieutenant, now awakening to the situation.

"Well, almost," answered Tabby. "About twenty minutes ago I took a phone call from Traypart Artamus."

"Really," interrupted the major. "I know Mr. Artamus. He's more of an engineer than a journalist. Why on Earth did he call you?"

"He called us and asked if any of our A-10s were flying as we spoke," said Tabby. "He's one of the few journalists Hans-Peter allows inside the gate. They even let him inside their mission control area for the rescue mission. So I think that means he can see the flight telemetry as it's coming in, in real time."

"It also means he can see all the tracking data coming from ground up," said the major. "So we have an engineering journalist, inside their mission control, calling us to see if our A-10s are flying while the Rebel was in the air. And that question only makes sense because we flew A-10s along with the Rebel on their other two flights, but we didn't know about this flight, and so we didn't fly."

"I think the corporal's on to something, sir," said Martinelli. "They probably have some pretty good equipment at their mission control and they picked up an electronic shadow that was the same size as an A-10. They had a pretty good image of something flying along with their bird, but they couldn't see it. If that radar image wasn't really good, they wouldn't bother to call us, but they did call us. If we had told them that we had at least one A-10 up and following along, they'd probably forget the whole thing. What did you tell them, corporal?"

"The truth," said Tabby rather uneasily. "I told him we were not flying at this time of night."

"That's fine, Tabby," said the major, "we're not at war with anybody." The major turned his attention to Martinelli. "You want me to believe there's a UFO out there about the size of an A-10 that's shadowing the Rebel?"

"I don't want anything, sir. I think Tabby's made a very good call, and I hope he's dead wrong. The only reason that journalist would call us was if he couldn't identify something flying along with the Rebel."

The major turned his attention to Tabby. "What's the status of our A-10s?"

"Two are ready to fly now; however, as usual, they are not armed. The next two can be in the air in about an hour. Our last two are in routine maintenance and would need at least three days to be airworthy."

"Do you have any idea when they're going to reenter the atmosphere?"

"No sir."

"Are you sure they'll be coming back to San Bernardino?"

"No sir."

The major shifted back to Martinelli. "Hans-Peter has risked his neck to rescue those people, and I don't want some prankster messing around with his return flight. Is there any reason I shouldn't fly out there and escort him home?"

"Sir, I cannot answer that question, but I know how to get an answer for you."

"Okay, you stay here with Corporal Tabby and get me that answer. Corporal, I want to know when they'll reenter and where they're going to land."

"Yes sir." The corporal immediately began to query a different part of his system.

"I will be in my office," said the major. "Don't call me. When you have all three answers, I will expect to see the lieutenant in my office. As I leave, I'll have the sergeant secure this area. Gentlemen, please find those answers quickly."

Milo Schotts and Sandy had stepped back from the control stations to a place where they could talk privately. "How could Max possibly know that the Rebel could fly into orbit?" asked Sandy, "He's no engineer."

"He got lucky," answered Milo. "He just got lucky. Listen, I've known this guy for years. I don't think he can always tell the difference between science fiction and science fact. Before you came aboard he got it wrong big time more than once. So what's your angle?"

"He told me to read about Tesla and some old Nazi rocket guy that said he received engineering help from people 'from other worlds.' He also told me to watch the UFO stuff that Ruthiebell put on the Internet. What's happening here, Milo? The Rebel made it to the space station, just like Max said it would; and there sits Ruthiebell with Traypart at one of the control computers. Max said there was a UFO angle to this story and look at her. There she sits, Ms. UFO, at a control station right here in mission control."

"Ruthiebell isn't controlling anything," said Milo. "She's part of the press corps like you and me; and she's over there with Traypart Artamus, who is the only other journalist they let up here. They're letting them sit there to see the story as it's unfolding, the same way they let us inside to see the story."

Sandy surveyed Milo's face with great skepticism. "Shouldn't we be over there with Ruthiebell? I don't think she even knows we're here."

"I'm sure she knows we're here," said Milo. "She doesn't miss much. She and Traypart look pretty busy."

Sandy grimaced and said, "Milo, they're not telling us everything."

Milo started to laugh. "You got that right, kid. No question about it. Let's go get you and Ruthiebell and that Traypart guy on video. Show them a lot of respect and ask them what they think. While you talk to them, I'll make a video. Come on, let's go give it a try."

Hans-Peter was pleased with the way the Rebel was handling. From the flight-engineering seat, he could see as much of the Rebel as TC-Control could. He spoke into the open frequency. "Hailing the Johnson Space Flight Center. This is the Rebel spacecraft. Is there someone on this frequency that I can speak to?"

"Rebel, that's affirmative. This is Elliot Dover at the Johnson Space Flight Center. We have been tracking your aerospace craft from the time you lit your fancy hybrid rocket engine. Congratulations on obtaining orbit on your third flight and successfully rescuing all six members of the International Space Station crew. How can we assist you?"

"Are you tracking our precise orbit?"

"Rebel, that's affirmative. We are tracking your orbit."

"Are you also tracking most everything else in orbit?"

"Affirmative Rebel, that is a big part of our 24/7 job."

"Are we on a collision course with anything?"

"Rebel, that's negative. Your current orbit will be clear for at least several months. That's the question we continually worked for the ISS. When your last RCS fire ended, we went to work on your new orbit. If we had found anything, we would have called you."

"Thank you, Elliot," answered Hans-Peter. "It is very good to know that you and your colleagues are looking out for us. Is there anything about our orbit that you can see, that we should know?"

"Rebel, that's a negative. Your part of the sky is totally clear."

"Mr. Dover, that is good to know. My best to you and your colleagues, this is the Rebel signing out."

Eleanor was back with her passengers. She had taken to zero-g flight like a duck takes to water. "Yes," she said, "our restroom is through this door and fully operational. Now then, is anyone hungry? We have wonderful food, ready-to-eat. Who would like something?"

Nancy left her seat and started forward. Her face was as pale as death. She passed Eleanor and kept going up to the cockpit and then sat sideways in Eleanor's place. Hans-Peter turned and gave her his full attention. She asked, "Is it likely that the collision with the Soyuz has damaged our heat shield badly enough to jeopardize our reentry? Are we just as dead as the crew of the Columbia was?"

"I admire the clarity of your question," said Hans-Peter with no hint of concern. "We have no problem. The Rebel doesn't reenter like the space shuttle did. We won't experience the same extreme heat that they did."

She shook her head. "I'm not following you. How can we reenter without extreme heat? Any object reentering must dissipate the kinetic energy it accumulated going up when it comes back down. Everything reentering must endure extreme heating."

Hans-Peter broke into a relaxed smile. "The main rocket on this bird still has enough propellant to decelerate us to zero velocity before we hit the atmosphere. The kinetic energy will all be gone. In the free fall that will follow, I doubt we will even reach Mach 2. We will be much too slow to heat up."

"That's a nice idea, but it's impossible. You're either kidding me or you're mad," she said. "Have I been rescued by a lunatic? You can't do that unless your rocket can give us at least 3,000 seconds of impulse and you still have about a third of your rocket propellant." Speaking from both anger and despair she asked, "How much is in the tanks?"

"Our propellant tanks are about half full. So how many seconds of impulse do you think we needed to get to the space station?"

Nancy considered the fact that she was inside a new kind of spacecraft that had rescued her from the ISS. She sighed a long thoughtful sigh and moved over to Hans-Peter. She kissed his cheek. Pulling away from him she said, "I sure hope you're right. There's nothing I can do anyway, is there?" She then floated to her place in the aft-cabin. Angelo and Eleanor had brought out the pizza and everyone was relaxed and enjoying the flight. Nancy took some pizza back to her seat. She thought it best not to say anything about the ride home and the fact that they all may be dead. All I can do, she thought, is enjoy my last few hours with these good people.

From the cockpit, Larry and Hans-Peter saw the same UFO they had seen on the assent. At the same time someone in the back had told a joke and everyone was laughing. Hans-Peter could see an odd frequency setting and low power setting floating in front of him as clear as day. He adjusted an auxiliary radio to those settings. "Visiting Friends, is this the channel you'd like to communicate on?"

"Yes," said the same voice he had talked to on the way into orbit. "You are much more telepathic than you thought you were. Let me congratulate you on safely rescuing the six astronauts."

"May I ask who you are?"

"Not just yet."

"May I ask where you are from?"

"Not in a specific way, but I can tell you I am from a star system in your part of the galaxy. We are neighbors in a galactic sort of way."

"That would make you an alien from another world."

"In your mind, is that a bad thing?" asked the voice.

"I have no experience to answer from, but I doubt your story. You sound like an American. We all know our government has totally black projects. You're either Air Force or Navy, and you're flying a secret spacecraft."

"That's very unlikely. If this was a secret spacecraft from your government, I would have been instructed to stay away from you and never make contact; clearly that's not the case."

"When you contacted us on the way up, do I recall you saying you wanted to help us with the rescue?"

"That's an 'affirmative,' as you like to say," said the voice. "You have done splendidly without our help, but let me assure you we have been with you all the way."

"If you were with us, why did you let the Soyuz crash into us?"

"We determined any damage would be minimal, and we wanted to see how you would handle the problem."

"Can you give me some pictures of the damage?"

"Yes, we can do that. I will use this frequency to send my survey of your outer hull. Use an isolated monitor for my video."

"Okay, I'm ready."

"Yes, I'm maneuvering under your craft. Are you receiving my image?"

Eleanor had come back to the cockpit. She was watching and listening without saying a word.

"Your video stream is very clear," answered Hans-Peter. "From my monitor it looks like we were hit at an angle. It looks like we have several long gouges all at an angle to our centerline. Are there two rather deep depressions two thirds of the way back along the gouges?"

"That's an 'affirmative,' Rebel. I'm taking a closer look."

"Those are now weak spots," said Hans-Peter. "If they go through to the pressure hull and break, we could have explosive decompression."

"That's another 'affirmative,' Rebel. Can you determine the structural integrity of your pressure hull?"

"No. When we fire our rocket for deceleration, the forces it creates could break open the weak spots. My first thought is to get everybody autonomous in their pressure suits and let the cabin go back to a full vacuum. If the pressure hull cracks open and we are already at full vacuum, we won't feel it."

"Affirmative, Rebel. If I were in your airplane, that's what I would do."

"Who are you talking to, Hans?" asked Eleanor.

"I'm not sure," he said and pointed to a still image of it he had captured on another monitor.

Eleanor moved forward and looked at it. "That's the same craft we saw as we ascended and the same voice. Oh my," she said, "Do you know who they are?"

"No."

"Hans, let me talk to them."

He pulled a microphone on a cord, out of his panel that was isolated from the other electronics, and handed it to her. "This is Eleanor Scribble of the FAA, please identify yourself."

"Hello, Ms. Scribble, I'm one of Hans-Peter's new friends."

"You sound like an American. We all know our government is flying classified aircraft that have not yet been revealed to the public. Let me thank you for assisting Hans in appraising our damage. Now, according to regulation, you need to give me the 'established black noncompliance waver'."

"Oh, golly," said the voice. "I don't know the secret password, but getting back to business, be prepared for the hull damage to give your craft a strong starboard turning tendency. If you pay attention, your control surfaces should be adequate for the correction."

"Alien creatures don't use the word 'golly.' I would like to thank you again for your observations and a reasonable suggestion," said Eleanor with just a touch of anger in her voice. "I am flying with this craft to insure its compliance with FAA flight regulations; and since you have made yourself known to us, you need to be in compliance also."

"Can you identify my spacecraft?" asked the voice as the UFO floated back up in front of the windshield.

What she saw looked solid. "You really are there, aren't you?"

"Yes, I am, and can you identify my craft?"

"I'm afraid not. For now, you are an Unidentified Flying Object, and on behalf of the Federal Aviation Administration, I'm requesting an identification."

"But then if I identify myself," said the voice, "I'll lose my UFO status. I have the ability to move in and out of different dimensional spaces. I'm going to move into a different set of dimensions. From your perspective, I will simply disappear."

Eleanor, Larry, and Hans-Peter were the only three in the cockpit. They were all watching the UFO to see what it would do, and then it just disappeared.

"This is the Rebel to the visiting spacecraft," said Eleanor, "do you copy?"

No one said a word for three or four minutes, and nothing came back over the frequency.

"That turkey is not following civilian/military protocol," said Eleanor. "Were you able to capture that spacecraft on video as well as that still photo?"

"Yes," answered Hans-Peter. "In fact I have quite a bit of his spacecraft and everything he said in a file."

"Excellent," she answered. "That guy sounded as American as you or I. I think it would be best to keep this encounter between the three of us. Let's not tell anyone else on board what happened. When we get home, I'll see to it they toast his butt."

"Don't worry about me," said Larry. "I thought it was just some swamp-gas."

Eleanor couldn't help but smile with considerable skepticism. Her watch now read 1:40 a.m. Pacific Standard Time.

Chapter Twelve
In Orbital Space

Through the wee hours of the night, mission control at Titanium Composites had become a brewing sea of concern. No one knew how much damage the slow speed collision with the abandoned Soyuz spacecraft had done. Until today, no one outside Titanium Composites even knew the Rebel could fly into orbit; but that accomplishment was meaningless if they couldn't get back. Apprehension was spreading among the mission control team. They knew there was very little they could do. The next Soyuz wouldn't be ready to launch for at least several weeks and if the Russians could get it into orbit empty, it could only bring back three people.

Ruthiebell and I were still at the engineering station off to the side of the control area. She seemed to have complete mastery of the equipment and had recorded every second of the Rebel's ascent until the radio blackout. She was fascinated by what she thought was good evidence for a UFO and was replaying the image the Rebel's aft-looking radar had caught. The image was much smaller than the Rebel. She pointed to it on her monitor. "It's the right size for an A-10, but it's moving much too fast. Look at it, Traypart. That's an alien spacecraft. That's the only thing it could possibly be."

"The image is not clear," I said, "but I agree with you; it looks very real. I think we're looking at a small, totally classified, military aircraft that no one outside of the black world knows anything about."

"That's a wonderful explanation, Traypart," she said cynically, as she imported various analytic programs from somewhere outside the company into her computer. "I'm sure the Project Blue Book guys would be very proud of you."

"What are you doing?" I asked.

"I'm patching into the, 'objects in orbit,' data base at the Johnson Space Center. They've been tracking the Rebel since Claudius told them Hans was attempting to rescue the ISS crew. If that UFO is still flying with Hans, we might see it here in their data stream. Okay, here it comes. Let's see what we can find."

Hans-Peter had told Nancy that the Rebel didn't need the same kind of heat shield for reentry that the space shuttles did. The Rebel had the same metallic thermal protection that had been invented by BF Goodrich for the VentureStar, but it really didn't need it. The concern was for structural integrity. If the fuselage had been weakened in the collision, then the Rebel might break up during reentry.

The structural loading that the long retrorocket burn would create, and the aerodynamic loading that always occurs during flight, would demand a high degree of structural integrity for a safe return. Hans-Peter thought the guys in the UFO were probably telling him the truth about the damage they saw, but how could he trust guys who wouldn't even give Eleanor the correct 'established black noncompliance waiver.' He had never heard of the noncompliance waiver; but then he had never flown a secret airplane from the black-world side of the government. He was, however, quite sure you shouldn't mess around with someone like Eleanor. She had, after all, the entire federal government behind her.

While everyone on board was enjoying the relative safety of the Rebel, Hans-Peter was determining what he would look for when he went outside.

Six of them onboard were freely enjoying the comfortable atmosphere, the cool spring water, and as much pizza as they wanted. Only Hans-Peter, his copilot Larry, Eleanor, and Nancy understood how tenuous their status might be. Hans-Peter left his place in the cockpit and floated back into the cabin. They were telling jokes and laughing.

When Hans-Peter stopped at the entrance and didn't take anything to eat, the cabin fell silent. "It's so good to see that everyone's comfortable here inside the Rebel. As you remember, we had a slight collision with that free-floating Soyuz. Before I choose a reentry time, I'd like to go outside and have a close look at the impact area. I don't think we have a problem, but I'd like to make sure. Please enjoy the cabin while I suit-up, and make sure your pressure suits are ready to support you independently. If you need some help, Angelo can show you how to fill your oxygen from the ship. I'm not sure if the impact has damaged the seals on our doors. So far they have been holding tight, but to be on the safe side, when I go outside we'll bring the internal pressure down to the space vacuum."

The party atmosphere slipped away as everyone remembered the collision. Each one had thought about death long before they had signed on to fly into space. This moment demanded that those thoughts be revisited. The only thing they could do was take comfort from their fellowship and wait for Hans-Peter's return.

Sandy and Milo approached their senior executive with all the appropriate respect they could muster. Their driver, on the other hand, stood as far away as he could. Sandy waited for Ruthiebell to look away from her monitor and recognize her, then she spoke, "We had no idea you were here. Milo and I were out on the runway and were able to make a good video of the Rebel's takeoff."

"Yes, I know," answered Ruthiebell, "I saw it when you sent it back to

Max." She shifted her attention to Milo. "Your choice of f-stops and focal points were excellent, Milo. You made some of the best footage I've ever seen. You make me proud to be part of the *Herald Express* team." She looked back at Sandy. "Have you met Traypart?"

"Yes, we had breakfast together with Keith Wiley the day of the rollout."

Ruthiebell grimaced a bit. "Keith's probably asleep, unless one of Max's friends tipped him off about the night takeoff. As we speak, Keith may be driving out here right now. Let's hope not. Are you two tracking the Rebel's progress?"

"Yes ma'am," answered Milo with a lot of friendship as well as respect. "Right now I'd like to shoot Sandy interviewing you and Traypart. The Rebel isn't reporting anything right now, so I think this is the best time." Milo then looked at Traypart and then back to Ruthiebell. "Would you like to do that?"

"Sure," said Ruthiebell, "That's a good idea. Are you up for an interview Traypart?"

"I'm usually the one doing the interviewing," said Traypart. They all looked back toward the center of the mission control area.

"Those guys look pretty busy to me," said Ruthiebell. "That collision with the Soyuz has everybody pretty worried. They're probably trying to help Hans-Peter deal with more damage than they've reported. I think we better leave them alone for a while. What sort of question would you like to start with?"

"Well," said Sandy testing the water, "Max told me there should be a UFO angle to anybody flying out into space." Not that question, thought Milo. He looked at Sandy, not believing his ears. He knew that topic was sudden death.

"Really," answered Ruthiebell. Her tone of voice, suggesting that Sandy had lost her mind. "Milo, would you put the cap back on your camera lens."

꒰ഒ꒱

Down at Cactus Patch, Lieutenant Martinelli had just entered Major Hayes's office. He was still wearing his bathrobe over his uniform.

"Do you have three answers for me?" asked the major.

"No sir, but the corporal and I think you would like to hear what we are receiving. Tabby's managed to get a real-time patch into the downlink to the Johnson Space Center. That electronic shadow is back with much more resolution."

Even as the lieutenant was speaking, the major was up and heading for the door. "Does anybody else on base know what we're following?"

"No one to my knowledge except Raymo. He's hanging around outside Tabby's door, but the sergeant won't let him in according to your order." The major was one step ahead of Martinelli and moving quickly. Martinelli reached forward and grabbed the major's left arm to stop him. The major stopped and turned with an expression that said, this had better be good. "Sir, before we proceed," he said in a hushed voice, "I want you to know that I'm sure that Raymo knows much more about this than he's letting on."

One doesn't grab a superior officer. Major Hayes, however, instantly understood that Martinelli didn't want anyone else to hear what he had to say. "Thank you, lieutenant, that means we must let him in on what we're doing because we can't afford to miss what he might be able to contribute."

"Yes sir; that would be my call."

When they reached the entrance to Tabby's area, Lieutenant Raymo Woodburn was pacing outside. The major spoke to the sergeant first. "Sergeant, I am now giving Lieutenant Woodburn access to the operations area. There are now only four of us you may let pass. Is that understood?"

"Yes sir," snapped the sergeant. "That would be you and Lieutenants

Martinelli and Woodburn and Corporal Tabby."

"Yes, exactly," said Major Hayes with a pleasant nod as he passed.

When they were inside, Martinelli closed the door. The major looked over Corporal Tabby's shoulder at the screens and then spoke to Raymo while still standing. "Raymo, you were here pacing outside this restricted area, so now I've let you inside. Do you know things about our current situation that you haven't told us?"

"Not exactly, sir. I haven't had the special training or the clearance that Martinelli has; but I have read everything on UFOs I could get my hands on, and I have taken the time to talk to a very credible man who claims to have been abducted. My unclassified knowledge may prove to be an asset, and even a complement to Martinelli's classified information."

"I gather that means you've finished reading Caruso Phillip's book?"

"Yes sir," answered Raymo a bit defensively. "I have been reading UFO literature for years. Caruso Phillip's book is just one of many."

The major looked back and forth at Woodburn and Martinelli. "Okay, I like that. Let's take a look at what Corporal Tabby has and see if we can figure out what the electronic shadow really is."

On one screen, Tabby had the official Johnson website that was showing a global representation of the world with the positions of both the Rebel and the ISS. On the map, they were very close together, but out in orbit they were actually more than ten miles apart. On a second screen, Tabby had the telemetry data the Rebel was transmitting and on the third screen was the secure Air Force mission surveillance. At the moment, the Air Force had no data and was only displaying their logo.

Angelo's voice came over the audio from orbit, patched through from Johnson, "Hans-Peter is now ready to go extravehicular. Yuriy Brominkov is still in his extravehicular space suit from the ISS and is standing by ready to assist. Our copilot Larry Stevens is also at the hatch to assist with egression and entry. The cabin pressure is now down to zero. All systems are functioning correctly. We will continue to transmit over this frequency in real time."

Standing between the double doors of the hatch, Larry was helping Hans-Peter to get outside. Everyone had their helmets back on. Their pressure suits, including Yuriy's space suit, were all re-pressurized. Hans-Peter had asked Yuriy to come to the hatch as a backup, but to stay inside unless needed. Angelo and Eleanor were up front in the cockpit keeping an eye on the controls and any ground communication.

Speaking over the frequency that everyone could hear and was patched to the ground, Angelo spoke. "I'm reading the hatch open. Is Hans-Peter outside?"

"Yes, he's extravehicular," answered Larry.

When Hans-Peter went outside, he saw the UFO. It was quietly keeping a position about fifteen feet under the Rebel. It startled him and he could feel it pulling him toward it. He grabbed his safety line to stop his fall.

"Be at peace Hans-Peter, we are here to help," came that same voice from the UFO that they had heard before. "I'm going to move up slowly beneath you. Let your feet stand on my vehicle."

Hans-Peter knew he didn't have any choice, so he relaxed just a bit and straightened out his legs. The vehicle came up so slowly he hardly felt the impact. Then he realized his feet were stuck. He couldn't lift either one. He felt a surge of panic. He was trapped like an animal.

"Calm down, Hans-Peter," said the voice. "I can read your vital signs. You are not trapped. I put what you would call a tractor beam on your feet. This way you don't need to worry about floating away. How do you feel?"

"Fine, I guess. It's clear I have no choice."

"Good. Now get out your camera. I'm moving you back to where the damage is." Hans-Peter began to relax even more. The UFO moved to the best possible position to evaluate the damage. "Are you getting good images?" asked the voice.

"Yes, actually I am; but I could use some more light."

"We can do that. I'll put the light source behind you. There, how is that?"

"Perfect, that's just right. Will you take me back to where the impact damage started?"

"Yes, of course; how's that?"

"Oh, come on. Creatures from other worlds don't say 'yes of course.' You sound just as American as I do."

"Thank you, Hans-Peter. I've been working hard at mastering your simplified version of Galactic. Of course, I'd rather you didn't refer to me as a creature. Creature sounds even worse than being called an 'Extra-Terrestrial Biological Entity.' Would you mind calling me your new friend? Now, once again, have I put you in the right position?"

"Yes. It's very good. Now let's move forward slowly along all the damage."

"That will make the same video I gave you when you were inside," said the voice with a hint of irritation.

"Let's move back to the two-thirds spot where that piece of skin was ripped open." At this point, Hans-Peter was sure the voice was human and probably military. His vital signs went back to normal. "Would you move me up to where I can get a hold of it?"

"Yes, I can do that, but don't grab it. It looks very sharp and it will rip open your glove. Get out the pair of pliers you're carrying and test it with them."

"I was thinking of doing it that way, but I certainly appreciate the word of caution." The UFO positioned him perfectly and he carefully extended his pliers to the ripped open the skin. It was ripped partly away from the fuselage, but it wasn't loose. The large piece of the metallic thermal protection that had been over this part of the skin was missing entirely. "I plan to reenter the atmosphere slowly so I won't get too hot; I won't need what's missing. What do you think? Can you tell if my structure has been compromised?"

"I have evaluated your structure, and it looks fine; but you may lose cabin pressure. When you reenter, keep everyone on his or her own air; and you'll be fine. Are you ready to go back inside?"

"Yes."

"By the way," said the voice, "no one else could hear our conversation." The UFO moved him near the hatch and then released his boots, pushing him ever so slightly toward the hatch. When Larry extended his hands to help Hans-Peter back inside, he saw the UFO. From inside, Hans-Peter spoke to the UFO through the open hatch as though he was calling from one boat to another. "Thank you very much for the best assistance I could ask for. May I please know your first name?"

"Why sure, old buddy, my name is Daypart," said the voice. Then the UFO disappeared again.

"That's not your name. You're playing games with me. You've probably read Traypart's editorials in *Aviation Week* and you just modified his name. If you want to play games with the truth, you're going to have to do better than that."

Larry couldn't hear what Hans-Peter was saying. He helped him inside enough to close the outer door. Before closing the door, he looked outside and saw nothing. When he closed the outer door, Hans-Peter's communication was restored. Larry didn't know it, so he motioned for

Hans-Peter to move on inside.

"I'm moving, Larry. Can't you hear me?" asked Hans-Peter.

"Now I can. Your communicator shut down when you went through the outer hatch."

Yuriy had moved back to his seat to clear the way. Once fully inside, Hans-Peter helped Larry close the inner door and spoke to the cockpit. "I'm inside, Angelo; bring back the cabin pressure."

While most of Cactus Patch slept, Tabby was scanning the images that were coming through. The major and the two lieutenants stood behind him watching the screen. Then Tabby was able to catch the one good still of the UFO. "That's it," said Raymo with great anxiety. "That's it, that's the one that guy told me about. The abductee I talked to described a UFO that would look just like that one; and there's a reference. I don't remember where, but other people, I think somewhere in England, described a UFO like that one. It landed somewhere in the woods near an Air Force base, maybe forty years ago."

"That was the Rendlesham Forest incident back in December of 1980," said Martinelli as he turned his attention directly to Major Hayes. "Oddly enough sir, the Rendlesham incident happened next to the RAF Woodbridge field. At the time the US Air Force 81st Tactical Fighter Wing was based there. The 81st was flying A-10s just like ours."

"Look at the screen," blurted Raymo, "it's unbelievable! Tabby's got the damn thing on his screen. Do you know that one, Marty? Is that one one of the 'Identified Alien Crafts'?" demanded Raymo.

"No. At least it's not one of the IACs I've seen before."

"What are you talking about, Raymo?" said the major with building exasperation. "Did you just make up that acronym? I never heard of an

IAC before. Are you telling me our government has actually identified more then one kind of UFO and when they know what they are, they call them IACs?"

"Yes sir, that's my understanding," said Raymo.

The major shot a glare at Martinelli.

"Yes sir, Raymo has used the correct acronym. The one we are looking at, however, is one I have never seen before. To the best of my knowledge that one is a UFO."

Major Hayes was beginning to feel like a grade school kid talking to postdocs in a national laboratory. He spoke to Martinelli, "Is there any chance we're looking at a totally classified spacecraft that our government is flying?"

"Yes sir, that's always a possibility; but as I said, I don't recognize that one. Our people that fly classified equipment are never supposed to let it get so clearly photographed. If that one is ours, those guys are in trouble."

"So why didn't we hear anything from Hans-Peter when he went outside his craft?" asked the major.

"We heard Larry, the copilot," said Tabby, "tell Hans-Peter his communicator shut down when he went through the outer hatch."

"Corporal Tabby, are you copying all this in one of our own files so I can review it later?" asked the major.

"Yes sir. I'm putting it in the most secure place I have," said Tabby and then continued. "Lieutenant Martinelli, the Air Force screen is displaying 'eyes-only' access. Would you like me to leave the area?"

The major put his hand on Tabby's shoulder. "Stay put, son, you're doing just fine. Martinelli, don't keep them waiting. Bring up their message."

Martinelli got out his black security card and swiped it to open the message. The, 'eyes-only' message came up in oversized black print. It read, 'Instruct Major Hayes to escort the Rebel back to its landing with recon pods only. Fly as many A-10s as possible, and fly an extended open formation. Record everything possible and be prepared for multiple UFOs. Record each one. Acknowledge, M-Type-One.'

Martinelli acknowledged with his black card. Then, the screen snapped back to the Air Force logo. "There's your answer, Sir. HQ doesn't want some prankster messing around with the Rebel's return flight either."

"Yes, I can see that, lieutenant."

"Sir," said Raymo intensely. "We've been told to fly with recon pods on the rails, but we need ammunition if we're going to stop anybody from blocking the Rebel's safe landing. If that thing really is a UFO, missiles will never stop it. Only the A-10 has an armor-piercing weapon that can bring down a UFO. We must, therefore, fly with ammunition."

"There is nothing wrong with your thinking, Raymo, but the 'eyes-only' order said recon pods only."

"Yes sir, that means recon pods on the rails only. That says nothing about ammunition for the cannon."

The major didn't answer Raymo, but spoke to Martinelli. "When will Hans-Peter reenter?"

"I don't know. If it was me, I'd want to come down in sunlight."

"Tabby," said the major. "Have you heard any indication when they're coming home?"

"No sir."

"What do think, Raymo?"

"The Rebel is in a 90-minute orbit. If I knew when the Rebel had completed its first orbit, I could give you the likely landing times plus or minus 10 minutes."

"No problem," said Tabby. " Air Force Surveillance said the first orbit was completed at Zero Hundred Hours California time. At midnight they were directly overhead."

"The reentry orbit will be 110 minutes instead of 90," said Raymo as he looked at his watch. It's 0205 now; that means the next possible landing is at 0320 give or take 10 minutes."

"You're probably right, bro," said Martinelli, "but it's still dark then."

"The next three windows would put them here at 0450, 0620, or 0750 Hours."

"Okay," said the major. "We prepare for the 0620 intercept, but we understand it might not be until 0750. I will fly lead on this one. Who are the next three to fly?"

Both Woodburn and Martinelli stepped forward.

"Okay, that makes sense. Tabby, find me a third man, and notify him for the flight." The major looked at Martinelli, "How does that sound?"

"That sounds right to me, sir," answered Martinelli. "I think Raymo has just made a very good call. Sometime over the next hour or two, Corporal Tabby should be able to get their exact time."

"Very good," said the major. "Tabby, hit the alert and start your clock now."

The peaceful desert night was rudely violated by the noise of the pulsating alert horn.

"Get me that third pilot," barked the major, "I'll go wake up our maintenance Captain myself." The major looked directly at Raymo, "I'll have him load the cannons."

Lieutenant Raymo snapped to attention and saluted the major saying, "Yes, sir."

Tabby spoke over the base P.A. system. "Attention all personnel. Prepare A-10s for a recon engagement sortie. This is not a drill! Repeat, this is not a drill!"

Ruthiebell had managed to copy the one good still photo the Rebel had taken of the UFO. She knew the UFO in the photo fit the description of the UFO of the Rendlesham Forest incident. There were no photos from that incident, at least none that were published; but there was a fairly good written description.

She had dismissed Sandy and Milo before the photo had come up on her screen. She smirked at the irony of using the standard government tactic of implying that anybody suggesting UFOs was totally crazy, on her own employees, while she had in fact the newest and best UFO photo to be had. She moved the UFO photo off the screen and put the Johnson Space Center in its place.

Sandy and Milo had wandered into the back room looking for some coffee and something to eat; dinner was a long time ago.

Ruthiebell knew if a UFO like the one in the photo was flying with the Rebel, then Hans had probably seen it when he went extravehicular. She had heard Larry say that Hans had lost communication when he was outside. She must talk to Hans.

Ruthiebell exhaled dramatically to get Traypart's attention; then she gave him the expression of helplessness that all women have rehearsed for controlling men. She had his undivided attention. Using her most engaging smile, laced with a tapestry of her personal charm, she said, "I'd like to stay at this terminal for a bit longer. Would you mind trying to find an iced tea for me?" She had let the, 'for me' words linger seductively in the air as though she was flirting with him.

"I need to stretch my legs," said Traypart as though they were at a picnic table. "I'll go see what I can find." He was gone immediately.

Ruthiebell took the microphone on a cord from her control panel and stood up. She turned toward Claudius and the senior company controller. When she depressed the send button, a red light came on at the controller's desk. Both Claudius and the senior controller turned and faced her. They were too far away to hear her. She patted her chest and pointed up. The controller gave her an approving nod and threw a switch that opened her access to the Rebel again.

"This is Ruthiebell at TC-Control hailing the Rebel, do you copy?"

"Yes, Ruthiebell, we copy. This is Hans-Peter."

"Your telemetry stream is very good. We missed hearing from you when you went outside. Apart from the damage report, was there anything else that might be of interest?"

Oh yes, thought Hans-Peter, Ruthiebell can be so delightfully vague. "Let me first say that the damage is probably not serious enough to be a problem for re-entry. That said, I think the chickens have come home to roost. Oh, and I have the word for your puzzle. Try the word, 'part-day.' So very good to hear your voice Ruthiebell; please patch me over to Trajectories."

"Rebel, this is TC-Control Trajectories, are you ready to come home?"

"TC-Control, I'd like to land under sunlight. I calculate the end of the fifth orbit brings us down around 6;00 a.m. The reentry program we planned was for a rocket burn at 94% thrust starting just over Hawaii. How should I correct our current orbit to be in the right place?"

"Rebel, with your airframe damaged, we would like you to burn at just 58% for a longer time."

"TC-Control, that sounds like a good idea. Less thrust will put less structural challenge on the airframe," said Hans-Peter. "Have you worked up the new numbers for me?"

"Rebel, that's affirmative. For starters, we will need an orbit correcting RCS burn for 44 seconds. Please change your craft orientation 21 degrees to the starboard."

Ruthiebell turned the volume down on her workstation. Hans had said it, 'the chickens have come home to roost.' She knew that meant Hans had seen the UFO. This was no longer hypothetical. He had also used their code to give her the name of the alien he had contacted. Hans had said 'part-day' and that meant Daypart. Daypart was the name of the alien Hans had talked to.

I looked at Ruthiebell from across the room. I could actually 'hear' her thinking. 'Oh my God, she thought, Hans has actually made contact. He's talked to an alien. A surge of excitement and curiosity rolled over her. Then the dark reality of it began to sink in. This wasn't a game anymore. If aliens were real, she knew they couldn't be overwhelmed. The dark fear of utter helplessness began to fill her being. It was a sensation she had never encountered before.

Several appropriate UFO stories ran through her mind. The aliens in the stories she remembered always did whatever they wanted. What kind of alien was Hans-Peter talking to? Most of the stories she knew talked about, 'Grays,' 'Reptilians,' 'Nordic Aliens,' and occasionally a, 'Humanoid Shape-Shifter.' She knew all of them had more technology than she could even dream of; and she understood clearly what that meant. I could feel the deep fear Ruthiebell was feeling. She knew that if aliens were real, they couldn't be overpowered.

I had found some iced tea and Danish. I had also heard her talking to Hans-Peter. These two humans are much brighter than the average. I had other ways of communicating with Daypart and I knew he had been called a creature. Apparently Hans-Peter and Ruthiebell were now calling him a chicken. Well, I wonder how long it will take Ruthiebell to see the similarity in my name and Daypart's?

I could see Ruthiebell was still standing at her station. My guess was that she was hoping Sandy and Milo would come back; but she had brushed them off so soundly that she couldn't expect to see them anytime soon.

In my refreshments box, I had two iced teas in unopened glass bottles and Danish pastries wrapped in linen napkins. I also brought extra napkins and unopened straws. When I reached her station, I tried to lessen her anxiety with the mundane and I said, "I found some good-looking apricot Danish. I brought two. I thought you might like one." I extended the box to her.

As she took the linen, the tea, and a Danish, she didn't look at me; but with all her might, she thought, 'are you from another world?' Of course, I could 'hear' her.

"I saw Sandy and Milo," I said. "They fixed them up with a station on the other side of the room. Milo's learning the monitor with one of their people, and Sandy is interviewing anybody she can catch on a break. Has anything developed while I was gone?" I hoped she couldn't see in my face that I knew what she was thinking.

Ruthiebell opened her iced tea and drank some from the bottle. "That electronic shadow has morphed into a spacecraft." Once again she thought with all her might, 'Do you have a brother named Daypart?'

I wasn't ready to reveal who I was just yet, but I was impressed by how strongly she could project her thoughts. "Really," I said. "Can you put it back on your screen?"

She sat down and brought up the photo of the UFO. "Have you ever seen anything like that before?" she said with a taunting tone of voice.

Good grief, I thought, she has a very good photo of Daypart's craft. In fact you could read all of his insignias on the side. I had better be careful. I try never to lie, and as I said, I try to follow my father's advice and never be completely open with anyone. "Yes, I have. I've seen things like that posted on the Internet, but their credentials always seem rather dubious to me."

Her eyes narrowed as she unwrapped the Danish. She drank a little more of her iced tea. Being so near to her, I could also feel her intense anxiety. She was asking herself, 'How could this be? I have written about UFOs for years and I'm now sitting next to an alien pretending to be a human.'

What could I say? I realized it would be best to 'listen' a little more and try to learn which way she was going. Then she thought, 'If Traypart is an alien, then surely he is telepathic. Look at him sitting there pretending to be human. This isn't the way it was supposed to happen. An alien should step forward from a dazzling spacecraft dressed in otherworldly splendor and ask to speak to our leader. He shouldn't be sitting at my terminal eating Danish. Can you hear me?' she thought with great energy. I was tempted to put my hands over my ears as though she had yelled at me. Tempting as it was, I didn't.

Her thinking continued. 'This is pretty good Danish. What can I do? What can I do? What can I do? I'll test him. So far nothing bad has happened. He's either a Humanoid Shape-Shifter,' – the mere thought of being next to a shape-shifter, fired her adrenaline to a near panic – 'or a Nordic alien. Nordic aliens allegedly look like humans and don't do evil things.' Thinking I was a Nordic, or should I say hoping I was a Nordic, calmed her blood back down. 'I'll just test him,' she thought. 'His information can't be any more misleading than the government is. He's probably not all that smart, anyway.'

Chapter Thirteen
Orbital Realignment

After leaving the impaled and failing space station, the Rebel assumed a natural orientation to the Earth as it coasted effortlessly along its new orbit. With no gravity to give the astronauts a sense of direction, they could rely on the floor to be down and the ceiling to be up. Looking out any of the windows, they would see the Earth was down and the endless blackness of space was up. Little things can be comforting.

Hans-Peter was still in his Extra Vehicular Activity space suit as he stood by the flight engineer's station in the cockpit. Eleanor had come in just before he had and was in her seat. Angelo was still in the aft cabin. Hans-Peter and the other two in the cockpit had their helmets off. "Larry," he said, "we need to correct our orbit as soon as possible. I would like you to do it. Alert our passengers."

"Passengers and crew please return to your seats and buckle up," announced Larry to everyone. "We need to change our orbital orientation 21 degrees. I am doing that now." He fired the smallest of the RCS thrusters. "There, we have it. The orientation has been changed. It was so slight you may not have felt it. Next we need to fire the two big RCS rockets for 44 seconds. My display is not yet showing that everyone is secure."

Angelo was standing in the aisle in the aft cabin between Nancy and Valentina's seats. He reached forward and took hold of the grab bars on the back of Rodney's and Aleksey's seats. Angelo called forward. "I'm secure Larry. Everyone in the aft-cabin is secure."

Hans-Peter put his gloved hands on the grab bars on the back of his seat and Eleanor's; then he spoke to Larry. "I'm secure. Fire when ready."

Larry spoke again, "I'm starting the rocket burn now." The two big Reaction Control System engines lit simultaneously. Hans-Peter could feel the force, but it was much less than he thought it would be. Withstanding the force was not a problem. The RCS rockets burned for 44 seconds.

When the burn was over, Hans-Peter carefully scanned the monitors at his station. "TC-Control, this is the Rebel. Do you copy?"

"Rebel, we copy. Your telemetry looks good. Local time is 3:08 a.m. and your third orbit is complete. Set your retro ignition time for 5:58 a.m. You will be over the Philippine Islands. At 58% thrust you will reenter over the Pacific. Then, after about 17 minutes of jet-powered flight, you should be landing here in San Bernardino at about 6:22 a.m. Were you able to copy those numbers?"

"Roger, TC-Control. We will ignite our retro burn at 5:58 a.m. California Time."

With roughly one and a half orbits left to go before the deorbiting rocket burn would start, Hans-Peter had plenty of time to get out of the bulky EVA space suit and get back into his flight suit.

Everyone on board knew that Hans-Peter and TC-Control had worked out a slower retrorocket burn that would be less demanding on the Rebel. None of the passengers had guessed that somebody named Daypart, in a UFO no less, had also helped Hans-Peter evaluate the Rebel's collision damage.

"We will be up here a little less than two hours before we start our reentry. You may leave your seats and move about the cabin." Larry made it sound like they were flying from LA to Boston. Everyone heard the humor in the announcement.

After Angelo moved forward in the cabin for more pizza, Rodney Ellis, the Australian, took Chris, one of the Americans, to the back of the cabin to apparently check how well the two cargo containers were strapped down. "Listen, mate," he said in a hushed voice. "I trust you more than my own mum."

"Well, thank you, Rod. I've enjoyed working with you on the space station. Is there something bothering you?"

"Struth, there is, mate!"

Chris frowned, trying to understand what Rodney had said. "Let's see, 'Struth' is your colorfully perverse Aussie way of saying, 'good heavens,' without being colorfully perverse. That means something is bothering you big time."

"Right-o, mate! Just take a gander out your window."

Corporal Tabby had heard every word that was said between the Rebel and the ground. By this time, Tabby had begun to genuinely care about the ten people aboard the unproven Rebel and what might happen to them. The major and Raymo had left the operations area to check on the A-10s. Tabby spoke to Martinelli. "What do you think, sir? If they're planning to be back in San Bernardino at 0622, should we be airborne at 0550 hours?"

"No, that sounds too soon. Wait a minute, something's coming in."

The Air Force monitor read, 'Printable Information.' Martinelli got out his black security card and swiped it to open the message. The message said, 'Instruct Major Hayes to be airborne at 0545 hours local time. Each A-10 flying must be fitted for reconnaissance pods. Repeat; A-10s should be airborne at Zero Five Forty-Five hours, Pacific Standard Time. Fly as many A-10s as possible and fly an extended open formation. Record everything possible.' The system let Tabby print two copies. Then the screen displayed, 'Acknowledge, M-Type-One.'

Martinelli acknowledged with his black card. The screen snapped back to the Air Force logo. Then he asked for Tabby's microphone. "Please give me the P. A." Tabby threw a switch. "This is Lieutenant Martinelli. The next A-10 sortie needs to be airborne at Zero Five Forty-Five hours."

As the lieutenant returned the microphone, Tabby said, "Lieutenant Martinelli, I have a problem."

"Okay, so what's your problem?"

"If you fly this sortie, I will have no way to open the next secure AF message that may come over that screen. I will be unable to keep our major informed."

"I can't give you my card. If I did that, I'd never fly again."

"For this sortie, I believe it's absolutely critical that our major be kept informed of anything that comes over that screen."

"Well there's nothing I can do about it, corporal," said Martinelli rebuking him.

"Lieutenant Potash can fly in your place and you can stay here to insure our major is informed of everything they may want him to know."

Martinelli was growing angry. "I'm not going to miss this one. He got his black card out. "Can you handle this with complete secrecy? No messing around, I'm talking the real thing, and you keep your trap shut. This is between you and me. Can you do that?"

"Yes sir, I can."

"Okay, then I'm authorizing you to use this for this sortie only; and you will tell no one about it. Not even the major. Do you understand?"

"Yes sir, I understand."

Martinelli gave Tabby an approving nod and as he left he said, "We'll stay in touch, bro." Martinelli left in a hurry, taking one copy of the newly printed orders with him.

Ruthiebell and I were finishing our tea and Danish. For the lack of anything more interesting to look at, we were studying the picture of Daypart's spacecraft. Sitting next to her made it very easy for me to 'hear' her thinking and 'feel' her emotional state. There was now no question in her mind that Hans-Peter had made contact with an extraterrestrial that called itself Daypart.

The unimaginable part for her was that she thought I was also an extraterrestrial rather than a human. I could 'feel' her relaxing as she began to doubt that I was really an alien. My unusual name, Traypart, was her only clue to who I really was. I knew she wanted to look at me closely, so I looked away from her at the big screen on the wall. I could feel eyes focus on my ear and then my skin and hair. 'He sure looks like a human,' I 'heard' her think. 'His hair isn't very blond for a Nordic alien. He's certainly no Gray. He's no alien at all. Just look at him. He's just a lazy engineer who would rather write stories than work like other engineers.'

Lazy engineer! I had to stifle an impulse to laugh. I'm not going to make this easy for her. I knew this would all play out in a few hours. For now I would just play dumb, and watch her grope for the truth.

"We were lucky," I said. "Both the Danish and the iced tea were really good."

"I can't remember," she said. "Were you doing journalism back in 1980 when the Rendlesham Forest UFO story was breaking?"

"Not really. The first time I was published was in 1982."

"But you were around in 1980, you just weren't published yet. Do you remember that story?"

"You know, I don't really remember it back then, but recently I have seen the retelling of that story on the Internet."

She tapped on the monitor. "Look here, this is a much more believable spacecraft than the artist's rendering made from the eyewitness accounts at Rendlesham."

"Yes, it is," I answered, "but Computer Graphic Art is getting much better."

"Hans has no reason whatsoever to create a CGA image of a UFO. Do you think this is real or not?"

She had a very good photo of Daypart's spacecraft. I was careful not to let the expression on my face show that I recognized it. I was still amused from 'hearing' her think that, 'she would test me,' and that 'he's not that smart.' Please don't think that I see myself with any special brilliance. I see myself as having a good healthy mind, but my people have had advanced technology for much longer than you have. I know how things work that you haven't even thought of yet. Therefore, I did have an advantage over Ruthiebell. "I think what you have on the screen is a real spacecraft," I answered. "Hasn't one of those anonymous 'whistle blowers' you talk about all the time told you what that really is?"

"What kind of remark is that supposed to be? Are you forgetting whom you're working for? I put good money in your pocket to work for me. I don't need any smart remarks about my 'whistle blowers'."

Oh good, I thought; she's forgetting I might be an alien. Let me see, what would a human say at a time like this? I'll be defensive. "I gained access to this story when I came out for the rollout; and I did that long before your money appeared in my pocket. Frankly, I really don't know how you gained access, but since we're both here, let's stay focused on the story. Shall we?"

Then, rather unexpectedly she said, "Okay. You have the reputation of being a journalist with a better than average understanding of the sciences. So, you can make a much better guess than I can. Is that a homegrown spacecraft developed in the deep black world or is it a UFO from off the planet?"

"If I were going to bet some of that new money in my pocket, I'd bet it's a real alien spacecraft that was built off the planet."

"How could you possibly know that?"

"It's a bet. So how could you possibly know what you're talking about?"

The party spirit from the successful rescue was reemerging in the aft-cabin. Eleanor came back for some more pizza and a break from her post. For the lack of anything to do, Valentina, one of the Russian cosmonauts, had fallen asleep with her arm floating freely in the aisle. Eleanor gently moved Valentina's arm back across the small pack she had in her lap.

In the very back of the cabin, Rodney and Chris seemed to be checking the two cargo containers. Rodney had just asked Chris if he had seen anything unusual out the window.

"After we were all onboard and were moving away from the space station, I stopped looking out the window. What was I supposed to see?" asked Chris.

Rodney pulled out his smart phone and showed Chris a short video of the small UFO maneuvering along near them and then slipping under the Rebel. "Wha da ya think o' that, mate?"

"That looks like some Computer Graphic Art that you had in memory. By showing a little optical distortion from the window and part of the window frame, you have made it look very real. Are you going to enter it in some kind of CGA competition when we get back home?"

Rodney narrowed his eyes and said, "Right-o! I reckon you're always a straight talker?"

"That may be why you trust me."

"Chris! You know I don't do CGA. I saw this thing out the window. I take heaps of pictures. That's why I carry my phone all the time. It's my notebook."

"Oh yes, I know that for sure," said Chris. "Did you ever erase the video of us putting that apparatus together backwards?"

"Don't be a drongo, mate. That's to show them how badly designed it was." The Aussie's accent thickened as he remembered what a problem it had been.

"And do you still have the video of us taking it apart and then putting it together correctly and getting it to work?"

"I'm not sure. That wasn't very interesting," said Rodney, and then with real frustration, "Chris, this isn't a game. It's fair dinkum. This here is a true blue UFO! Don't take a smoko now, you have to pay attention."

"That was pretty persuasive, Rod. You ought to sell used cars when we get home. There's no question you made some great CGA. I've never seen another UFO quite like that one. You're an artist."

"You telling me you've seen other UFOs?"

"I'm talking about the movies, dude. Did you know Mark Twain once said, 'It is easier to fool people than to convince them that they have been fooled.' Now if you'll excuse me, I'm going to get some pizza before it's all gone." Chris floated forward and was carful not to awaken Valentina as he passed by her.

Rodney drifted around the front of the containers, but stayed in the back of the cabin. Eleanor could tell Rodney was up to something and moved back toward him. She stopped next to him and grabbed one of the handles of a container for stability. "Rodney, as my dear aunt would say, you seem to have a bee in your bonnet. What would you like to tell me?"

He didn't say anything as he showed her his video. "Chris thinks I made this UFO with Computer Graphic Art and it's a stunt for a contest; but I don't know how to do CGA. I'm no artist, I can hardly sign my name."

"May I ask you not to get too excited if I tell you what I think?" asked Eleanor.

Eleanor's words were shocking, Rodney instantly understood. "You actually saw it too, didn't you?"

"Yes. We saw it up front through the windshield. We even had a brief communication from it. We don't think anybody on the ground knows about it yet. I personally haven't said a word. Hans talked to it. I'm letting Hans take the lead on this and I'd like you to do the same."

"You seem awfully calm about this. We're talking 'alien' contact here and your acting like it's no big deal." Rodney scrutinized her, looking for evidence of yet another government cover-up. "Have the chaps over at the FAA already made alien contact and they're keeping it to themselves?"

"I'll not go that far, but I happen to know several reliable rumors from within the FAA, that a number of reasonably good photographs of UFOs have been taken from both the Space Shuttle and the ISS, and we have them on file."

"That's news to me," he answered indignantly, "and I've been through astronaut training in both the US and Russia, and I've lived and worked on the space station. Nobody, but nobody ever talked about UFO sightings."

"I haven't had any of those experiences," answered Eleanor calmly. "You're the one that shot the video. What do you think you shot?"

"This isn't a game, is it?" Rodney felt the same cold sinking feeling come over him that he had felt when he realized the ISS was toast. "You're twisting the reality I live and don't like it. I worked on the space station for many weeks and I never saw anything like this. So how many lies have we been living with?"

"We really don't know what it is," answered Eleanor. "The video you caught is real, but it might be a classified government craft with one or two airmen on board. If you get too carried away with this and it turns out to be one of ours, you're going to look pretty stupid."

Her words gave Rodney a different kind of jolt. "Eleanor me love, it's a pleasure to have you along. I was missing the most obvious interpretation."

She gave him an approving nod. "Just be cool until we know what's going on."

✑✑

Lieutenants Woodburn and Collins were in a Quonset hut hanger with Major Hayes. Raymo's A-10 with the callsign, RAINDROP, was pulled forward. The major and the lieutenants were watching the airmen load the 30-millimeter rotary cannon magazines.

Raymo was smoldering with anxiety. "You giving me a maximum load?"

"No sir," answered the sergeant overseeing the loading operation. "Occasionally a maximum load will jam on the first round. I'm loading each aircraft to 92%. There has never been a jam at 92%. If you need the cannon, it'll be there."

"Excellent," said Major Hayes. Then surveying his lieutenants, he said, "Gentlemen, let us leave the sergeant to his work."

✑✑

On the other side of the TC-Control Room, Sandy and Milo were at a control station with a TC employee. Milo was at the keyboard.

"Okay," said Sandy. "Can we look at what Ruthiebell has on her screen?"

"Yes," said the employee. "Hold down the control key, and type TC-11. Ruthiebell and Traypart are at terminal '11'. All the terminals can interact."

Ruthiebell still had the UFO on her screen and when Milo typed in the request, the UFO came up perfectly clear. Both Milo and Sandy took the image to be a joke.

"So what's that supposed to be?" asked Milo. "Are you guys playing games with Computer Graphic Art?"

"At last," said Sandy, "I was wondering when the Jungian archetype would appear, but I think Carl Jung would have expected a more traditionally shaped Flying Saucer. Are you guys trying to play on the collective psyche with a UFO stunt?"

"Not to my knowledge," said the employee as he reached forward and turned off the screen. He then took a key from his pocket and locked the switch off.

"Hey man," said Milo, "if that's CGA, you guys get the prize. I'd sure like to have a copy of it."

"You two would be a lot better off," said the employee intensely, "if you don't remember seeing that."

"You're being way too melodramatic," said Sandy, "but then that's all part of the game, isn't it? Are you guys making up your own episode for *Project Blue Book*? You know, nobody believes in weather balloons, I mean UFOs. If you want to play games, why don't you let us play along with you?"

"We've done more of that than you have," said Milo with a truly phony wink.

"Listen you two, please listen to me," said the employee. "Our own military is flying things that virtually no one has ever seen. I'm not going to be the one that reveals a totally classified military spacecraft and you don't want to do that either."

"So you're telling us we just saw something our own government built?" asked Sandy.

"Some questions are better not answered. Like I said, you don't remember seeing it, because you never saw it. This terminal is now inoperable. I need to have a word with Ruthiebell and Traypart." The employee then left them.

Sandy stood up. "Let's go hear what that TC guy says to them."

Milo extended his hand to her. "Please sit down. I don't think Ruthiebell wants us around while she deals with him."

She sat down. "Okay, I'm calling Max. You keep an eye on them. They say you can't fool that Traypart guy. He might give the whole game away. Go on over there part way. Get close enough to hear what they're saying."

There were three windows along each side of the Rebel's aft-cabin. With no gravity, it was easy to float to one side or the other and look out. The passengers were all veterans of the International Space Station, and as time passed the Rebel's crew was becoming more accustomed to the zero-g environment. Hans-Peter came back into the aft-cabin leaving Larry, their copilot, to manage the cockpit.

"And a G'day to our flight commander," said Rodney. "Are you here to come clean and tell us the low down on the UFO that's shadowing your lovely aerospace plane? The one we can see just outside the window."

Hans-Peter shot an inquiring look at Eleanor.

"Check out the video he has on his smart phone," she said.

"Attention, everyone," said Larry over the internal system. "We are now only 42 minutes from our retrorocket burn. Please be mindful of the time."

Hans-Peter looked at the video, then at Rodney. "That little gadget did a pretty good job of catching our visitor. Has everyone seen the UFO that's been flying with us?"

Valentina didn't wake up, but she smiled. No doubt enjoying her dream.

"This is no time for games," said Chris. "We should be thinking about re-entry, not Rodney's computer art."

Eleanor directed Chris to look out one of the portside windows. The cabin fell dead silent as everyone looked out the portside windows. There, not forty feet away was the UFO Rodney had recorded.

The UFO was nothing like anything they had ever seen before. Rodney picked up his helmet and spoke into the microphone. "Good on ya mate, we can now see ya. I was starting to think you were a bit camera shy. Your ship looks to be smaller than ours, and nothing like anything I've ever seen before. May I ask what you call your ship?"

"In your terminology," said the now familiar voice of Daypart, "this is a 'short range reconnaissance craft,' and it is smaller then your Rebel aerospace plane."

Hans-Peter and Angelo had made their way forward to the cockpit. Eleanor moved back toward Rodney waving her hands for him to stop talking to the UFO. "Put your helmet down," she said. "I told you that Hans would handle the communication. Now button it up." Her voice was alarming, and Rodney did as she said. He found her voice reminiscent of an elementary school teacher he once had.

As Rodney put his helmet back under his seat, Eleanor moved forward to her place in the cockpit.

"This is Hans-Peter of the Rebel. Am I speaking to Daypart?"

"That's affirmative, Rebel. This is Daypart. Please be advised that your orientation is incorrect for your retrorocket burn.

"Yes, we know that," answered Hans-Peter. "We haven't turned around yet. We plan that maneuver in 15 minutes. It is a great pleasure to communicate with you. May I ask what your intentions are?"

"Yes, you certainly may."

"This is the Johnson Space Center hailing the Rebel. Do you copy? We have lost your telemetry signal and all radio communication. Rebel! Do you copy?"

"This is the Rebel to Daypart. Have you cut our communication to the ground?"

"That's affirmative, Rebel," said the voice. "We have cut your communication. Please don't be alarmed. We would rather communicate unobserved. Have you lost interest in our intentions?"

"No, I'm very interested in your intentions."

"We plan to fly in formation with you back down to beautiful San Bernardino. May I recommend that you turn your aerospace plane around before you start your retrorocket burn? If you turn to your portside, you will need 192 degrees of flat rotation. If you rotate to the starboard side you will only need 168 degrees of flat rotation."

"You know, I really do understand which way to fire a retro burn and those are the same numbers I calculated," said Hans-Peter, "but if it will make you happy I'll do the turn now." He then spoke to his passengers. "Attention, please prepare for a flat 180 rotation. I will turn rather slowly, but you should be able to feel a little of the turning motion." Hans-Peter executed the maneuver with the RSC rockets, and as he did, the UFO turned with them staying in perfect formation.

"Most excellent, Rebel. Your rotation was correct."

Suddenly Eleanor was quite sure that Daypart was a military prankster. "This has gone far enough," she said from her seat in the cockpit. "You have become ridiculous. You were beginning to fool me, but your voice and conversation is what I would expect from an American who is playing games. We know our government is flying classified aircraft that have not yet been revealed to the public. It is apparent that you are an American astronaut, and as you know, you need to give me, or any other FAA Controller, the 'established black noncompliance waiver'."

"As I said before," answered the voice that was calling itself Daypart, "I don't know your secret password."

"You have told us your name is Daypart," continued Eleanor. "I happen to know a journalist named Traypart and there's no question in my mind that he's as human as I am. I think it's a cheap shot on your part to take a well-known name and concoct a variation for yourself. That's the sort of thing a human would do, and you're not fooling me one bit."

Hans-Peter reached across the aisle and tapped Eleanor's shoulder. When she turned, he motioned her to stop talking. "Daypart, this is Hans-Peter. When you told me what you were planning to do, you said 'we plan to fly in formation' with us as we reenter. Does that mean there are two of you in your spacecraft, or does it mean there is another spacecraft we haven't yet seen?"

"I am flying with two other space crafts. There will be three of us that will land with you in San Bernardino."

"Do the other two crafts look like your craft?"

"No, they are much bigger. I am going to leave now and coordinate with the two others. We will all appear when you start your retrorocket burn. Don't try to use your radio. For now we are blocking your ability to transmit. When your reentry has taken you over Catalina Island, we'll release your radio and let you talk to Air Traffic Control in Los Angeles. This is Daypart signing off."

Daypart had maneuvered his spacecraft so that it was floating crossways no more than fifty feet in front of the Rebel's windshield. The UFO didn't fly away; it simply disappeared.

From the pilot's seat, Angelo had recorded the UFO in great detail, including the undecipherable writing on the side of it.

"Can you guys still see his radar profile?" Asked Eleanor with alarm.

"No," said Hans-Peter. "He's gone. There's nothing out there, but you can bet he'll be back with his buddies when we get near the Philippine Islands."

"I thought he said Catalina Island," said Eleanor.

"We get our radio back when we reach Catalina," said Hans-Peter, "but I think we'll see all three of them over the Philippines just before we fire our retro burn."

Eleanor had been around airplanes forever and was beginning to realize the UFO visitor was really not of this world. Now comprehending the nightmarish realty, she felt fear spreading through her. Her mind was clear and she was very anxious. She was ready to fight or run, but there was no one to fight and there was nowhere to run. She was determined not to let her fear show. She would see this through with Hans. She would not let him down.

"Hailing the Rebel. This is the Moscow Control Center. Rebel, do you copy?"

"Affirmative Moscow, the Rebel copies your transmission."

"Hailing the Rebel. This is Moscow Control. We can see your position, but we are no longer receiving your telemetry. Rebel! Do you copy?"

"Affirmative Moscow, we are receiving your transmission." For exactly two minutes there was nothing over the radio. "They can see us, but they can't hear us," said Hans-Peter.

"And that's what Daypart said he would do," said Angelo.

"My clock says 18 minutes to retro fire," said Hans-Peter, "Let us start our countdown. "Attention all passengers, we are counting down the last 17 minutes to our retrorocket burn."

Eleanor unbuckled and said, "Hans, you better stay here. We don't know what that Daypart guy will do next." She then started back into the cabin.

"Remember, I will pull a vacuum on our cabin before I light our rocket engine," said Hans-Peter over the system. "Eleanor is coming back to make sure your oxygen supplies are full. Larry, Angelo and I can handle this. Go on back and help Eleanor."

"Hailing the Rebel. This is Moscow Control. If you can hear us, we wish to confirm that your position is correct for re-entry. We calculate your best retrorocket ignition time is in 14 minutes. We see your altitude at 147 miles. We are with you. We will call out when we think you should start your 7 minute countdown to retro rocket ignition."

Addressing everyone from the cockpit, Hans-Peter said, "Don't worry about the telemetry. When we fire the main engine, they will not be able to hear us anyway. Let the record show that my instruments show the same numbers Moscow has recommended and we appreciate their confirmation. I am now ready to count off those last 7 minutes."

"Please put your tray tables and seatbacks in their full upright and locked position," said Angelo. "We are preparing to start our approach into beautiful San Bernardino."

Eleanor and Aleksey gently awakened Valentina and helped her with her helmet. "Wake up comrade," said Aleksey, "we're going to California."

Nancy overheard what Aleksey said and thought; I sure hope we make it to California. She knew, as well as Hans-Peter, if the Rebel started to heat up or the fuselage started to fail under the rocket's thrust, they were all dead.

"Hans-Peter, this is Chris. I'm on the starboard side and out my window is a very big, old-fashioned flying saucer. It's gray and looks like it came out of an old 'B' grade science fiction movie. If you have CGA images built into your windows, you're not very creative."

"The other saucer can be seen out the port side windows," said Hans-Peter. "They look like twins to me."

"Is that Daypart guy out your windshield?" asked Rodney.

"Yes, he just took up his favorite position high and directly in front of us. There is absolutely nothing more we can do. My instruments show the main rocket engine is almost ready to fire. I have set it for the 58% thrust as planed. In a minute or two we should hear from the Russians. If we do not hear from them, it makes no difference; I know exactly when to start our retro burn."

Eleanor and Larry came back up front.

"My instruments show that everyone is independent," said Hans-Peter. "I'm now decompressing our atmosphere down to a vacuum."

Two or three minutes can be forever. Each member of the ship's company was isolated in their own pressure suit. There was not a word to be said. Looking out any of the windows, they saw what looked like alien spacecraft. The big flying saucers didn't have windows and if they had lights, none of them were turned on. Nancy considered what Chris had said. She thought the big gray saucer she could see out her window looked a lot like a low budget prop from a cheap 'B' movie. Surely, she thought, the hoaxers could do better than that. In fact the irony of it made her smile. The interior of the Rebel had become silent, completely silent. She wondered if they'd ever hear from the Russians.

Chapter Fourteen
An Escorted Reentry

Holding a perfect formation in orbit, four spacecraft silently sped toward the western skies of the Philippine Islands. Their altitude was 147 miles and they were travelling at just over 17,500 miles per hour. The Rebel aerospace plane, the only recognizable vehicle, was in the center of the formation. Relative to each other, they moved in perfect unison.

Hans-Peter was monitoring the Rebel's orbit from the engineering position in the cockpit. With great care he was controlling the lithium heater for the main rocket engine to prepare it for the re-entry burn. He didn't think flying in orbit with a UFO was a first. He had seen stories on the Internet of UFOs shadowing Space Shuttle flights. Allegedly famous astronauts had said that every space flight that has ever flown was under, 'constant surveillance by UFOs,' but then, Hans-Peter doubted most of what he saw on the Internet. If the unidentified escorts were really from the government's totally black world, then nothing of any real note was happening. There was no communication. The four craft moved along so peacefully, they appeared to be asleep.

The interior atmosphere of the Rebel had been pulled down to the same vacuum as orbital space. Each member of the ship's company was independently supported by their own pressure suit and helmet; but while their life support systems were isolated, their helmets let them hear and speak to each other freely.

Chris was sitting in the front of the aft cabin near the hatch because he had been the last one to leave the space station. He was becoming increasingly skeptical about the genuineness of the big old-fashioned looking flying saucer he could see through his window. It never moved relative to the window and he knew that holding a perfect, unwavering, formation was impossible. There should always be just a little movement, but if it were actually a CGA image inside the glass, it would never move relative to the window. He could only look at it through the visor of his helmet and then through the window. The two layers of reinforced transparence made the saucer look even more suspect. He was beginning to think Hans-Peter had a very elaborate sense of humor. Chris knew he had no options. If he were still aboard the space station, by now he might well be dead. Come what may, he was grateful to be aboard the Rebel.

Across the aisle from Chris sat Yuriy Brominkov in his bulky EVA space suit. He just barely fit in the seat and his belts were stretched to the limit. Back home, he and his Russian countrymen had enjoyed a much more open dialog about UFOs than the average American did. When he signed on for the ISS, he had actually hoped he would get a good photo of a UFO from the space station. That hadn't happened. Now, like Chris, he found the simple gray saucer out the window rather suspect. There was nothing he could do. He was quite sure that reentry in this seat with its big window would be much better than being crammed in a Soyuz spacecraft. In fact, he thought, this might be even better than reentry aboard the old American Space Shuttle.

Behind Cosmonaut Brominkov sat Rodney Ellis, the Australian. Twice he had made additional smart phone videos of the gray UFO, but neither one was as interesting as the first one he had made of the smaller spacecraft that Daypart was flying. The big saucer out his window was beginning to look suspicious to him. He had bought into Daypart's smaller craft. The big gray flying saucer, however, could easily be a hologram that Daypart was projecting for some incomprehensible alien reason; and speaking of holograms, if they did make it to California he wanted to go to Disneyland and see the dancing holograms in the Haunted Mansion.

They had to be infinitely more interesting than that gray thing out the window. He smiled, thinking that if the aliens were twice as trustworthy as politicians; he wouldn't believe a word they said.

Cosmonaut Aleksey sat across from Rodney and behind Chris. He had been one of the youngest members of the Communist Party in the Soviet Union before it fell apart. He and Rodney played chess at about the same level. They weren't bad players or really good players either. They were evenly matched and never knew who would win. From the friendship that had developed over the chessboard, Rodney had learned that Aleksey was a secret admirer of Xi Jinping, President of the People's Republic of China, and longed to reestablish the Communist Party in Russia. Whenever Rodney won, he would inflict a little pain by claiming a victory for 'Capitalism,' and of course whenever Aleksey won, he would claim a victory for 'The People.'

Cosmonaut Valentina sat behind Aleksey. This had been her second expedition to the ISS. She was a physical chemist by education, and fascinated with all the stories of alien materials that were supposedly part of crashed UFOs. Under the guise of working on 'Foreign Technology' she had spent her entire career working in the most secret laboratories in Russia. It was never clear to anyone what exactly she was doing aboard the ISS, but she pushed her experiments relentlessly. She liked Aleksey a lot, but after winning each of the only four chess games they had played, he seemed to lose interest in her. The emergency effort to repair the meteorite impacts and then the dash to prepare for evacuation had left her exhausted. She was absolutely practical and understood that for now there was nothing more she could do. Her pressure suit and chair were as comfortable as a cradle and she had fallen asleep.

Nancy sat across the aisle from Valentina. She was a biochemist who, in defiance of the status quo, had proposed that a 'fifth' protein structure type that had never been seen on Earth could be grown in zero-g. She would be the intelligence behind a new biological design. A few million years of undirected evolution could never lead to the intricacies she had dreamt up. Her protein needed a creator.

Nancy had been the first one to escape the ISS to the apparent sanctuary of the Rebel. She was also the only one who clearly understood how grave a problem the damaged heat shield could be. Nancy had signed up for her six-month expedition in space, to work in a zero-g laboratory. The small pack she held in her lap contained samples of the protein she had theorized and then managed to grow. Visions of a Nobel Prize danced in her head if she could only get her stuff down safely and into a lab. For Nancy, the alien spacecraft out her window was little more than an annoying distraction. She hoped it would just go away.

Hans-Peter scanned his instruments. Everything was green. The numerical clock was counting backward to ignition. The clock showed 10 minutes and 42 seconds, make that 40 seconds, make that 38 seconds. He hoped the Russians wouldn't call again. He knew exactly when to light his rocket engine.

"TC-Control, hailing the Rebel. Do you copy?" He recognized Ruthiebell's voice, but he knew he couldn't transmit an answer through the UFO blockade. "Hans, TC-Control is not receiving your telemetry. We know where you are. We concur with the retro fire data from Moscow; we can hear them too. Traypart and I are sharing a computer station in the TC-Control room. I feel fortunate to be with the journalist who has always had such extraordinary insights. I have concluded that Traypart must have an extraordinary perspective. We are now reading less than 10 minutes to your rocket ignition. Best of luck."

Oh yes, thought Hans-Peter. Ruthiebell is trying to tell me that she thinks Traypart is an alien just like Daypart. Of course, Daypart may be nothing more than a computer program set up to emulate a human. I have a few minutes with nothing to do, thought Hans-Peter. I must try to talk to Daypart. "Visiting spacecraft, do you copy?"

"Rebel spacecraft, this is the visitor and yes, we copy."

"Daypart, we have a few minutes before I fire the retro. Would you care to tell me what you would like to accomplish with your visit? I would like to help you in any way that I can. From the ease of our conversation, it is apparent that you know a great deal about our world."

"Shouldn't you be flying your airplane?" answered Daypart's now familiar voice.

"Angelo and Larry can fly this thing home as soon as the retrorocket shuts down. My job is almost done. May I ask how long you have been here in the Earth/Moon system?"

"No, that's not where I want to start. Tell me, Hans-Peter, why do you think I'm interested in your planet?"

"It's beautiful. The photographs that came back from Project Apollo were more beautiful than anything anyone was expecting. I would guess that our technically advanced neighbors, from nearby star systems, would be drawn by its beauty and come by for a closer look."

"That's not a bad first guess," said the voice that was allegedly an alien named Daypart. "I think we would use the word interesting instead of the word beautiful, but you're on the right track." Then after a dramatic pause Daypart said, "Tell me, grasshopper, why would the people of old, technically advanced civilizations want to come and visit the toxic mess the Earthlings are creating on their beautiful blue planet?"

"Grasshoppa," exclaimed Rodney letting his Aussie accent get as thick as it could. "Did you catch that mates? Daypart, whoever or whatever he is, thinks our flight commander is a Kung Fu novice. Tell me, Daypart, does your data bank show that Lockheed actually built your little spaceship?"

"Can it, Rodney," rebuked Eleanor. "Whoever Daypart is, he has been completely civilized. Your rude remarks will not be accepted. From now on, you will only speak when spoken to, or you can float home."

"To my way of thinking," answered Hans-Peter with no hint that he had even heard Eleanor rebuke Rodney, "your question is the most fundamental UFO question there is and I have thought about it. To put myself in your shoes, I would come here looking for two rather different things. Given the complexity of DNA, I would imagine the variations it can assume are almost infinite. I would come here to see what kinds of plants and animals were flourishing. The other reason to come here is to listen to our music. Once again, given the almost infinite number of ways one can create and blend sounds, there is probably no way to predict what the Earthlings would come up with. From your extraterrestrial prospective, I would imagine, you see us on Earth creating the unthinkable. "

"Officially," said Daypart, "DNA profiling is the reason for my visit; but we may also look for pleasant expressions of the local arts, and for me that is music."

"So, how do we stack up?" asked Hans-Peter. "How would you rate the best of our music against the old galactic standards that you know and none of us have ever heard?"

"Well, of course I'm not a musicologist," answered Daypart, "but I think Earth's best composition is very fine by what you are calling galactic standards."

"I knew it," said Hans-Peter, "the best of our music, unlike the best of our technology, is most excellent even by galactic standards. Tell me, what kind of music has caught your attention?"

"I like classical music the most. I find Beethoven's seventh symphony astonishing and as you would say, beautiful. I have an analytic, diagnostic instrument in my ship that can read your CDs and create the sounds encoded. For the past few weeks, I've been comparing parts of the seventh with various excerpts from the music of Handel."

"CDs? Really? May I ask how you obtained your CDs?"

"I get them the same way you do. I bought them in West LA, but more to the point, did you know that Beethoven had copies of most of George Frideric's music?"

"I have heard that a time or two. I'm not surprised. I have a number of the lesser-known pieces that Handel wrote. Astonishing is a good word. Much of the beauty that I hear in both Handel and Beethoven is astonishing. So have you just told me that you have several of our CDs in your spaceship?"

"Yes, that's what I've just told you."

"Then this is not your first visit to or planet."

"That is also correct."

"Have you actually walked into a music store and bought a CD?"

"Not recently. Nowadays I use Amazon; but years ago, I did go into music stores. Of course, I never wore my spacesuit."

"That was very thoughtful of you, but in West LA it probably wouldn't make any difference."

"I'm sure you're right," said Daypart, "but I didn't want to talk to people that would want to know where they could get one like mine."

"So where does Amazon mail your CDs?"

"I have a post office box. They'll rent one to most anybody; and my friends and I love the junk mail that it seems to attract."

"Stop this," interrupted Eleanor rather loudly. "This is ridiculous and it's gone far enough. An alien visitor from another world doesn't buy CDs in West LA, or rent a mailbox at the post office. You are either Navy or Air Force, and I represent the Federal Aviation Administration. Let the log show that I am requesting the correct 'established black noncompliance waiver.' As you know, I am directed to enter the waiver in my log, and your noncompliance has gone far enough."

"Oh golly," said the voice. "I don't know the secret password. Eleanor Scribble of the FAA, I, Daypart request that you write up and file the appropriate document for our three space crafts to land with the Rebel in San Bernardino."

"You've got to be kidding," she said. "You may be nothing more than a computer image being displayed in the windows."

"I'm sure I have more substance than that. Would you please file the appropriate flight plan for the three of us to land with Hans-Peter?"

"Attention, passengers and crew," announced Hans-Peter. "Right now it is 7 minutes and 30 seconds and counting down to retrorocket ignition. At zero seconds I will ignite the engine. Just as a reminder, when you hear 5 seconds, press your helmet and your head against the back of your seat. It will not be violent. The force will increase over twelve seconds; then the burn will be steady. I will give you the countdown when I start it. Should Moscow call back, you will be able to hear them also." Once again, Hans-Peter hoped Moscow wouldn't call back.

"Hailing the Rebel. This is Moscow Control. We have no transmissions from you. If you can hear us, we wish to confirm that your position is correct for the calculated 58% thrust burn. Please mark 7 minutes to your optimum retrorocket ignition."

"There you have it," said Hans-Peter. "The Russians have the same time I do. We now have 5 minutes to ignition. Please check on each other."

Nancy unbuckled and reached across the aisle and tapped Valentina to awaken her. "Valentina, if you're awake please raise you hand." She raised her hand, but didn't open her eyes.

"Hailing the Rebel. This is TC-Control Trajectories. Please mark 3 minutes to your ignition."

"Their clock is in sync with mine," said Hans-Peter. "I'll not duplicate their countdown, but I'll fire our rocket according to our onboard clock."

Eleanor determined that the Daypart encounter, what ever it might actually be, wasn't covered in the FAA regulation book. "This is Eleanor Scribble of the FAA hailing Daypart. If you would like me to write up a flight plan for you and your friends, I will need to know your point of origin."

"Eleanor Scribble, you may show our point of origin as the backside of Luna."

"Daypart, at what time and date did your flight originate?"

"Eleanor, please show our departure at high noon Greenwich mean time, five earth days ago."

"Daypart, it is your intention to land, terminating your flight, at Norton Field, today at six-twenty a.m.?"

"Yes Ma'am," said Daypart. "I would be grateful if you would file the appropriate paperwork on our behalf. Please include the two large interstellar spacecraft we are flying with. We all plan to land with Hans-Peter. I will hold my position in front of the Rebel, and the two large craft will come in behind us. Would you make your flight plan show four of us landing at the same time?"

At this point, Eleanor had given up on established procedure and said, "Why sure old buddy, I'd be happy to."

Hans-Peter and Eleanor looked at each other across the aisle. She extended her open hands as if to say, 'what else could I do." He smiled and shrugged his shoulders and then turned back to his instrument panel.

"We are very close to retrorocket ignition," announced Hans-Peter. "Remember, it is best to be facing forward during the retro burn. Okay, here we go. Ignition in 20 seconds, , , mark 10. . 9. . 8. . 7. . 6. . 5. . 4. . 3. . 2. . fire.

At the same time Moscow said 'fire,' Hans-Peter lit the rocket engine. "We show a successful ignition," he announced. "My instruments look 'A-OK.'"

"This is Nancy. What is your delta-V objective?"

"17,100 miles per hour. When we have burnout, we should have a velocity of 410 miles per hour due east relative to the surface of the Earth. At that point we should be about two hundred miles west of Southern California."

With the word California, everyone in the aft cabin applauded with their gloved hands. The fancy new tri-propellant rocket engine was working perfectly; and while they could feel the force of deceleration, it was much less than the acceleration they had felt during the Soyuz launch.

"My compliments, Hans-Peter," said Nancy into the intercom system. "Your main rocket engine is burning just as smooth as silk. Do you have any way of measuring the structural integrity of this bird while we are decelerating?"

"No, I don't; but with no problems emerging so far, it's likely the fuselage will hold just fine."

Nancy became just a little less intense. It looked to her like Hans-Peter was going to pull this thing off. If there was actually a UFO or two that landed with them, she wondered how quickly she could get out of the airport with her pack of samples. Alien contact was not one of her objectives.

"Congratulations, Hans-Peter. This is Daypart and you and your rocket ignition look very good. As you can see we are decelerating with you. Did Eleanor file the right paperwork for our arrival at San Bernardino?"

"I have written a flight plan for you, but I can't file it until you free up our radio transmissions," Eleanor spoke with all the authority a good bureaucrat could muster. "What do you say, Daypart? Why don't you take off the interference?"

"We will turn the screen off when you get near Catalina Island. For now bear in mind that your rocket plume is much too energetic to penetrate. Your own engine has you blacked out."

"If your radio screening device is on, and we also have a blackout from our own rocket engine, how can we talk to each other?" she asked.

"I have technology that lets me do whatever I want to."

Eleanor didn't like that answer. It reminded her that if these UFO guys really were extraterrestrials, they were in complete control. This encounter may not have a happy ending. Cooperating with Daypart was probably a very good idea. She felt cold fear returning. She could only pray, 'Oh dear God help us through this.'

The rocket engine had now completed its main burn and started to taper off. "Angelo, Larry, heads up," said Hans-Peter. "I'm reading an altitude of 95 miles. . . There, we have flame out. Use the RCS to turn us around and keep the nose 20 degrees high. Initiate the turn now."

As the Rebel turned around to its reentry position, Hans-Peter said, "Attention, passengers and crew, our retrorocket burn was a success. Our velocity relative to the atmosphere is 414 miles per hour due east; and we will not experience any reentry heating. I am starting to re-pressurize our cabin slowly. Please keep your pressure suits independent of the cabin until I confirm our atmosphere."

Nancy exhaled her anxiety with a long steady sigh. Reentry was turning into an airplane ride home. She now felt certain they would land safely.

With small amounts of thrust, Angelo turned the Rebel around.

"The atmosphere is very thin up here," said Hans-Peter. "Use the RCS to maintain our orientation. That's it; that looks good. We'll fall for about 4 minutes before you'll feel any atmosphere. My instruments show us right on course. Everything looks good."

"Not bad, Hans-Peter, not bad at all," said Daypart. "I calculate 4 minutes of free fall before you can feel the atmosphere. Now for Angelo and Larry, be prepared for the hull damage to give your craft a strong starboard turning tendency. If you pay attention, your control surfaces should be adequate for the correction."

"Thank you for the reminder," said Angelo, "We're prepared for that possibility."

"You know, I'm a humanoid creature like you are," said Daypart.

"I didn't think you liked being called a creature," answered Hans-Peter.

"I don't, but in this case I'm sharing the title with you."

"Are you actually a creature in a Navy or an Air Force uniform?"

With that question, Eleanor turned toward Hans-Peter and shook her helmet with a 'yes' gesture. She didn't say a word, but Hans-Peter saw her and gestured back with his open hands indicating there was no way to know.

"Rebel, if you can possibly copy, this is TC-Control Trajectories. Your position and speed tell us your retrorocket burn was successful. If you can hear us, you are exactly on course and we are anticipating your arrival back here in San Bernardino."

"Hailing the Rebel aerospace plane. This is the aircraft carrier Nimitz. We know where you are and that you are experiencing a Loss Of Signal. Be informed that the LOS is not preventing our ability to track you. We have sent two Super Hornets to escort you back to the coast. Your radar image is very confused. Please turn off any specialty radars you may have. You should see the F-18s in 5 or 6 minutes. They can let us know how you look, and we will report your status to the FAA on your behalf."

"I didn't know you had specialty radars," said the UFO voice.

"We do, but they're not on. I'm sure the Nimitz is getting at least part of your big saucer crafts in their radar. Will those folks flying the F-18s be able to see the big saucers?"

"Yes, of course."

"Can you cloak the two big saucers? With one on each side, the Navy might think you're trying to capture us. We don't want them to try and rescue us by firing their missiles at the saucers. Your small craft, on the other hand, flying in front of us isn't very threatening. Letting them see only your small craft should be a good way to test their reaction."

"Hey there, Mr. Hans-Peter, the saucer out my window just disappeared," said the Aussie. "Tell the truth, lad, was it ever really there?"

"Is the other saucer visible?" asked Hans-Peter.

All three voices on the other side of the cabin answered, "No."

"Hailing the Rebel aerospace plane. This is the USS Nimitz. If you can copy, our radar image of you has improved significantly. Apparently you can hear us, and you have turned off your specialty radars. Two F-18 Super Hornets are closing on your position. Your current altitude of 75,000 feet is over the service ceiling of the F-18s. Look for our intercept when you reach about 50K. They will let us know how you look. Perhaps, at close range we can re-establish radio contact."

The Rebel was still falling and the air speed had moved up to Mach 1.5. The atmosphere was still very thin. Angelo was starting to feel response from the control surfaces. Larry was preparing to start the two inboard jet engines when they fell to 50K.

"Hailing Daypart. Do you copy?" asked Hans-Peter.

"Loud and clear, as you like to say."

"Will the F-18s be able to see you on their radars?"

"No, not on their radars, and they may not see my craft either. My craft is very nearly the color of the sky. Since they are not looking for me, they may not see me until we are much lower and you start flying subsonic powered by your jet engines."

"How about the two big saucers?"

"They will stay cloaked until you put down your landing gear on final approach. I completely agree with you about cloaking the big ships. We want to make this contact as nonthreatening as possible."

"By saying, 'this contact' are you telling me you have made contact before?"

"You got to be kidding," answered Daypart sounding a little more human than usual. "Don't you people on Earth talk to each other?"

Down on the high desert, at Cactus Patch, four A-10s had been pulled out near the runway. Airmen were with each aircraft and the canopies were open. Major Hayes and his three lieutenants were ready to fly and had all gone back into the operations area where Corporal Tabby was following the radar data for the Rebel.

"Does it look like they're going to make it?" asked Martinelli.

"Yes sir," answered Tabby with a smile. "For some reason the Rebel still has a LOS. Both the radio and the telemetry are not working, but they've had a perfect retro fire and they are on course. They just fell through 54,000 feet and they are at Mach one."

The radio Tabby had tuned to the Rebel's open frequency interrupted them. They all heard TC-Control call out to the Rebel anticipating their arrival back in San Bernardino.

"There it is," said Tabby, "they're coming home to San Bernardino."

"How far west are they?" asked the major.

"About 140 miles west of the coast," answered Tabby. "The Nimitz has sent two F-18s to escort them."

"What about that still photo of the UFO you found, has somebody posted it again or has it been talked about?" asked the major.

"Nothing has been said on the open frequency, but I've got a bad feeling about it," said Tabby reluctantly.

"A bad feeling? You can't take that to the bank. Go off the record," said the major. "Just tell me what you're thinking,"

"Hans-Peter and his people know what they're doing, and his airplane is coming in like there is nothing wrong. Sir, the Rebel is exactly where it should be. So there is no reason in the world for them not to be able to transmit. My gut tells me that little UFO we saw is real and it's flying with them and it's messing up their transmissions."

"You can bet on it, Tabby," said Raymo ready to fight. "The Rebel has at least three radios on it and they can't all be broken. Those little bastards in that UFO made the Rebel's LOS."

The major raised his left hand to silence Raymo. "Please put that one good photo of the UFO back up on one of your monitors."

"That's it," said Raymo with great anxiety. "That's it, that's just the way I remember it. It had a dull shine and a bank of blue lights. The abductee told me about the very UFO you have on your screen."

"Can you hear the F-18s?" asked the major.

"Yes, but they're not saying much. I don't think they have a clue about the UFO."

"Is it possible the Navy will force the Rebel down at the Point Mugu Naval Air Station?"

"The Navy has said nothing to that effect so far," answered Tabby.

"Okay," said the major, "we fly. When do we take to the air, corporal?"

"Right now would be a couple of minutes early and very good."

The major then addressed his three lieutenants. He focused his attention on Lieutenant Raymo Woodburn. "We are carrying live ammunition. There is only one chance in a million we will need it. This is a recon mission. You will fly a tight formation behind me. Only when we see the Rebel will we break formation and start taking pictures. If we see the UFO, we are here to photograph it. We are not here to engage it. We are not here to try and shoot it down. Is that understood?"

The three voices snapped back with, "Yes, sir."

"As tempting as it may be," said the major off the record, "let's not take any shots at the Navy either."

The Lieutenants and the corporal enjoyed the major's humor.

The major gave his attention to Tabby, "I'll send the two captains back here to keep you company. Are you up to this?"

"Yes sir, I am."

"Very good. Let's go." The three lieutenants ran out the door. When the major stepped through the door he stopped and spoke to the sergeant. "Starting right now you may also admit both of our captains. I am going to ask them to assist Corporal Tabby."

"Yes sir, understood."

Then the major broke into a run out to his A-10 Thunderbolt.

On the big flat screen up on the wall at TC-Control, the global map had been replaced with a map of the ocean and landmass that the Rebel would fly over returning to San Bernardino. With the Rebel now out of orbit, the feeling of the room had become relaxed and even jovial. Sandy and Milo were sending the right kind of stuff back to Max, and the *Herald Express* website had gone viral.

The Rebel was being tracked along with all the commercial aircraft in the area. The USS Nimitz was also being plotted along with her two F-18 Super Hornets flying toward their intercept. The large electronic map on the wall looked more like air traffic control for the FAA than something from NASA.

I was still with Ruthiebell at her computer station. She was displaying the same map on her screen that was on the wall, but she had enlarged the Rebel so that we could only see about forty miles around it. My guess was that she was looking for the two F-18s to show up.

Ruthiebell's thinking was evolving. She had known of my editorials for years and we had met at several aviation events. The first panic she had felt realizing I was probably an alien was now mostly gone. I had after all done nothing more than bring her some iced tea and a Danish, and of course I was eating a Danish just like the one she was eating. Ruthiebell knew that the sinister Gray and Reptilian aliens didn't do that sort of thing. I hoped she liked the shirt I was wearing.

Without saying a word, Ruthiebell thought a question in my direction. She didn't imagine yelling at me. She simple thought a very clear question at me. 'When Daypart lands, do you think he would like to join us for lunch?'

I almost answered. She thought her question so correctly at me, that it 'sounded' like her voice. "Doesn't the Rebel aircraft have backup radios?" I said as though innocent of the lunch proposition.

"Of course they do," she said matter of factly. "Bear in mind that we're not receiving their telemetry either. Do you think some stinker calling himself Daypart is blocking their transmissions?"

I couldn't pretend I didn't hear that one. "Well, most anything is possible. You've been reading and writing about UFOs for a long time. What do you think? Do you think some alien is using the name Daypart to hide a sinister agenda?"

She looked at me with the intellectual fatigue of a long life of uncertainty. "I think there are other civilizations, in other star systems, in our part of the galaxy. You tell me, why don't you just land somewhere in the daylight and let us video an interview?"

"Today might be that day," I said, not pointing out that she had just referred to me as though I was an alien. "You have asked a good question. Today, my best guess is that three UFOs, and I mean three ET spacecraft, will land with Hans-Peter."

Her eyes flashed with anger. "You know everything, don't you? Why don't you just come clean, and tell me who you are?"

I shrugged with open hands. "And you too will know everything when we go outside."

Chapter Fifteen
Landing A Paradigm Shift

"Hailing the Rebel aerospace plane. This is the USS Nimitz. We have your radar echo without a transponder signal. While you are not transmitting, we hope you can copy our message. We are offering a closer landing strip than San Bernardino. If it is to your advantage, you may land at the Point Mugu Naval Air Station. When you encounter the F-18s, they will escort you to Point Mugu. We are here to help. Best of luck."

"They can't do that," said Ruthiebell angrily. She and I were still in the TC-Control room where everyone could hear the Rebel's communication. "The Navy just wants to steal his technology." She then changed her screen image to focus on the aircraft carrier. "Hailing the USS Nimitz. This is Ruthiebell at TC-Control. Please be advised that the transponder for the Rebel is currently not working. When in working order, the Rebel continually transmits a full band of telemetry."

"TC-Control, this is the USS Nimitz. Thank you for the telemetry information."

After hearing the Nimitz, I said to Ruthiebell, "Maybe his radio will start working when he gets closer to home."

"There's nothing wrong with his radio," she snapped. "That Daypart guy, in his fancy little UFO, is generating the radio interference. Do you think Daypart will also interfere with the F-18s?"

"I'm sure that depends on what the F-18s try to do." I could 'hear' her thinking. Her mind was drifting back and fourth between the F-18s and how to prove that I was an alien. The thought that I was probably an alien had triggered a surge of adrenaline and panic that she was repressing as best she could. I could 'feel' the fatigue she was enduring from the all-nighter we had just worked through. I knew she was looking at me, so I looked only at the computer screen. "I'll bet the F-18s can see the Rebel by now." I pointed to the screen with an unopened straw. She focused her attention back on the screen. My speculation about the F-18s distracted her and I could feel her adrenaline response go back down.

"Hailing the Rebel aerospace plane. This is the F-18 lead from the USS Nimitz. We are on either side of you and we will come in close as you fall just a bit more. Don't be alarmed. We will come in close to inspect your fuselage. So far you are looking pretty good."

"Daypart! Materialize those big saucers before the F-18s fly right into them."

"Roger that, Hans-Peter," answered Daypart.

"Oh my God, where did they come from?" said the voice of the lead F-18.

"Daypart, do you copy?"

"Yes, I copy. This may get interesting," answered Daypart.

"We're getting closer to Catalina, would you please open my radio back up?"

"Roger that Rebel, you may now talk to your world."

"Hailing the F-18 lead. This is the Rebel. Do you copy?"

"Loud and clear, Rebel. This is the F-18 lead, so good to hear your voice. I see 'Unexplained Aerial Phenomena.' For now we will stay low and outside. Can you tell us anything about the UAPs? Are you being threatened?"

"F-18 lead, that's negative. They are not interfering in any way. Did you see where they came from?"

"Rebel, that's negative. They just materialized from out of nowhere. Do you also see a small UAP high and leading you?"

"Affirmative, F-18 leader. That one is quite a bit smaller. The three

UAPs are holding a very consistent formation."

Inside the Rebel, Eleanor read the cabin pressure from the data display in front of her seat and turned off her pressure suit. She opened the visor. The cabin pressure was fine and she said, "The cabin pressure is back, everyone. I'm taking off my helmet."

"Hailing the Rebel. This is Los Angeles Air Traffic Control, do you copy?"

"Los Angeles Air Traffic Control, that's affirmative. This is Eleanor Scribble aboard the Rebel. Our radios seem to be working again."

"Welcome home, Rebel. Please let the F-18s guide you to a safe landing at Point Mugu. We estimate your landing time at Point Mugu to be in 8 minutes."

"This is Hans-Peter commanding the Rebel. We decline that offer. As you know we are carrying six astronauts who have been in zero-g for many months. There is specialty equipment in San Bernardino to accommodate them and handle our landing. We can see the coast and will fly over the Santa Monica hills due east, staying north of the LAX traffic."

"Negative. That is not an option. Rebel, you are directed to land at Point Mugu. We do not want the 'Unexplained Aerial Phenomena' over the LA Basin. Point Mugu medical personnel can handle the six astronauts. Failure to comply will be a major infraction on your part. Rebel, please confirm your compliance."

Daypart's small craft and the two large flying saucers blinked out and totally disappeared.

"Los Angeles Air Traffic Control. This is the Rebel. There is no 'Unexplained Aerial Phenomena' in our vicinity. Please describe the phenomena you are seeing."

"F-18 leader, this is Air Traffic Control. Please describe the aerial phenomena you reported."

"Air Traffic Control, we see nothing unusual. The UAPs have evaporated like swamp gas. I see nothing on my targeting radar but the Rebel aerospace plane. The Rebel's image is solo."

❧

Back down at Cactus Patch, the four A-10s took off climbing with full power. Major Hayes and his three lieutenants were racing to a high holding position just north of the Rebel's most likely course back to San Bernardino.

"Hailing Cactus Patch. This is Major Hayes. Do you copy?"

"A-10 recon group, affirmative. Cactus Patch copies loud and clear."

"Cactus Patch, please report status and position of the Rebel."

"At its current speed, the Rebel aircraft is now 5 minutes from landfall. They have declined a landing at Point Mugu. I estimate they will land at Norton Field in 12 minutes. Your intercept should be north of Pomona in 8 minutes."

"Cactus Patch, A-10 recon group copies. We are now switching to their open frequency."

"A-10 recon group, be advised that the Rebel is now being escorted by 2 F-18s," warned Corporal Tabby.

Down at TC-Control, Ruthiebell was fuming with anger toward the Navy. She looked at me as though I was an accused criminal in a courtroom. "I don't really know who you are, but your technical writing is always the best. So, do you think Hans has built a rocket engine the Navy wants to steal?"

"Yes. His orbital flight has proven he has something at least three times better than anything in the 'white world'."

"Did those extraterrestrials give him the design?"

"No, definitely not."

"How could you possibly know that?" she said as though cross-examining me.

"I'm a remote viewer."

"Right," she snapped cynically. "If you're a remote viewer, I'm Tinker Bell."

"Yes, of course. Looks like you've gained a little weight."

"You better watch your mouth, mister. My weight is none of your business."

One didn't need to 'hear' her thinking. One could see her thoughts written on her face. She left her monitor and walked over to the TC Senior Mission Controller sitting next to Claudius. She talked to him for just a minute, then came back quickly. Apparently, Hans-Peter had given her more authority than I had thought. She picked up her mike and said, "This is TC-Control hailing the Rebel. Do you copy?"

"Yes, TC-Control, we copy."

"Rebel, TC-Control is now analyzing your reopened telemetry stream. Hans, you're looking very good. We confirm the Rebel is fit for a safe landing at Norton Field. Do you copy?"

Eleanor spoke before Hans-Peter could say a word. "This is Eleanor Scribble. We copy. Is Claudius Thud still available?"

Claudius was following every word and answered immediately. "Roger that, Rebel. This is Claudius Thud. Your flight plan is approved for landing here at Norton Field. Welcome home."

"This is the USS Nimitz, hailing the escort F-18s. Your mission is complete. You are now directed to return to the carrier."

Pulling away from the Rebel and turning toward the north, the F-18s began climbing. Continuing to turn until they were headed due west, they accelerated until reaching their cruise altitude. Once out over the ocean they went supersonic to speed their return to the aircraft carrier.

At altitude, Major Hayes and his men could see the F-18s leave the Rebel and head for home. "Okay, let's spread out our formation," he said, "but stay with me." They were higher than the Rebel and about a mile north and still heading west. As they approached their target, Major Hayes started a long 180 turn to fall in behind the Rebel. Lieutenant Raymo was high and a few hundred feet behind the major. The other two were out a hundred feet on either side.

I thought I heard those Navy guys identify 'Unexplained Aerial Phenomena'," said Lieutenant Collins, callsign CALLBIT, from the A-10 off on the major's starboard side.

"You did," answered Martinelli, callsign VINO, "but keep in mind that Navy guys have also identified mermaids a time or two."

The major couldn't help but smile as he said, "Okay, we're in line. CALLBIT and VINO move out farther and stay higher then I am. Where are you, RAINDROP?"

"I'm 400 feet behind you and about fifty feet higher."

"Excellent, RAINDROP. Can you see any mythical sea creatures?"

"No sir, my radar is only tracking you and the Rebel. Please be advised that UFOs have much better stealth technology than anything we could even dream of. I believe those Navy guys got a good look at a real UFO and once they locked their targeting radar on it, the UFO turned on its stealth and seemed to just disappear. My money says they're still out there and they're laughing at us."

"If they were really there in the first place," said Martinelli, "then they may have just dropped into another dimensional space."

"What are you talking about, VINO?" snapped the major. "What's 'another dimensional space' supposed to be?"

"If there are other dimensional spaces," answered Martinelli, "they may be like radio frequencies. To move between them, all you have to do is change your channel. RAINDROP's intuition may be one hundred percent correct. They may still be here, or they may be very far away. Nobody really knows how dimensional spaces work, at least not in the white world."

"That's not real helpful, VINO," said the major. "We can only photograph what we can see, and I don't want a hundred pictures of the Rebel. Stay sharp. If RAINDROP is right and their stealth breaks for even a few seconds, I want pictures."

"You want pictures?" answered Raymo, "My money says if I fire a cannon round or two where they used to be, that'll break their stealth and you can get all the pictures you want."

"Don't you try it, RAINDROP. I think your stealth idea is a lot better than VINO's dimensional space idea, but we don't engage things we can't see. You keep your hand off that trigger. I don't want even one round hitting the city below. Do you hear me, lieutenant? Not! One! Round!"

"Yes Sir."

"Hailing the Rebel aerospace plane, this is Major Hayes leading an A-10 recon group now closing on your position. Do you copy?"

"Hello there, Major Hayes," answered Hans-Peter. "Are you and your boys carrying your fancy cameras?"

"We are. How would you describe your flight status?"

"Very good. As you can see, all four jet engines are operating normally. We have plenty of jet fuel to make a normal approach and landing at Norton Field. As you can see, our control surfaces are rotated for a turn, but we are flying straight. If one of you would like to check out the lower surface of our fuselage, you can see we are correcting for some angular damage the Soyuz caused in space."

The major dropped down a bit and checked it out. "Your skin is dented and scarred in several places. I even see one large hole in it. I gather the skin is not the major bearing element of your fuselage?"

"Major Hayes, that's affirmative. This bird is built up with bulkheads and longerons. Do you see any signs of fuel leaking?"

"Rebel, that's negative. You look dry as a bone."

"Hailing the Rebel. This is Norton Field, do you copy?"

"Affirmative Norton Field. We are now east of Pomona and over Rancho Cucamonga. We are descending in our approach to Norton Field. Are you reading our position?"

"Affirmative, Rebel. Your position is correct for your final approach. We expect your touchdown in 4 minutes. Hailing the A-10 group leader. What are your intentions?"

"Norton Field, this is the A-10 group leader. We are creating a video log of the Rebel's approach. We will fly in with her, but not land. We plan to hold a minimum altitude of 100 feet. Does this pose a problem?"

"No, A-10s, but please stay at least 200 feet away from the Rebel."

Collins and Martinelli moved farther away from the Rebel and stayed in formation. The major fell back and then pulled up to Raymo's place. As the major fell back, Raymo fell back further and took an even higher position.

"This is the Rebel; I'm lowering my gear. A-10s, how do they look?"

"Oh my God, look what just showed up." Collins and Martinelli were only forty feet from the enormous saucers and moved another hundred feet away.

With a blink, and appearing from nowhere, two large flying saucers had materialized flying along with the Rebel in a close formation. The saucers were a light metallic gray and very near the color of the sky. There were no windows and they were showing no lights.

"That's just 'Unexplained Aerial Phenomena'," answered Hans-Peter. "How does my landing gear look?"

"I can't see your gear," said Collins. "The big gray 'Unexplained Aerial Phenomenon' is in the way. That baby's at least 170 feet across. He's flying just under your wingtip and in-between me and your landing gear. I can't see a thing."

"Roger that, CALLBIT," said Martinelli. "Rebel, you've got another one on this side. The UFO on my side also looks about 170 feet across. It's gray and I see no markings on it."

"Rebel, this is Lieutenant Woodburn. Do you see another small UFO high and in front of you?"

"That's affirmative, lieutenant," answered Hans-Peter. "They are flying with us, but not interfering. We will land with or without them. I don't think we have a problem. When this is over, I want to see your videos."

"To hell with the videos," snapped Raymo. "That little turkey is my target. If I nail him now, the broken pieces might hit your windshield, so I'll wait for you to land."

"That's a negative, RAINDROP," yelled the major, "and your language is not becoming an officer. You watch your mouth, lieutenant. I want you to pull up and out right now. I want you to go up to 1,000 feet where you can see everything at once. Start making videos that capture everything. Do you understand me, lieutenant?"

"Yes sir." Raymo pulled up and away, climbing as fast as he could.

Inside the TC-Control room, the approach of the four spacecraft and the three remaining A-10s were on the big screen in color and in high-resolution. Ruthiebell was on her feet and so was I. She turned to me and pushed her microphone into my chest. "Traypart, you tell your friends not to pull any monkey business while Hans is landing his airplane."

Ruthiebell was now sure who I was, so I spoke to her without being vague. "They won't cause any problems. Let's go down and greet them. I will introduce you to my brother Daypart." I could see a surge of anger enveloping Ruthiebell. She gritted her teeth and headed for the door.

Downstairs, a TC jeep and driver pulled forward to us. Ruthiebell took the passenger seat and I jumped up in back. Several Army jeeps, with armed uniformed soldiers, were also parked near by. Two of them followed us as we pulled out. We could see the Rebel at the far end of the field just about to touch down.

"Attention Rebel. This is Claudius, senior FAA controller. Your approach looks very good. As you roll out of your landing, please taxi to the center of the big open space between the two largest hangars. Do you copy?"

No sooner had Angelo put the main landing gear down, than the three A-10s roared overhead taking pictures as fast as their recon pods could manage. "We've got-em, we've got-em all," called out Collins. "We've got-em next to an airplane of known size, and in full daylight. Those turkeys can't hide from us! "

Angelo had put the Rebel down in exactly the right place. "Welcome home Rebel you're looking good," transmitted Claudius from mission control. "And congratulations. You just broke Shuttle Challenger's record for the largest crew landing of eight. Landing today with ten aboard gives that record to the Rebel, but then landing with UFOs is certainly another kind of record. Do we have a problem?"

As the Rebel slowed, Angelo lowered the nose gear. The two large gray saucers had gained altitude and were now about thirty feet higher than the Rebel's wings and staying in perfect formation. Daypart also held his place high and ahead of the Rebel.

A fire truck and an airport emergency vehicle raced along the runway in pursuit. Instead of taxiing to the usual place in front of the Rebel's hangar, Angelo taxied out to the big open space where he had stopped on the last flight.

"This is Hans-Peter commanding the Rebel. We have parked and are shutting down our engines. We are reading no hazards from the Soyuz collision. There is apparently no problem with our equipment."

As the TC jeep Ruthiebell and I were in approached the Rebel, we saw at least 300 soldiers and their equipment ready to keep the crowd away from the airstrip. It was truly eerie. The sight of three UFOs had caused everyone to fall silent. There were no disagreements between the soldiers and the crowd. Everyone stood in silence; amazed by something they thought they would never see. The soldiers had opened up several places for people with good cameras and tripods. No one was in a hurry to get any closer. A strong sense of comradeship was developing among the soldiers and the civilians. There was no question that they were watching very large, very real UFOs.

Without moving forward or back, Daypart's small spacecraft turned 180 degrees as though to be facing the Rebel, but held its altitude of about forty feet. There were no windows on Daypart's vehicle. The two big saucers moved forward of the Rebel about fifty or sixty feet. They each extended five metallic legs and landed so gently that one could not hear them touch down.

The fire truck pulled up near the tail of the Rebel and prepared for the worst. A very large forklift tractor carrying a personnel platform large enough to accommodate four wheelchairs and several medics pulled up to the Rebel's hatch. When the Rebel's hatch opened, Eleanor was the first one to step out. Her eyes focused on the large flying saucer she could see from her side of the Rebel. No one was talking. Soldiers were quietly forming a large circle around the entire area.

Eleanor went back inside and helped a medic get Yuriy out and into a wheelchair. Nancy and Valentina, both clutching their small experiment packs were helped out next. The fourth chair was given to Aleksey; and

Eleanor hopped back on before the platform was lowered. Nancy was taken to the jeep Ruthiebell and I had come in. She told the driver her pack contained perishables and she needed to get inside as quickly as possible. The driver took her and her medic away, not losing a minute.

Valentina, not in a hurry to leave and carrying her small pack, had her wheelchair pushed nonchalantly over to one of the big saucer's five metallic legs. She was pushed close enough to touch it. She removed a small scanning device from her pack.

High above the San Bernardino basin, the A-10s made a long turn getting ready for another pass over the airfield. Raymo was already at altitude and about a mile ahead of the others. "I told you they were still there," he said rather loudly. "Look at them, they're up to no good. You can't trust those little SOBs."

"Things look pretty calm down there, RAINDROP," said the major. "Okay VINO, you're the expert. What's going on? Do you recognize any of those UFOs?"

"Yes sir. The two large saucers have been reported and photographed for the last forty years, but we still don't know where they came from or what they want. The small craft still hovering has a design that's halfway between the recovered Roswell craft and the UFO photographed in the Rendlesham Forest back in 1980."

"You mean to tell me, lieutenant, that something actually crashed at Roswell?"

"Yes sir, that's my understanding, and the Air Force has confirmed that it was a weather balloon."

"That little UFO doesn't look like a weather balloon to me," scowled the major.

"Total BS," yelled Raymo. "That little turkey is just like the one that abducted me; no I mean the people. It's time to even the score!"

"Lieutenant Raymo Woodburn," called out the major. "Are you hearing me, lieutenant?"

"Yes sir, I am."

"Your recon data is so valuable, I want you to take it back to the base right now. I don't want you or your data at risk from the UFOs. Do you understand me?"

"Yes sir. I'm heading home right now."

Back down on the ground, Daypart's small spacecraft extended four legs and lowered to a landing. When the forklift raised the platform the second time, Hans-Peter was the last one to come out the hatch. As soon as he appeared, everyone nearby cheered. The crowd out on the Santa Ana Wash couldn't see what was going on, but were still astonished and rendered speechless by the size of the big gray UFOs they could see.

Ruthiebell was nearby. She had been up all night working and thinking hard about what was happening. When she realized I was really an alien and hiding my agenda, the ISS rescue seemed trivial. Were that not enough, even as she tried to come to grips with who I was, her anger toward the FAA and the Navy for trying to force the Rebel down at Point Mugu was still smoldering. The thought of some government contractor stealing the Rebel's technology burned up every drop of emotional energy she had left. She no longer had the strength to repress how she really felt. When Hans-Peter stepped off the platform, she threw her arms around him. She needed to hug him to be sure he was there. Her eyes filled with tears. She then saw me to the side and was emotionally pulled back into the astonishment of alien contact. As she stepped back from Hans-Peter, I handed her my perfectly clean white handkerchief. Inaudibly, she said thank you.

I then extended my hand to Hans-Peter, "Welcome home, Commander."

"Your voice is reminiscent of Daypart's," said Hans-Peter, "Is that a coincidence?"

"No, not at all. Would you care to meet Daypart? He's my brother."

Hans-Peter turned and looked at Daypart's spacecraft. The legs held the spacecraft about ten feet off the ground. As everyone looked, a hatch on the bottom of it opened and a column of blue light shone down to the ground. I extended one hand behind Ruthiebell and the other behind Hans-Peter. "Come along, my friends, let's go meet Daypart."

Behind the trio, by only ten feet or so, two TC security men followed along. Sandy and Milo came along with the TC security men, but stayed off to the side to get a better camera angle. An Army captain with two armed men followed one of the TC security men and a lieutenant with two more men followed the other TC man. As they walked closer, a man in a dazzling otherworldly suit appeared, slowly coming down within the blue light. Once on the ground, the light turned off.

The man bore a striking resemblance to Traypart, but he was not a clone or what we would call his twin. The man walked forward and met the trio. My brother and I shook hands and he said, "You're looking well. These must be the friends you told me about." Then turning slightly and extending his hand again, "You must be Ruthiebell?"

She took his hand, and said, "Yes, may I ask which star system you are from?"

Daypart and Traypart both smiled and laughed slightly. "Oh yes," said Daypart, "You're not one to waste even a minute. So, to be equally straightforward, that is a question I will not answer on this visit."

She pressed further, "May I ask if more than one kind of extraterrestrial has ever visited our planet?"

"You may, but I'll not be specific. More than three kinds of extraterrestrials have visited your planet, and I can also let you know that they come and go."

"So why did you come here today?"

"It's time to bring Traypart home. He's completed his hitch on your planet. He also suggested we meet him here in San Bernardino. He said this small city, east of Los Angeles, would be a safe place to meet out in the open. I know we're being filmed." With that remark, Daypart waved and smiled at Sandy and Milo. "We all thought retrieving Traypart this way could be a consciousness-raising event for those interested in extraterrestrial visitors."

"So you're telling me you've been here before?" asked Ruthiebell.

"What do you people say?" said Daypart seeming a bit exasperated. "Give me a break! How do you think Traypart got here in the first place?" Then un-expectantly, both of the human-like extraterrestrials looked skyward.

"Everybody take cover," I yelled. "Get under the big saucers. We're being attacked." Another alien man dropped out of Daypart's small spacecraft and ran for one of the big saucers.

"What'd you do," yelled Ruthiebell. "Did you bring some alien enemy of yours down here for a fight?"

"No, it's an A-10 and he's coming in fast."

Everyone could now hear the A-10 coming in, and ran for cover except Ruthiebell. "Yeah," she yelled, "I'm not going to fall for that one. You're just trying to abduct us all." With profound arrogance she stood her ground.

The primitive Neolithic urge to protect women overcame Hans-Peter, and at his own risk he picked up Ruthiebell in his arms and ran for cover.

High in the sky and bearing down on the UFOs, Raymo yelled out, "I can see you. Why don't you turn on your damn stealth and try to hide?"

At that moment, the gray dome atop one of the saucers lifted about 8 inches and split in half, revealing a nasty-looking weapon. The dome could now move like the turret on a tank, but Raymo was already there.

Raymo opened fire and a line of thirty-millimeter armor piercing bullets hit the big saucer with the closed dome first. There was no apparent damage other than a line of dents. Leaving the saucer, his line of bullets ripped open the concrete between it and Daypart's spacecraft. The rapid-fire Gatling cannon hit Daypart's craft twenty-three times before Raymo started to pull up. The bullets ripped the small UFO in half and hit some kind of power source that exploded with just enough force to blow it apart.

Everyone, including the three aliens, had run under the big saucer and were crouching down near the ground. Hans-Peter had shielded Ruthiebell with his body. Fragments from the explosion flew everywhere. One piece, about the size of a cellphone, hit a glancing blow to Hans-Peter's back and fractured three of his ribs. Ruthiebell was untouched. He had protected her.

The weapon on the other saucer, now on target, shot an orange light ray at Raymo's A-10 and stopped it in midair. Raymo ejected safely and was thrown to the other side of a big hangar. The orange light ray held the A-10 steadily and ripped its two wings off in midair. It then pulled all the jet fuel from the A-10 and threw it up into the air in a single great mass. At about a thousand feet, the jet fuel burst into a huge fireball. Everyone along the Santa Ana Wash saw it and started for home. The Army oversaw a very fast but orderly exodus. People were sure they had just seen the beginning of the war of the worlds.

The orange light ray split in half and put the two A-10 wings neatly on the concrete. The other half of the light ray held the A-10 fuselage out over the dirt at the edge of the concrete. The Gatling cannon was fired into the dirt until every shell had been spent. The aliens emptied the weapon as though they were removing caps from a toy gun. The light ray then put the fuselage down on the concrete neatly near the two wings.

Medics ran to the aid of everyone with injuries. Fragments had hit both of the aliens in their extraterrestrial suits, but in both cases the fragments hadn't penetrated the cloth. Traypart, who was wearing some of his newest human clothing, hadn't been hit.

The three human-like aliens started to walk out to Daypart's broken in half and thoroughly wrecked ship. The airport fire crew was spraying water on the hot spots. A medic and Ruthiebell helped Hans-Peter over to the wrecked spaceship and joined the aliens. As they walked over, the other big saucer retracted its five legs and floated over the damaged craft. The bottom of the saucer opened up a space the same shape as the wreckage.

"That rotary cannon you people put on the A-10s is something to be reckoned with," said Traypart to Hans-Peter. "You need to pay close attention to who you let fly those things."

"We saw one man escape your spacecraft before it was hit. Was there anyone else inside when it was hit?" asked Hans-Peter.

"No, fortunately. None of us were injured," answered Daypart as the three aliens started walking back toward the saucer they had all hidden under, "but I see you were hit rather hard."

"Oh, it's not too bad, I'll be fine in a few weeks."

Blue light came down from the large saucer that had been hit and dented. The blue light lifted the broken parts of Daypart's craft up into it. As the two big pieces lifted, all the small fragments were swept up with them. "Looks like you're taking everything home," said Hans-Peter.

"Of course," said Traypart. "We don't want to be part of your vast planetary littering problem. What is it they say? Visitors should take only pictures and leave only footprints."

Overhead, the three remaining A-10s flew over in a friendly way. The alien weapon tracked them without igniting its orange light. The A-10s rocked slightly back and forth making their wings go up and down. The wings were meant to be waving good-by as the A-10s flew away.

"Can you possibly stay a few days and be my guests here on my grounds?"

"Thank you, Hans-Peter, but this place isn't as safe as we thought it would be. It would probably be best for us to go home now."

"Wait," said Ruthiebell. "How about leaving us with just one little piece of that broken spaceship?"

Traypart and Daypart looked at each other, obviously engaged in a serious telepathic conversation. "I'm afraid not," said Traypart. "As you saw, we collected all the broken pieces. We know how to identify our stuff and pick it all up."

"We're not authorized to leave anything behind on this trip," said Daypart in a very sympathetic way. The aliens, now sure the A-10s were really going home, folded their weapon back into its turret.

Everyone had moved back under the big saucer. From where they stood, they couldn't see the turret closing and lowering back onto the big UFO. A fairly large hole opened up in the saucer's underside. Traypart and his brother and the other alien stepped directly under it. Everyone else moved farther away.

"What should we call you?" yelled out Ruthiebell to the aliens.

"You've been calling us 'Nordics.' That's close enough, but you might also start calling us your friends."

A blue light came down over the three aliens and they ascended up into their craft. Valentina's medic pushed her wheelchair away from the leg she was examining. Without moving, the big gray saucer retracted is five legs. The two saucers rocked back and forth imitating the way the

A-10s waved their wings to say good-by. Without a sound, the two saucers rose and climbed into the eastern sky. As they moved, they accelerated, and in very little time, they were gone.

As usual, there was not one piece of tangible evidence left behind. The twenty-first century, now just one-fifth over, was replacing many paradigms that had appeared rock solid a mere thirty years ago with new thinking. But then a real paradigm shift needs tangible evidence. Everything that had happened could have been masterfully created inside a computer, except that Ruthiebell was now certain she would not let anything come between her and Hans-Peter again.

CPSIA information can be obtained
at www.ICGtesting.com
Printed in the USA
LVHW110844071120
671027LV00054B/1309